THE KNIGHT'S
SCARRED MAIDEN

Nicole Locke

MILLS &
BOON

Published in Great Britain 2017
by Mills & Boon, an imprint of HarperCollins*Publishers*
1 London Bridge Street, London, SE1 9GF

© 2017 Nicole Locke

ISBN: 978-0-263-92598-2

Printed and bound in Spain
by CPI, Barcelona

An unearthly growl resounded as a man leapt out of the darkness.

'Let her go!'

His cold voice raised the hairs on the back of her neck. Terror gripped her even harder and the two men tightened their grips. Through her watering eyes she saw a supplicant expression now masked Rudd's face. She knew that unctuous curve of his lips when he wanted to appease a customer.

'Here, now, this is none of your concern,' Rudd said. 'We only want a bit of privacy.'

'You harm a woman, you'll get no privacy except in death.'

The words were menacingly calm.

There was a whoosh of breath and the sharp thump of one captor's body, as if someone had kicked him down.

She watched Rudd's smug face draw white with fear as he ran towards the trees and disappeared.

The man crouched near her, his elbows resting on his legs, his hands hanging between them. Empty hands. His scabbard was bare and there was no sword at his feet.

'

Nicole Locke discovered her first romance novels in her grandmother's closet, where they were secretly hidden. Convinced that books that were hidden must be better than those that weren't, Nicole greedily read them. It was only natural for her to start writing them—but now not so secretly.

Books by Nicole Locke

Mills & Boon Historical Romance

Lovers and Legends

The Knight's Broken Promise
Her Enemy Highlander
The Highland Laird's Bride
In Debt to the Enemy Lord
The Knight's Scarred Maiden

Visit the Author Profile page at millsandboon.co.uk.

THE KNIGHT'S
SCARRED MAIDEN

Ode to a house right next door. So handy to pop over for nibbles, a chat, copious amounts of champagne.

Ode to a stairwell landing propped with pillows and treats. For my kids, made comforting like a warm hug, adventurous like a magic carpet.

Ode to David and Cydonie.
This book wouldn't have been written but for you and those chats and that champagne.

I treasure our friendship more than the longest of hugs and the grandest of adventures.
More than all the bubbles in every raised fluted glass that ever was…or will be.

Chapter One

He was here.

Helissent let out a breath and rearranged the flagons on the tray. Again. This was the second night he'd come in, which wasn't the only reason she'd noticed him.

'Hurry up, girl, customers are thirsty.'

Helissent didn't glance at Rudd. She never glanced at the innkeeper's son, now owner. She tried not to notice him at all, but it didn't help. His eyes grew more calculating every day as if she was in a trap and he was merely fattening her up.

'If you stand there much longer,' he said, snapping a towel in the air, 'I'll add another flagon to that tray and make you carry it over your head.'

If he put one more flagon on the tray, she'd make sure to dump it on his head.

Then where would she be? Out in the streets.

Pasting a smile that only deepened her scars' appearance, she gave him her most guileless look. 'I'm simply ensuring that everything is in its place, so the customers have what they need.'

Rudd didn't have any reaction to her scarred and distorted smile. And that fact frightened her most of all. The fact she couldn't frighten him. Her deep scars that spanned the entire right side of her body from her temple to her feet made everyone frightened. It's how she kept the travelling customers away.

'If you give me any more grief I'll ensure you give them what they *truly* need…' he answered, twisting the towel around his fist.

She lifted the tray and suppressed the anger and fear she couldn't afford to expose. Her village didn't have many streets to live on and there were certainly no others who would take her into their homes.

The only reason her tiny village survived was that it was on the road between London and York. People mostly travelled through and never stayed. If only she didn't have to stay. But she had nowhere else to go.

Here, at least, they knew why she was disfigured. Any place else, people could think she was cursed. Or worse, they would pity her.

Here, she was just ignored. Except for Rudd, the prodigal son, who had returned a month after his parents' death. He didn't ignore her at all.

It was up to her to avoid him and focus on the inn's patrons. Some travelers, mostly regulars… and now *him*, who she could feel watching the altercation between Rudd and her.

Sidestepping the narrow counter, she dodged a stumbling patron on her way to the patrons by the large window and set the tray in the center of the table. For a brief moment, she closed her eyes to soak up the bit of warming sun slanting down. Often it was the only sunlight she felt during the daytime.

Then she gave a genuine greeting to the patrons at the table. Regular customers, who met her eyes and exchanged pleasantries. Patrons, who knew her family and the former innkeepers, John and Anne, who'd taken her in after the fire destroyed her home and killed her family.

She'd take any kindness thrown her way. It was probably why she kept skirting her eyes to him. He, who sat at the shadowed table in the rear. Sat in shadows, though he never lowered his cloak's hood.

He watched her, which usually made her angry, made her tilt her chin so that those gawking could see every grueling angle of her physical and personal pain. She liked it better when they winced or flushed and turned away.

She liked it not because it hurt them, but because it reminded her of her shame, her cowardice, and all the hurt she deserved.

But she didn't tilt her head with the man in the shadows because he'd told Rudd her honey cakes were exceptional. It was why he'd returned today. He'd ordered more and paid in advance. He was here to collect them.

Unaccountably nervous, she passed him to get to the kitchens out the back. His head was partially bowed and she still did not see his eyes, but she nodded her head in greeting. She woke up early this morning to make twenty-five cakes. She often received compliments on her baking, but was never requested to make this many cakes before. She'd never known a man with such a sweet tooth and she'd dared to ask Rudd about him.

Rudd didn't know the man's name, but he did know his business. He'd come in a couple of days ago and was staying in the lodgings at the edge of town, him and almost twenty other men. Travellers, but two had spurs. This man with his hood, and another man, who was immensely tall and ducked his head to avoid the ceiling rafters.

The first day, he and the other men sat at the different tables. There was much talking, sometimes in languages she didn't know. All of them addressed the man in the hood. She never saw his face nor heard his voice, though the men did.

Whatever he said made them laugh, made them nod in agreement. They deferred to him. Fascinated, she watched when she could. She wondered who these men were, where they were going next. Not for her to know, but it was a small bit of entertainment she made for herself.

On the second day, it was only him and the giant. On that day, she swore he watched her.

She didn't see spurs when her shadow man came in, but she thought he must have been a knight. His travel clothing wasn't particularly fine, but it was his bearing that he couldn't hide beneath his cloak. Tall, with a lean grace not many people possessed, and certainly none in this mostly farming community.

He couldn't hide the sword he carried, like it was a part of him, either. Natural, predatory… lethal.

He returned alone on the third day. On this day to retrieve his order. Carefully placing the cakes in the travelling sacks, she turned again to the inn. She wondered if this time, he would raise his head so she could see him.

Rhain peered at the customers in the ramshackle inn. Nothing made this one any different than the hundreds he had occupied over the last five years. For a mercenary like himself and his men, only location and information mattered.

This inn had neither. What it did have was sheep…lots of sheep. Even with a stiff breeze, there was no mistaking the smell or din.

A few days' ride north of here lay the comfortable Tickhill Castle, a strategic motte and bailey now held by the King himself. He and his men would be welcomed at such a castle, and when he started this journey, it was his intention to oblige himself of their company, sumptuous bedding and fair.

Castles had location…they also had information, but he could no longer indulge himself of such. Not any more.

Instead, now, he opted for obscurity. An obscurity that had nothing to do with his occupation as a mercenary. Hence he'd stopped at this wreck of village meant to accommodate the local farming community and the occasional poor traveler.

The lodgings down the street were adequate protection from the rains, but this inn—

Rhain lowered his head as the woman passed by his table. Even so, he noticed her greeting. It was difficult not to notice her. When he first came to the inn two days ago, he almost lost his protective hood.

She'd been standing at the counter, arranging cups. He'd opened the door and the sunlight had hit her. He only had a profile of her, but it was enough to stun him and his men had slammed into him before they'd stumbled around him. She was absolutely exquisite. The pale perfection of her skin, the thick eyelashes. The room's light wasn't bright enough to see the exact color of her hair, but it was close to chestnut and waved luxuriously down her back. Then she lifted the tray and he could see the curves of her body, the graceful way she moved. In this hovel of a tavern was someone who belonged in a king's bed.

And he should know, having grown with wealth and privilege, knowing the King himself, he knew the quality of the woman. But that wasn't all that surprised him.

It was the wide berth of patrons around her. The inn was crowded at that time of day and a beautiful woman should have been pressed against, or been fighting, some of the more inebriated customers. If nothing else, if she was some wife, or sister, there would have been some camaraderie, some familiarity with her. Instead, she was ignored...

No, in a crowded inn, she was ostracized, the berth continued though she was done arranging the goblets, had lifted the tray and was turning to serve them. Everyone's back was to her. As the door behind him closed, she hoisted the tray and then he saw what he had not from the profile of her left side.

As she turned to feed the customers behind her, he saw her right profile. Then he understood why, while in a crowded bar, she was left alone. Scarred beyond any repair. Old and healed burns from what he could tell. She had suffered some time in her past and suffered greatly.

He watched her. It was as if that moment had locked something inside him. She made him... curious. He didn't know what side of her compelled him more. It wasn't just her physical differences, it was her personality. Wary with the innkeeper, friendly with regulars. Defiant as if she insisted on showing her scars to travelers like him.

So he watched her while he sat in the back of the inn and drank poor ale, but waited for food that should never have been produced in such a hovel.

The innkeeper was a giant oaf of a man, whose unctuous manner grated on Rhain. Though he'd seen enough cruelty in the world, the innkeeper taunting the woman angered him. More than once he found himself reaching for his dagger to throw. A disquieting impulse, since he'd been able to shrug off such behavior before.

Yet he came back since he and his men enjoyed food he'd never expected to taste here. The cuts of meat in the stew were poor and often the vegetables were not fresh. But instead of grease and gristle, herbs and flavors had been added. Fine, arduous sifting of flour had been done to the rolls, which also had a sprinkling of herbs, making them both light and delicious.

It was a tiny village with no information. Completely useless to him for his business. No one would expect for him to be here and his men could be dry and fed well. More to the point, none of them protested when he said they would stay a few days.

And that was before he ate the cake which was light, but dense with honey that dripped and glossed over the top. He might be a giant oaf of an innkeeper, but the man's cooking was unmatched.

Two sacks set on the table in front of him. It was the woman who delivered them, one hand perfect, the other gnarled with scars. Ravaged from fire like the entire right side of her face, neck and no doubt, by the way she moved, her body as well. One side exquisite, the other disfigured.

Slowly, he tilted his head up so as not to dislodge his hood, but enough to meet her eyes, which were a color he could not guess—green, grey or brown. He couldn't determine their exact color, but they were clear, straightforward with intelligence, wariness and just a bit of pride. The fire had tilted down the corner of her right eye, and marred just a hair of her full lips. Her nose was left perfect, but her cheek and ear were deeply grooved.

This was the first time he had dared look at her fully. He of all people knew what it was like to be stared at. Compelling though she was, he tried not to keep watching this woman. Still…

Her voice was melodious, and cultured, with a hint of French, her teeth white and even. It was just as conflicting as the rest of her and this inn. A hovel of an inn, sumptuous fare, a woman both beautiful and disfigured. A voice that should be filled with laughter instead of sorrow.

It was the sorrow he heard. His hands almost shook as he grabbed silver coins from his pouch and set them on the table. Too many, perhaps, but he didn't dare check or she'd noticed his momentary weakness. He didn't let anyone see his weakness.

'I'll require fifty by tomorrow morning.'

A slight flutter of those hands like he surprised her. 'Twenty-five can be done by morning, another twenty-five by afternoon. The ovens are too small for fifty.'

'I'm leaving tomorrow morning, and I require fifty. I'll pay you double.'

She darted a glance before she slid the money off the table with her perfect hand. Her movements were graceful, but more importantly, they were silent. She acted like she didn't want anyone to know she was pocketing such money.

He dared to look at her again, although it gave her an opportunity to see his own features. No one could see him now. It wasn't for his safety, but for his men's. For that he wouldn't appease her curiosity though he recognized it since he felt the same about her.

Her expression was unreadable, almost as silent as the scraping of the coins on the table. On closer inspection, her face wasn't badly scarred, the scars were softer, white and a light pink. But the deep gnarled grooves on her hand spoke of another story. She hadn't been subjected to fire for a short time. Only prolonged exposure could cause that kind of damage.

Another coin hit into her hand, then to her pocket, and she left the rest. 'It's too much. This is more than double.'

Ah, she'd been counting as she took. Cultured voice and educated. Contrasts, and his curiosity was more than piqued. It was good he would be gone tomorrow. He hadn't been curious about anything or anyone for many years. He didn't have time to be curious now.

'I just want the cakes done on time,' he said.

She didn't take the coins on the table. An honest tavern keep, too.

'Take the rest for you.' He wouldn't raise his head, but he saw her shake her head.

'Double will be enough,' she said. 'I'll talk to the innkeeper, but I have no doubt you'll get your cakes.'

Pleasure coursed through him. Another emotion he didn't have time for. But if a few coins would give him such delicious pleasure, albeit briefly, he'd take it. He hated coin at the same time he used it to his advantage. He'd use anything to his advantage. It was his nature and even more so now.

'Thank you,' he said as she walked away. He untied one of the sacks in front of him and released a cake. It was warm and the smell of butter and honey were extravagant in the musty, almost putrid smells of the tavern. It fit perfectly in his hand and he reveled in the color, and the springy texture of his first bite.

He knew the taste would be better out of the darkness of the tavern. For a man of his wealth and status, a man who made his money on his mercenary skills and diplomacy, he knew the art of patience. He could wait until he reached the lodging and his men, but he didn't want to.

Cakes. Such a little pleasure to most, but to him all the more precious since a price went on his head.

Chapter Two

'It's late. I'll take first watch.' Nicholas, Rhain's second in command and oldest friend, finished his loaf of bread and brushed his hands against his legs.

'No, it's mine,' Rhain said, finishing the last of the cakes. Two of his men didn't want them. Fools, he thought them, but he already knew they would refuse, which was why he'd bought them. 'You trained the men hard today, you'll have no watch tonight.'

'Any less than you?'

'I had that break.'

'Ah, yes, your leisurely trip to the inn.'

'I had to wait until the cakes were finished.' None of it was true, but Rhain knew Nicholas understood that. They carried a conversation that would be heard by the other men. His men he paid well for their loyalty for the last five years.

A long time for mercenaries to stay together, even longer to keep loyal.

As far as he knew, they were still loyal and he'd trusted them up until two months ago.

Now because of his own actions in London, he could trust Nicholas because they fostered together at Edward's court.

As for the rest of the men, and as was true with any mercenary, they could be bribed. Consequently, he trusted them up to a point. For now they travelled north to meet with King Edward's men collected there. Then they would part ways. If he was killed before then, he trusted Nicholas to pay them well for their services. He didn't expect them to mourn. They were not friends; he wanted no friends.

At first, he had tried to get rid of Nicholas, who joined him a year into his travels, but finally gave up. He allowed him some privilege into this life, but not everything. Trust, loyalty, friendship could only go so far since the life he lived was a lie. That was something he wouldn't burden Nicholas with.

A lie and a quest. When he set out five years ago from his home in Wales, he burned with hatred and with a vengeance to set the past right. To find his father for answers.

He didn't know who his father was. The irony

was he hadn't known who his true mother was until five years ago either. It had been a terrible and deadly secret. All his life, Rhain had thought himself the second son of William, Lord of Gwalchdu, and Ellen, his wife, and the younger brother of the current Lord of Gwalchdu, Teague.

It was a gifted life, wealthy, privileged and, as a second son, one without responsibilities. One he had always reveled in. It was his older brother Teague who had to make the difficult choices. When Rhain was born, their mother, Ellen, had died in childbirth and his father, William, had been killed only moments before.

So at the age of five Teague became Lord of Gwalchdu and a Welsh Marcher Lord. When Teague was betrayed by a Welsh prince, he went to the English King Edward and gave him his loyalty.

Rhain was too young to make such decisions, but he worshipped his older brother and never questioned his loyalty, which was always to his family and to Gwalchdu. Therefore, Rhain fostered with King Edward before he returned to Gwalchdu and his brother, who was being threatened by an enemy.

Only after much adversity was it revealed that Sister Ffion, Ellen's sister, was the one threatening his brother. Sister Ffion, who suffered from episodes of madness, of fervency, of seizures.

Such illness she'd been fighting all her life with rumors that the Devil's blood ran through her.

After being caught, Sister Ffion had died, but not before she revealed the terrible secret. That she was Rhain's true mother. In her dying words, she did not say who his father was. Only telling him the clue was in a necklace she gave him.

And that was what he had been doing for the last five years: finding clues along the way. That his father, most likely, was the captain of the former Gwalchdu's soldiers. That from a piece of needlework the necklace was not only links of silver, but that a large inlaid pendant had once belonged to it.

Thinking his father had taken the pendant, Rhain attempted to discover in which direction he'd travelled. When that trail went cold, he followed the jewelers who could make or sell such a necklace and pendant. Spain, France, further along Wales and London.

Along the way, he'd earned money and a reputation by his sword. He'd earned men, who followed him when his reputation increased. All the while, he asked questions. He wanted, needed answers. Why was Sister Ffion his mother; why did his father abandon her? Did his father know the Devil's blood ran through her veins? And— the one question that plagued him, that drove him on—did his father suffer from seizures, too?

Simple questions. A golden life turned to rusting iron in one moment. A privileged carefree life. Where he had no worries on money, or family. Where because of his looks, because of his wealth, he had friends, he had women.

Now, he had no family. His brother wasn't his brother, his mother was dead.

He was alone. Because of his Devil's blood, he would remain alone.

His life had been forfeit since that fateful day when he realized his mother was Sister Ffion, a woman plagued by seizures. Though he'd never suffered a seizure, he was all too aware the blood flowed through his veins as well. That he was tainted.

As a result, there would be no wife for him, no children. No future. But he'd carved a life for himself, such that it was. Until London.

Only Nicholas knew what stupidity he had done in London two months back. Only Nicholas would ever know because he had been there when he denied Guy of Warstone his services and then in one rash act had killed him.

Now, Guy's brother Reynold was after him. Rhain had a price on his head from one of the most powerful families in Europe. One reckless moment and he forfeited what was left of his life and jeopardized the lives of his men.

So that carefree man he was before was no

more and the purposeful life he'd made for himself was also gone. All he could do now was to set things right by getting his men under the protection of Edward's camp. As for Nicholas, who knew everything and most likely had a price on his head, too, he hoped he lived long enough to protect him as well.

This village was small, but was on the main road and would have travelers. He and his men took all the spare lodging and some of his men were in different accommodations. His priority was to Nicholas, but even now his enemy could be circling the village and setting a trap. He could stay here to protect, but it wouldn't give them enough time for the advantage he liked to have.

Rhain stood. 'I'm more restless than I thought. I'm going to walk the outer village first if you watch the men here. I'll return shortly.'

Nicholas raised one brow, but nodded his head. There was no good reason to search this sleepy village. It would take more than one man to take down their mercenary troop, but it would take only a trained assassin to take down one man. His life might be meaningless, he might be plagued with the Devil's own blood. But he would get his men to Edward's camp and do one good deed before he died.

Chapter Three

Helissent wrapped her shawl tightly against the cool breeze. It was spring and warm, but this time of night always brought a chill, which cut through her skin after the fires of the kitchens.

It was the one pain she welcomed in her day. In the beginning, those fires and her skin's sensitivities had almost kept her away from the ovens. But she knew how to protect herself now and had got used to the sting because it brought her joy. Like now even though she was exhausted after completing half the cakes requested.

Cakes she'd made almost completely in the dark. She had to make all fifty of them before tomorrow, but Rudd was meticulous when it came to the kitchen supplies and that included the use of candles to see by. She couldn't risk Rudd's wrath with the use of too many candles. He only gave her a small allowance to operate the kitchen and the food she fed to the travelers in the inn. It was all she had, but it was a matter of pride that she made the best food around.

She knew these cakes, slathered in honey, were some of her best. She could stay up later, but she risked the ovens overheating. Best to have them cool. They'd be warm enough to heat to the right temperature when she rose.

She stumbled and righted herself. Exhaustion didn't describe how tired her bones were. A full day's work. Not to mention she was up early making the original twenty-five cakes this morning. She was exhausted and Rudd wasn't letting up on her either. Since he arrived a few months ago, he'd worked her twice as hard as his parents had though they had been old and frail. She had done their work, plus hers in the end.

She'd also cared for them when both became bedridden. She'd do it all again for they had done much more for her. She missed them terribly. They'd taken her in and healed her when she had no one left.

Now they were gone and she had no one again. Except Rudd, and she desperately didn't want him. She prayed it would be late enough when she returned and he'd be asleep. In four hours, she needed to make more cakes and she needed to rest.

Fifty cakes for double the money. It still gave

her a thrill. It gave Rudd a thrill, too, if the lascivious gleam in his eyes and spittle in the corner of his mouth was anything to go by when she'd handed it to him after her shadow man had left. She hoped it appeased him at the least.

For one tempting moment, she'd thought to keep the money for herself. She'd do anything for that money. After all, her shadow man made the bargain with her and Rudd hadn't seen her take the money. She could have given him half and taken the other portion. It wasn't enough for her to get to another town, but it would have been a start.

But shadow man didn't know she made the cakes and she couldn't risk Rudd finding out. He was entirely too frightening now. His manner too familiar. But she knew his greed was great, consequently she'd given him all the money. If she could show him her worth was on her cooking, not on her living with him and being a servant, maybe he would leave her alone.

Her eyes burned now with the need to sleep. She was tired, but only a few steps more and she could rest.

'Where have you been?' Rudd said, low, soft as he stepped out of the dark side of her home.

She stopped suddenly and blinked. It was late, the village quiet. There was no need for him to be up.

'Why are you here?' she blurted out before thinking.

He scowled and the blunt slash of his lips turned cruel. 'It isn't any of your business why I'm here. But your being gone is mine, now isn't it?'

A strange relief swept through her tired body. She was exhausted, not thinking clearly. Rudd's parents worried for her when she came home late as she worked on a recipe. 'Sorry, I was in the kitchens. I should have told—'

'You think I don't know where you've been or how you earn your money?' Rudd held up his coin purse, though she knew he'd already hidden the coins given to her. 'You think I'm a fool. No one makes this kind of coin off cakes.'

Rudd's tone of voice was as sneering as ever, but what set her heart tripping was the choice of his words, the fact he held up the purse that she knew was mostly empty. Still she argued with him.

'Of course it was for the cakes. I handed you the coins; I explained how that man requested fifty cakes by tomorrow morning. I had to make some tonight.'

'Oh, I can smell the fires all over you.' Rudd sniffed. 'I know you were in the kitchens. But I don't see any cakes. I just see you, walking home.'

Home was feet away. They were on the dark and quiet side of her home now. If she had reached the front, she'd be surrounded by the lights of other homes, of the inn.

'It wasn't nice of you walking home this late, and making us wait.' Rudd took a step closer, his legs unsteady, but still upright. He had been drinking, but not enough to make him weak. Why would she care if drink made him weak?

But she did care. It was there in his suspicious words, in the fact he approached her on this side of the house where no one would see them. It was in the fact her heart tripped a bit more and the hairs on her neck prickled in warning.

'I left the cakes in the kitchens to cool. Check if you don't believe me. I have to make more in the morning.' She gathered her shawl closer and moved to step around him. 'I need to lie down and get some sleep now or else we'll have to return the money. We'll talk in the morning.'

A harsh chuckle escaped his lips. 'Oh, you'll lie down now…but it won't be to sleep.'

From the other side of her home, two men emerged under the moon's light. Two men she saw earlier at the tavern. The ones talking heatedly with Rudd, and giving her looks. Rudd looking smug. Too smug.

She pulled herself straighter, all tiredness gone. Her heart now hammering in her chest.

The men blocked her way around to the door of her home; Rudd blocked the other way. The only way to escape was to run the way she'd come, but that only led to the kitchens, to more darkness and further away from any one to help her. If there was to be help.

'What is this?'

'You know what it is. You do take me for a fool. I have to admit I had doubts when you handed me those coins for your cakes. But then these two men showed me the error of my ways. Showed me what more could be earned by having one such as you.'

She eyed the men, who held menacingly still. As if they were simply waiting for her to run. And she wanted to, but with her skin tightening up around her leg, she wouldn't get very far.

The only choice she had was to talk her way out of this. Perhaps appeal to their greed. 'I received that for the cakes, Rudd. Cakes I won't make again if you go through with this. I swear upon your parents—'

'Don't you mention my parents. Don't you ever talk about my parents again!'

Anger, fear. The men watching her changed stance like they could feel the trap they'd laid tightening on her. She could feel it, too.

Confusion entered her fear now. This seemed too personal. This was Rudd, the son who never visited, who returned only after their death to claim everything. The son the innkeepers spoke of once, his mother's voice breaking in the middle of the tale before the father told her the rest. He was an awful man, and hadn't cared for them. Yet he was angry now.

'I can get you more.' She gestured to the purse. 'Make more cakes, make more money. Just don't do this.'

'Don't do this?' Rudd jingled the purse a bit. 'It looks like you were already doing it. I'll merely profit more than I thought today. These kind gentlemen offered money as well. Not as much as you were being paid by that knight, but a deal is a deal. And you do need to pay your debt to my parents.'

This was personal. 'Debt?'

'You don't know?' Rudd laughed. 'All the better that I get to tell the tale. Get to see your ugly pious face as I break your heart.'

Rudd ran his eyes over her and his laugh turned ugly.

'You think they kept you here with a roof over your head, feeding you because they cared for you? That you worked all hours of the day, slaved until your fingers bled because you loved them back?'

They'd told her they loved her. So much pain she had suffered at the time, so many tears with the guilt of failing her sister, her soul, failing her family. She didn't love herself, but the innkeepers loved her. Of course, she worked for them until her fingers bled. She'd still do it.

'Oh! I can see you do believe it. They bought you. Two ageing failing innkeepers needed cheap help. Although I don't think you came cheap to them. I believe you owe more on your debt.'

'I don't owe a debt,' Helissent said, her eyes on the men who stepped closer. Too close. She took a couple of steps in the opposite direction and saw how their smirks increased. How had they become involved? 'Whatever these men told you, I owe no debt.'

'Oh, you do.' Rudd ran his finger down the right side of his face. 'My parents fixed you.' His mouth turned like he tasted something vile. 'Such as it is, but it was the best money could buy in these parts.'

He spit between his teeth. 'You think your possessions from the ashes of your home paid for that healer. No, it was my parents, who paid that healer with my inheritance.'

He reached back and pulled out of his breeches a small, heavily written-on parchment scrap. 'I have the evidence all here. Accounts from the healer and my parents. All about your treatment, and care, and healing.

'Oh, they were crafty, paying for your care.

But I know better. I was born and raised by those people, and everything became clear when this parchment was read to me. My parents were wondering if their slave would be working for them soon.'

For a split moment, she believed his cruel words for truth, felt the pain in them, but it didn't take away her sudden yearning and keen desperation. For in Rudd's hands was more treasure than she'd thought she'd ever see. A parchment, a few written words from two people she'd dearly loved and would give anything to hear from again.

She had nothing left of her own family, but Anne and John had become her second family. Now there was something of theirs, something she could read, to hold in her hand, to hear their voices again.

As he noted her fixation on the parchment, Rudd's eyes gleamed. Let him think he'd hurt her with the words and not with the denying of a scrap of paper. He could never know.

'The way I see it, you owe me, girl. And there's only one way a disgusting creature like you could pay me back.'

Two sets of hands clamped on to her arms. She cried out and kicked. Too late. Her eyes focused on the bit of parchment; she forgot the men.

'Is she ours now?' The one on her left sneered, his breath heavy with onions.

'Such a price you paid, how could she not be yours?' Rudd's snake expression turned to her. 'Can you imagine any man would pay a price to be between your legs? But these men paid plenty. They seem to like their women damaged. Your ugliness is lining my pockets.'

'Never had a burned one before,' Onion-breath said with glee. 'Last one was crippled and re-member the blind one?'

The man on her left closed his eyes like he sa-vored that memory, and she yanked her arm to hide her revulsion.

'Our agreement was I had her first.' Rudd tossed the parchment behind him, his hands im-mediately at his belt.

'I get the ugly half,' Ale man breathed.

'No, I get the ugly half,' the other argued.

In her struggle, Helissent yanked the men sev-eral feet before they dug their heels into the mud. Terror, like ice shards, struck underneath her skin. It was going to happen. She couldn't stop it.

Rudd laughed. 'I don't want any half except what's down below. Just shove her face in the mud. I don't want to see it for a moment before I get the skirts up and over her face.'

The men chortled, their manacled hands loos-ening. 'No!' She pulled her arms free and ran. Her heart pumped; she tasted the iron of blood in her mouth. As she feared, her right leg immediately dragged behind her. Pounding of feet on the cold dirt behind her, pain in her arms as the men grabbed and shoved her to the ground. The wet mud momentarily masking the taste of blood in her mouth.

More pain as a knee jammed into the small of her back. She threw her body to the left, kicked out, made some connection. Another hand on her ankle, yanking it to the side. Too far out, her legs were now widespread.

She screamed and tried to kick again. Grunts and harsh breath from the two men pinning her to the ground. She fought harder, a foot pounded into her ribs, a fist on to her cheek.

None of her struggles drowned out Rudd's laughter as he strolled up to them. His hands were at his waist, loosening his belt knot.

Waves of sickness crashed over her. Her lip was split open, but she wouldn't give in. Gathering what was left of her breath, she screamed again before a muddy hand slammed against her mouth.

An unearthly growl resounded as a man leapt out of the darkness. His cape swirled like a vortex of black; the arc of his sword glinted like shards in the moonlight before he went out of her line of sight.

'Let her go,' he snarled.

His cold voice raised the hairs on the back

of her neck. Terror gripped her harder. Let her go, let her go for what? The two men tightened their grips and laid heavily on top, suffocating what was left of her air. Through her watering eyes, she saw Rudd securing his belt. A suppliant expression now masked his face. She knew that curve of his lips when he wanted to appease a customer.

'Here now, this is none of your concern,' Rudd said. 'It's late and there's nothing to see. We only want a bit of privacy.'

'You harm a woman. You'll get no privacy except in death.'

The words were menacingly calm. He had a sword. Why weren't they getting off her? She yanked her mouth to get some air and a sharp prick bit into her side.

She was going to die. The men held her down with a knife. She prayed it would be a quick death.

'She's willing,' Rudd said, pointing towards her. 'See how she lays still?'

There was a harsh staccato of heavy breath from the men holding her down and one started nervously smacking his lips. She could feel they wanted to run, but the knife against her side held firm and they didn't move.

'I'll say this only once more. Call. Off. Your. Men.'

'See here…'

A whoosh of breath and a sharp thump of one captor's body like someone kicked him down. Then utter stillness as the knife released against her side. Onion Breath let go of her arm, scrambled before he slumped heavily on to her with a sharp cry.

Her eyesight dimming, she watched Rudd's smug face draw white with fear as he ran towards the trees and disappeared.

A yank of one body above her released her legs, another released the rest of her. She tried to push herself away, but her arms wouldn't work. Her legs jerking, she clawed the mud to flee from the man she hadn't seen, but who she was certain just killed two men.

A hand upon her back. 'Careful.'

She lashed out. Too slow to strike him. Too vulnerable on her back to run away. She froze, expecting a knife in her stomach.

Instead, the man crouched near her, his elbows resting on his legs, his hands hanging between them. Empty hands, his scabbard bare and no sword at his feet.

'You're safe now. They're gone.' The voice was no longer cold, but laden with an awkwardness in the cadence as if he was unused to giving comfort.

The full moon's light revealed his tall and angular shape coiled with predatory strength even in his relaxed stance. Shadows and a hood covered his face, but she recognized the distinct masculine chin, and full bottom lip.

'It's you,' she gasped.

Chapter Four

Holding her breath, she tried to sit up. Agony in her ribs.

'Stay still,' he said, a sharper tone to his words like he cut them against a blade, or wanted to cut another with it. 'Is anything broken?'

Pounding beginning in her head, her cheek throbbed, and she tasted blood on her lips. She kept her eyes closed and eased down in the mud again. Her thundering heart hurt her chest almost more than where they'd kicked her. But she could move her arms and legs, and the stabbing pain in her chest lessened when she didn't breathe deeply. 'I don't think so. I can't stop shaking.'

'I need to take you somewhere.' He glanced beyond her and cursed.

It was then she heard the hurried footsteps and the sudden stopping of them. 'Taking care of strays again?' said a dry, but friendly voice. It wasn't a voice she recognized, but she didn't dare move her head yet. The giant, perhaps?

'They're not dead; I hit them with rocks. But if they wake, and I'm like this, I'll use my sword.'

'Well, for your sake then I'll drag them into the forest—'

'There's another in the trees.'

'How unfortunate for him.'

'Make sure they're divested of wealth and weapons.'

The man gave an exaggerated huff. 'I'm a mercenary, remember? Is she hurt?'

They talked over her like she was dead. Parts of her were throbbing already, but she was alive and had suffered much worse. 'I'm fine.'

'She's hurt,' her shadow man said. 'Her cheek… perhaps her ribs.'

'Left cheek?'

'Does it matter?' her shadow man asked.

Helissent did risk moving her head as she heard the other man heave up the lax weight of one of her attackers. 'I wanted to be sure I left them in the same condition they left her. Except I think I'll take their…shoes…too.'

For one blazing moment, she wished he'd leave them worse off. But one look at her rescuers faces, and she knew they would be. Despite their easy banter, their faces were dark, their eyes

speaking of a violence she had never commit-
ted, but had almost been victim to. Whatever
happened to the men, they would be worse off
than her.

'Is there somewhere you can get help?' he
asked.

She turned her attention to the man still
crouched beside her.

Nowhere. Her home was with Rudd, who'd
just sold and tried to rape her. Her last view of
him was him fleeing. Would he stay away for a
night? 'My home is behind you.'

'Anywhere else?' he pressed.

'No, there's no one else.' His expression darkened. He didn't like her answer, but what choice
did she have? She pushed herself up, took heart
that she stayed up this time. 'I can get there myself.'

He adjusted his crouch. 'I'm going to lift you
now.' He reached out and suddenly stopped. 'This
is no time for propriety.'

At his unforgiving tone, she realized she'd inadvertently stiffened as he leaned over her.

It wasn't propriety that caused her to stiffen.
No one had touched her since John and Anne,
and before that, the healer, Agnes. No one. Not
even when money or drinks were exchanged had
she felt the brush of fingers. Travelers gave her
a wide berth because she horrified them, regu-

lars because they remembered her healing and didn't want to hurt her.

But this man, this stranger, hadn't hesitated. It startled her.

'I'm sorry, it's just—'

'That man's going to wake and we're not going to be here.' Without warning, he simply lifted her.

Held. She was being held as if her entire body was of little consequence.

No, he held her securely in a way she'd never been held before. She was acutely aware of the heat of his body, the smell of leather and evergreen, the way his chest rose and fell with his breath. Knew exactly where his arms touched her underneath and his hands. His hands—how they cradled her arm, the outside of her thigh.

All of it intimate suddenly as if they weren't outside with a vast forest at her back and clear night skies above. Her and only…him.

His hood partially fluttered when he lifted her. This close, she could see him if it wasn't dark. As if he could sense her scrutiny, he shifted his head away from her gaze.

'It is you, isn't it?' she said, before she stopped herself.

Almost imperceptibly, he tightened around her. 'Does it matter?'

Did it matter that the one man who gave her

a compliment on her baking, who rescued her from rape and maybe death, was the same? To her, very much. To him, probably not.

His long strides quickly covered the distance to her home, to her only sanctuary that wasn't any more. Stopping at the door, he asked, 'Are there any others here?'

She shook her head, and he opened the door. His only hesitation was as he took in the main living area, and the one closed door that indicated Rudd's room.

Thankfully, her pitiful home was dark and covered in shadows. 'You can put me down.'

'You need to lie down. I want to see the extent of your injuries, and if I can do anything. I have salves I can bring for you.'

There were hardly any candles. And she didn't want this man seeing her home, or her bed shoved under the crooked eaves in the back corner.

The only indication of privacy was from the coarse torn sacks she had sewn together and hung from the eaves. They were far too short, and hung only on one side, but they blocked her view of Rudd's door. She had once had a more proper room made by the innkeepers. Nailed-up boards and heavy quilts. When Rudd moved in, he claimed he was cold and took the quilts and yanked down the boards. He had been displeased when she made herself a cruder bit of privacy, but thankfully, he'd remained quiet about it.

'I have salves here.' Many of them. Her skin was sensitive to heat, to cold, and she often injured herself in the kitchens. Her skin could hardly take a scratch. 'I can care for myself.'

She hadn't had to take care of herself like this in a long time. Tonight reminded her how it felt to be helpless. She hated it more than the pain. She knew what it took to heal a body and straining it when it was already damaged wasn't wise. However, right now she just wanted him gone and she held her ground, though it was starting to cost her.

'I'm not harmed,' she said. 'Set me down.'

'It's the shock. You're trembling—when it eases, you'll feel the pain. We need to care for you quickly.' He looked around the room like he was trying to find an answer. It was too dark for him to see her bed and he slowly lowered her to the ground, but he did not let her go. One hand around her waist, the other at her elbow.

So easy to lean against him, and for an odd suspended moment that was exactly what she wanted to do. Instead, she stepped away from him. Only to stumble as her legs gave and his hold tightened.

'Your bed,' he said firmly.

She was trembling so much she couldn't hold herself up. 'I'll be fine.'

'We waste time arguing this. My man is out there.'

How could she have forgotten? One man against three. She nodded her head towards the corner and he half-carried her there, batted away the thin hanging sacks and set her down on the bed. Instant relief for her throbbing leg, but a sharp pain in her ribs. Swiping her tongue against the blood flowing from her lip, she tried to control her shaking body.

It was overwhelming to have this man in the same room with her. Rudd was large, broader, but somehow he didn't take up as much space. She hurt, felt sick, the last thing she wanted was to humiliate herself in front of him, and yet she simply sat as he stood over her.

She couldn't quite see him. Yet some odd pressure built between them and reverberated around the room. He was a stranger and yet familiar in a way she couldn't comprehend.

Silence held suspended between them as his hand went to the dagger at his waist, then his scabbard.

He glanced at his hand, then lowered it as if remembering what he'd left behind. The sword he pointed at the men. But he had knocked them unconscious with rocks when he could have easily killed them. It was another indication of the caliber of man he was. That he was well trained and honorable. But she didn't know the other man, who was a giant and sounded like he relished battering those men.

'Will he be all right?'

The room was dark, but not absolute. She could almost see the lifting of his arms, the untying of his cloak. Hear the heavy fabric pool to the floor.

'Your man, out there,' she explained. 'Rudd's unharmed. He could return and then—'

He made some sound, amusement and disbelief like her question surprised him. 'Nicholas can hold his own.'

There was something dangerous about his amusement and she was brutally reminded they were mercenaries. Hired swords. Men who made their living on violence and killing. Yet, she wasn't afraid of him. He had been kind to her and liked her cakes.

'Do you want them?'

He suddenly stilled.

'The cakes,' she explained around the split in her lip. 'There's twenty-five of them cooling in the kitchen.'

He jerked as if the words she gave were a blow he wasn't expecting—was he disappointed there weren't fifty?

Her stomach dipped. He'd saved her tonight and gave her enough money for fifty cakes. This was how she repaid him, by being a thief. 'I don't have the money to return it to you.'

'No money. No…cakes.' He stepped back, another, turned as he found the table in the middle of the room and lit the lone candle there.

For one brief moment the entirety of his face was lit, then he moved away. It was enough for her to blink. To wonder if tricks played with the shadows or if the pain affected her eyesight. No one could be that beautiful.

She moved to stand. 'I'll get the salves.'

'Stay. Direct me,' he said from the shadows.

The lone candle flickered in the small dark room. It illuminated enough so when she pointed behind him, he could find on a smaller table against the wall a pitcher, basin, and linens she kept there for her skin. When he stepped forward to pick up the small clay pot, the candlelight flickered against his half-turned body.

She'd only seen him in the dim light of the inn and while there she was too busy to linger, to watch. Now he was standing and all she could do was see him.

His face was still in shadows, but the rest… The rest of his body spoke of wealth and a masculine symmetry of strength that could only come from years of training. She'd never seen a man built like him. Elegant. Lethal.

He removed the lid, sniffed it and jerked back.

Her smile stung her split lip. 'It takes some getting used to.'

'Is this it?' He covered the top with his hand.

She nodded and couldn't hide her wince.

'Where does it hurt?'

She wasn't trembling at all now. In the quiet cocoon of darkness, her heart had stopped racing. She hurt everywhere. Her cheek had swollen, her cut lip throbbed. Her legs and wrists where they'd restrained her burned. Mostly she was having difficulty breathing. 'Here.' She pointed to her ribs.

Another hesitation on his part. 'Is there anyone else to care for you?'

'I care for myself. I can do this.'

'Not this.' She felt his frown. 'I'll need to feel if you have any broken ribs. I won't be able to feel it over that dress. You'll need to remove it.'

His words were suddenly firm, like he expected her to protest. He was probably used to women with modesty. He couldn't know she'd lost that as a child when the healer kept her naked for months, when the innkeepers applied the honey salve over the areas of her body she couldn't reach.

She wasn't modest, it had been burned away

from her, but she was very much aware of how she looked to others, who hadn't seen the worst of her scars. Along her torso, her scars were deep slashing grooves where the flaming rafters had pinned her before she could free herself.

A pounding on the door made her jump.

'It's Nicholas,' a male, muffled voice called out.

Her stranger opened the door. 'They're taken care of,' Nicholas reported holding out a sword. 'But the third returned and...'

'What did he do to you?' she gasped. Both men glanced her way.

'He...er...showed to the party.' Nicholas's grim expression looked almost amused as he returned his attention to her stranger. 'He'll be waking with a headache. When he wakes. It'll also take him a while to return.'

'How far?' Her shadow man sheathed his sword.

'To that thick of trees we passed to the South. I would have taken him further, but didn't know if there'd be any more guests.'

'There aren't any more,' she said.

Both men inspected her briefly. 'Give me a moment,' her stranger said, as he stepped outside.

She heard the men talk, but not the words. It was enough for her to know they'd spent many years together. Nicholas's voice was laced with amusement like he relished hurting his guests. Guests. Words she never would use with those men. But the word was significant because these men, these mercenaries, knew she was listening and used gentler words around her.

Kindness again. She was unused to it since the innkeepers passed away. Agnes, the healer, had cared for her, but hadn't shown her the same gentleness for her feelings.

She hadn't thought of the healer this much in years. But instantly knew why she was reminded. It was the men now talking behind the half-opened door.

Their words were efficient. Practical. The healer had cared for her in much the same determined manner. When the pain was bad, it was the healer's firm voice that broke through it and made her carry on. Like here. Scars or not, her ribs demanded she carry on and so she made a decision.

Her stranger stepped back into the room and closed the door. 'You won't have to worry about those men. They're gone.' He turned to her and stopped. 'Your dress.'

'I took it off. I'm having trouble breathing and I know nothing about broken bones. But it's sharp and stabbing me worse than their knife point. Will you be able to feel through my chemise?'

With the door closed, he was all in darkness. 'Yes. Sit, but do not lie down.' He grabbed the candlestick in one hand and the small table with the linens and water in the other.

The echoing scrape of the table as it was brought closer was unnaturally loud in the small room. Nervous, she ran her hands down her chemise and sat. It immediately constricted her breathing, but eased the shaking in her legs.

She wasn't prepared at all when he stopped pulling the table. Wasn't prepared as he lowered the candle so he could inspect her face…and revealed all of his. The lone candle flickered and dimmed with his movements, but she could see him and she was stunned.

Perfection. His hair was cut short on the sides and long on top. Blond, but with a gold tinge like honey in the sunlight, his brows were darker. His lowered lashes were darker yet and absurdly long and thick as he regarded the injuries to her lip and cheek.

His cheekbones elegantly framed the square jaw and slight cleft in his chin. And lips, light pink, almost full if not for the sardonic masculine curve to them. A man who knew humor… or at least once had.

His brow furrowed and there was a twitch to his lips before his eyes flashed to hers as if to determine something. She didn't know what because it took all she had not to react to the further reveal.

There was no way not to react. Her eyes widened and watered from not blinking. Her lips parted, her breath hitched and she experienced every surprise reaction anybody would under the circumstances.

Beautiful? He wasn't real. His eyes...they were amber colored. If his hair was light like the tips of a flame, his eyes were dark like honey heated by that fire.

As she watched, they darkened more, his chin tilting almost defiantly.

It was the defiance that broke whatever spell he cast. Defiance. As if he dared her to stare more. It was a look she had given many times when someone had gaped at her marred face. His made no sense to her. She forced people to look so they'd leave her alone.

Why defiance from him when he was perfection? He shouldn't need to be left alone. She didn't know the answer to that, but he had showed her only kindness and she was being rude. 'I'm Helissent.'

He quickly set the candle on the table and was again cast in shadows. But he hadn't set the candlestick aside fast enough. The defiance in his eyes had eased; however, his look remained guarded or trapped as if he didn't trust her introduction. It was an odd look coming from a mercenary, who just took down two men and made another run for his life.

Rhain almost groaned. Nicholas was right, he shouldn't be here. Neither in this part of the country, nor this tiny village and certainly not in this woman's home.

Restless, he kept his shift patrolling the town, which had no gates or walls for protection. Any of Reynold's men would have access to the buildings here. It was the perfect place for an ambush.

He should be proud he stopped an actual ambush even though it wasn't for him or his men, but this lone woman, who made cakes in the middle of the night when she shouldn't.

But he wasn't proud; he was a fool. He hadn't thought before he attacked. He reacted as he had in London. This time though he should have known better.

At first he did. The men's menacing voices meant nothing...until he heard hers.

Then he'd stopped. Her voice carrying on the wind. He shouldn't have recognized it because he'd never heard it above a soft whisper. But he did, and it wasn't just the tone of it, but the stridency. She was afraid.

Still, he intended to walk away. Nothing in this village was his concern. Especially not Rudd's more easily understood words about the innkeepers' debts.

When she screamed, when the piercing cry was cut short, nothing else mattered except getting to her.

But that led him to here. Alone in her home, telling her he would tend to her like he was some caretaker. Worse, she sat on the bed garnering full view of his face and all but asking for his name. He had enemies and his enemies had spies.

He was giving this poverty-stricken woman information that could make her rich, and for Reynold to find him that much faster.

He could rationalize his actions only so far. That she had no one else. That he had some skill with this and it wouldn't take long. Except he'd already been here in her room longer than logic or reason dictated.

Now she was introducing herself, and somewhere inside him insisted he answer. Maybe it was his breeding, certainly it was his manners; none of it was his instinct for survival.

'Rhain,' he replied.

Her wariness eased and her eyes lit. 'You're from Wales.'

More than foolish. He had not told her where he hailed from. Had purposefully kept the information, but she lived in an inn, and recognized his accent.

She probably expected him to talk of his homeland as he tended her injuries. As if all of this was some common occurrence.

Reynold on the manhunt to kill him aside, he felt no part of Welsh soil any more. He'd been gone only five years, but when he left, he severed that part of him. That home was dead to him. Should have been dead to him, except he carried a Welsh name, and carried the country in the cadence of his words.

He should have hidden it from her. His name was enough to harm him if he was caught. Hurt her if Reynold so decided. The irony was not lost on him. He'd saved her, only to get her killed. 'Have you no pillow?'

Not waiting for her response, Rhain abruptly strode to the other room before he emerged again with Rudd's pillow.

Helissent knew when to keep her mouth shut. She'd had years of biting her tongue against rude or cruel taunts, but she wasn't prepared for any of this.

She'd gone from elated exhaustion to abject terror. Then he'd swooped in like some avenging angel, who now insisted on caring for her. Her body felt like it was all real, but her mind felt that this must be some dream. Yet, his accent made him at least human, and she reached out for the little familiarity between them. To make sense of everything.

Now she feared she had made him angry. Her violent trembles had ceased but her entire body could not stay still. 'I'm sorry, I only meant... I do not know you and tonight has been...'

He cursed low and fast and threw the pillow on her bed. He did not finish her sentence or add words of his own to ease her tumultuous thoughts.

Pain stung her, and her breaths hurt more since she sat down. The silence between them stretched out as if he was coming to some decision. She felt the flickering of the candle on her and his studying eyes. The air between them thickened. She didn't even know what it was. Anger. Wariness. Danger...it felt dangerous. As though she was in the dark and her feet were walking a cliff side.

He let out a gust of breath. 'Your cheek is swelling. I may need to nick it to ease the pressure. Your lip will heal with salve. There are burns around your wrists. Any other injuries besides your ribs?'

He had not answered her questions, but talking of injuries was something familiar. She shook her head. Nothing serious. There were parts of her body that she could not feel. But when she took off her gown, she felt her body through her chemise and nothing bled.

'If you place your hands to your sides, I can check your ribs. I may hurt you.'

Did he think she'd balk at pain? She'd lived through fire. She placed her hands to her sides so her elbows stood out from her and he'd have more access.

He shifted his sword and sat next to her.

She'd only ever been this close to the innkeepers and healer. This man was neither of them. When he placed his hands flat on her back she felt every bit of that difference. Warm palms, elegant widespread fingers. All held flat, and steady. Maybe he was getting her used to his hands as if she'd claimed some modesty she had never felt. Then he slid his hands down her back, his fingers doing a fluttering walking movement, and she gasped. He immediately stopped.

'Did it hurt? Is it your ribs?'

No, it was his hands on her. Terror from Rudd, pain from the men, and now this suspended moment with this stranger. A moment that held even longer until she shook her head.

'Is it from the other injuries?'

Injuries, she had no other injuries, and then she remembered. He talked of her skin. Her *skin*. She had never forgotten it in the past. Every movement, every stray glance in the inn, every night when she used a salve she was reminded of it.

How could she forget even for a moment? Was it him? No, it couldn't be. Maybe she forgot because she was in shock or pain. It couldn't be because for a few moments in the dark, with him and his touch, her scars didn't matter. Right now her skin was fine, her ribs were hurting.

'No, it's not the other injuries.'

He moved his hands again, but watched more carefully for her response. Consequently, she tried to hold them in. Then his finger prodded and she couldn't.

'There,' she gasped.

He prodded again, maybe more gently, but it didn't feel like it. 'And there.'

He made some sound like distress or agreement. Then he fluttered his hands low around her front and the burning continued until she was panting to get air into lungs that refused to expand.

He yanked his hands away. 'Does the pain go further up?'

The pain was everywhere, she nodded her head.

'Feel them as I did.'

She hesitated, her body didn't want to move.

'I can't touch you there. Surely you know I can't touch you there?'

He looked more confused than she felt. Then she remembered, he worried for her modesty again. It wasn't something she had to practice, let alone realize she was supposed to feign.

'Of course.' She felt along her ribs, both her hands and fingers doing the spider-walking movement he had done.

'Nothing's moved?' he said. 'Your ribs, do any feel loose?'

'The pain radiates on my right. Am I to press harder?'

'No, don't. You'd know immediately if anything was broken.' He let out a breath. 'You're bruised, maybe fractured. We won't know that unless you are further harmed or the healing takes longer than a few weeks.' He stood and grabbed the pot. 'This salve is for your skin. Does it have other healing properties?'

'It helps with pain.'

He nodded his head. 'You can apply it to your front, but you're in no condition to apply it to your back.' He stopped, looked over her shoulder briefly. 'Will you permit me?'

His hands had seared through her chemise. Warm, large, unfamiliar and yet like everything about him, something that calmed and reassured her. A mercenary. A knight. So far from her realm of familiarity, she should be as terrified of him as she was of the men he chased away.

She felt no such fear, but she knew what her skin felt like. Did she dare let this man touch her?

'My mother…' He turned the pot in his hand. 'My mother was a healer. This smells familiar.'

Helissent licked her swollen lip. 'Did she work with burns?'

'Yes.'

'Like mine?'

He looked over at her then, his eyes locked with hers. 'No, but I watched her.'

What was he telling her? Nothing. He neither knew how to care for burns such as hers, nor had he ever done it himself. But there was something in the way he said it that put a sentiment she understood. Pain. He understood pain and that was enough.

She untied the lacing that bound her breasts within her chemise. When it was loose, she moved to shrug it off her, but his hand suddenly pressed upon her shoulder.

'Stop.'

She'd been avoiding looking at him when he had sat so close. When he touched and inspected her. She had completely averted her head as she felt along her breasts though she was sure he had not averted his eyes. She had been tended before, this should have been nothing but a normal everyday occurrence.

This wasn't like those times. *He* wasn't like those times. He was like no one she had ever met before and everything in her knew it.

Looking at him confirmed that now. The candle was behind him, but she caught glimpses of his perfect symmetry within the flickering flame.

He was stunning, he was standing close and his hand was on her shoulder. She was terrified, hurting, but whatever her body was feeling was none of those emotions.

'Your chemise is loose enough.' He poured some of the pungent mixture in one hand, as he peeled the chemise away from her back. 'Hold the front as I apply this.'

It was dark, the chemise would further shade her skin. He couldn't see her scars, but in a moment he'd feel them. Her torso was much worse than her face. Terribly worse and he seemed to sense it when he leaned a knee on her bed, laid his hands on her back and stopped.

He held his breath. She knew she held hers until she cleared her thoughts at being touched again like this.

She'd never been touched like this. But she needed to let him know he wasn't harming her.

'It's all right… You can't hurt me further. My skin. I hardly feel anything on that side,' she whispered frantically. She wanted this suspended moment over. It had gone on too long. His man was outside guarding the door. Rudd could appear and she shouldn't have a man in her home.

All of that didn't matter, because her shock was wearing off, but not the pain.

He made a sound as though he was stopping himself from saying something, then he slid his hands along her back, slowly, gently, efficiently. Practical.

It didn't feel practical. She lied when she said she couldn't feel anything. On her left, she felt everything. The roughness of his callouses, the heat from his hands. The gentle, gentle pressure that radiated something deep within her.

When he reached the lower part of her back, he let out a breath, but she couldn't seem to release hers.

Then she felt his studying gaze again and realized his hands had reached the deepest grooves of her skin. She was used to them, but she should have prepared him more. He confessed his mother hadn't treated anyone as bad as she.

'They don't hurt; it merely feels as though it does.' Her voice remained steady. Efficient, as his hands.

He huffed out another breath, but he widened his fingers and smeared the mixture until it started to stick, then abruptly he removed his hands.

Just as abruptly he stepped away and out of the candle's light only to loosen his belt and yank his fine linen tunic off. 'You need to apply the salve to your front,' he said as he began to rip his tunic into jagged strips. 'I need to bind your ribs. It'll help secure them if they're fractured; remind you that you're hurt before you move too fast. Tie your chemise's laces and stand.'

His request was kind, but his words were rough, like orders. Dipping her fingers into the pot, she wondered about his past that made him like this. She knew he wasn't always so rough or direct. She'd watched him for days. He had made jokes with the other men, drank ale from the goblet like it was wine.

Then there was an innate sense of elegance in every movement he made. Pulling her chemise away from her body and gently rubbing the familiar salve over her sore ribs. Refinement even in something as simple as tying his tunic scraps together.

He came back into the lone flickering light. The linen tied around his right fist, a strip in his left. A look of gentle determination about his face as he looked everywhere but at her eyes. Her eyes which took him in. It was as if the candlelight wanted her to see him for it flared brighter when she stood. The fit of his breeches, the low-slung angle of his belt and scabbard, the bareness of his torso. He was golden all over like heated honey. Like shadows, like light.

Eyes lowered, he kept his silence, though it

seemed troubled now. She remembered his wary defiant look from before and raised her arms so he could press the end below her collarbone. Then he took her hand to hold it there before weaving the fabric tightly around her.

He circled her while she kept her eyes straight, trying not to see, at the same time he kept his lowered as if he was trying to hide from her. But always, always his methodical movements flared the candle so that each swing around, his body was revealed to her more.

Utter perfection. Utter beauty. If a man could be called that. If a mercenary dared. Not even the few scars she glimpsed or one bruise that darkened his side marred the contours of his splayed back, the ridges of his abdomen.

She dropped her arms after the second turning. Saw him drop his shoulders as the linen bound tightly around her breasts, around her middle.

Collarbones that jutted. Shoulders curving with sinuosity even in the refrained movements of his hands.

All of it golden, all of it in shadows in the flared light. All of it too much as he finished the task and tied the knot.

'Your cheek is swollen, but not overly so,' he said. 'I will leave it.'

Then there was nothing else. He was done. *They* were done.

'It was you this entire time.' He stepped back, and grabbed his cloak. 'With the food, with the cakes. You're the one who made it all?'

She nodded.

'It was good. Very good.' He continued towards the door. When he reached it he said in a tone that was firm, but apologetic, 'I won't be here tomorrow. We're leaving early.'

She couldn't say anything. He wouldn't be here when Rudd returned, but she wasn't surprised.

As if reading her thoughts, he added, 'There's nowhere else you could go, no one else you could stay with?'

'My family died a long time ago.'

Though he'd never gazed overtly at her before, he did so now as his eyes roamed from her face down to her scarred and battered hand. His lips thinned as if stopping words from escaping before he said, 'You should rest now.'

She was tired and intended to rest. She needed it. She could no more stop Rudd than she could the fire, but she would survive both. She was only realizing how it could be done.

'Rhain,' she said through the tightening in her throat.

He stopped, looked over his shoulder.

'Thank you,' she said.

She'd surprised him; his eyes lit and she saw something restless beneath his steady gaze, then he opened the door. She heard Nicholas's words, a sound of amusement and Rhain's low rebuke before he shut the door behind him and all was silent.

But it wouldn't be for long. Before she released the breath she'd been holding, she knew what she had to do.

Chapter Five

Rhain heard the tethered horses and the jingle of tackle through the morning's drizzling air. His men's voices were low and unusually somber. There would be a storm today. He hated riding in the rain and it would be worse if the wind kicked up.

When he rounded the corner he saw his men who were no doubt wondering why they rode today. Before London, he never would have travelled on days like this. In inclement weather, many a wealthy and powerful family was forced to wait for their arrival. He wasn't soft, but wise. He valued his men, their safety and health, they were in turn valued by their patrons. It was a simple game of appearance.

Now, he couldn't take such a luxury as waiting out the weather. It was early, but already the village was wakening and many were loitering in the streets, watching them in curiosity. They had garnered enough attention in this tiny village.

He tried not to look over his shoulder at the inn behind him; he tried not to think of the woman he was leaving behind, and as his stomach growled he tried not to think of the best cakes he had ever tasted in his life wasting in the kitchens.

'You readied my horse?' he said, as he patted the horse's neck.

'You slept in late.' Nicholas shrugged.

'You were there; you know why.'

He and Nicholas hadn't slept but an hour or two. He left Helissent's home with a purse full of coin. It was considerably lighter after he and Nicholas knocked from door to door. Waking families, telling them what had occurred, paying them to protect Helissent should it come to it.

A troubled night and one where he had little faith in people. They should have already helped her before some stranger paid them to.

'Yes, but I didn't sleep late and miss all the excitement,' Nicholas said.

His thoughts plagued by a certain woman, who smelled of cakes, he couldn't fall asleep as Nicholas had. 'Excitement?'

'He means me,' a voice behind him said. A *female* voice.

Rhain spun around. Standing next to his men, wearing most likely all the clothing she had, plus the tattered blanket he'd spread over her, stood Helissent.

'What is she doing here?' he said.

Nicholas arched his brow. 'You gave her your tunic. I know how you like to care for stray dogs. This wasn't also part of your plan?'

'You know the plan and adding another isn't part of it.' Rhain waved his hand in her direction. 'Especially not a woman.' He didn't care what Helissent heard, but he kept his voice low. His men didn't need to hear his argument. 'What did you tell the men?'

Nicholas unclenched his fingers around the bridle. 'I didn't tell the men anything. They came to their own conclusions.'

Rhain looked to his men, who were no longer talking, but avidly looking at the proceedings. There was no amusement on his behalf or annoyance that a woman was in their midst. They were simply openly glaring at him. What conclusions had they come to?

Nicholas gave a saluting smirk before he walked the horse to the men and said a few words. Rhain swore he heard laughter, but his focus was on the woman staring levelly at him.

He still couldn't comprehend the color of her

eyes, even in daylight, but he understood the emotion behind them.

If she was stubborn, he would break her. If she was afraid, he'd keep it that way. He had precious little time left. He'd spent too much in the inn eating her food and too much time in her home, kneeling on her bed last night.

Last night... He'd slept in because he hadn't been able to sleep until exhaustion took him. Until he'd been able to stop his wandering thoughts of a scarred barmaid who'd stared with wide eyes at him in the flickering candlelight. Who'd sat stoically as he tended her. As his body shook with rage at what those men had done. Then he'd felt her back and he'd wanted to gather her to him, weep and rage some more.

His lack of sleep would deter him enough for the day if he didn't have distractions, which the woman who stood in front of him most definitely was. If for no other reason she extracted emotions from him he had no intention of feeling.

'What are you doing here?'

'I brought you the cakes.' She pointed to a sack at her feet. A large sack that matched the one next to it.

'I was going to leave them in the kitchen,' he said.

'I know,' she said.

He knew she knew. He could see in her eyes, and the tight bracketing around her mouth, she wasn't happy that he'd left the cakes.

'I only thought—'

'I told you to keep the cakes.'

She opened her clutched hand, revealing the coins he gave her. 'Then I'll have to give you back the money.'

'I told you to keep the money.'

'But I won't.'

An honest barmaid. A stubborn one, but a battle on the cakes wasn't one he wanted to win. He shrugged. 'So I'll take your cakes. You keep the money. You'll need it.'

'It's not mine either. It'll return to Rudd's hiding place as soon as we're done here.'

A moment of displeasure and frustration. He didn't want that vermin anywhere near his money. She made the cakes, she deserved the money. Especially since he fully intended to leave her in this village.

But his feeling of guilt wasn't what alerted him to something else she said. Guilt he could live with.

No, what caused him to look over her shoulder at his men and narrow his eyes, was that she acted as though they were bartering. As far as he was concerned, the transaction was over. He reached down and took one of the sacks at her feet.

'I want you to take me with you,' she said.

Rhain could feel his men's eyes on him. He most definitely could feel Nicholas's smirk even from this distance. How long had she been here before he arrived? Long enough for his horse to be saddled and prepared. Long enough for her to approach the men and ask to leave with them. And Nicholas, who knew what happened last night, knew he'd spent most of the time tending to her injuries, giving her his tunic for binding. Nicholas, who'd obviously come to the wrong conclusion.

Take her with them? Not on his life. 'No.'

'I won't be any burden; I can hold my own.'

Hold her own? He could barely look at her this morning, though it was the first time he saw her fully in the light.

The heavy shrouding mist made her look more bedraggled than ever before. Bedraggled? She looked like she was in pain. It pained him to look at her. It wasn't only the bruises on her face or the way she held herself protectively.

It was what was in her eyes. She didn't expect him to say no to her request and she took his refusal personally.

He couldn't have anyone on this journey, let alone a lone woman. No matter what she said next he would not take her. His men were openly glaring at him now and some of the Flanders men had stepped closer to her. He didn't care if they didn't like his judgement. His men would be better off without him as well, and if he made it to Edward's camp, he fully intended to leave them there.

'You aren't in any condition to travel.'

She winced as if he slapped her across the cheek. 'I'm stronger than I look.'

He knew she was stronger than she looked; her standing before him was testament to that. Her determination to be part of a band of mercenaries showed her bravery, but he could see the trembles beneath. Despite himself, he admired her standing firm.

If he didn't have someone after him, would he take her? Given his anger at just the thought of last night, he knew the answer. Unfortunately for them both, he didn't have the luxury of such questions. Though he had been taught a lesson, Rudd might try to harm her, but he was too much of a coward to kill her. Reynold would.

'Do you know what we are?'

'Mercenaries,' she said evenly.

'Then you know we murder and thieve for a living. Can you kill and steal?' He stared pointedly until her eyes turned mutinous. 'I didn't think so. You are of no use to us. You will only be a burden.'

* * *

Helissent forced herself to look directly into Rhain's gaze, clear as anything despite the hood he wore. Forced herself not to turn when his eyes roved all over her features taking in every old and new injury. Out of a lifetime of habit, she turned her head to display her scarred side. Felt his eyes there, but they didn't stay and he didn't wince or show pity.

It was probably because he already took his fill of her scars last night.

The moment Rhain left last night, she'd planned her escape. It didn't matter how much Rhain or his man Nicholas threatened Rudd. They would be gone and Rudd would seek his vengeance. She couldn't remain.

There was no home for her any more. She had to find a home of her own and the only way to do that was to get out of the village. But a woman travelling alone wouldn't get very far. She had to travel with this man. This man who told her he wouldn't take her.

'I was told you intend to travel north. I merely want passage to York. I can cook. I know you have no one doing that for you now.'

A certain light entered his eyes. A calculating disapproval. She wasn't sure as he eyed the men behind her. 'You were told our destination and told we had no one to cook for us.' Then he raised one sardonic brow and she felt all the mockery of all the ages bearing down on her. 'These men are not pampered and do not need fine fare.'

She wasn't prepared for him to say no, let alone a rebuttal, but she wouldn't give up. 'I can help with horses, or generally. I hardly eat anything at all.'

He slowly shook his head through her suggestions and his lips turned almost cruel. 'If there's a woman in the camp, there would be only one reason she was there.'

At first, she didn't understand. There was nothing in her history to allow her to understand. It was only how the men behind him suddenly stiffened and shifted. It was merely the cutting cruelty of his voice that reminded her about last night. Last night when he rescued her from those men, who'd almost raped her.

Did he believe she'd burst into womanly tears and run away? Never. He was telling her if she went with them she'd be a camp whore. She didn't blush because she wasn't capable. Even so, she wanted to laugh. Broken, brittle, but genuine all the same. Did he think his men would actually want her? Nobody would want her. She didn't even want herself. She hadn't saved her sister from the fire as she promised—like a coward she wanted the flames to consume her, too. Now she wore the deep scars of that shame.

And all of that, though true, wasn't at the heart of the matter. Because last night she was almost raped or worse and he had saved her. She did know one truth. He wasn't Rudd. 'Are you telling me I'll be treated worse than I was last night?'

The brackets around his tight jaw and mouth didn't soften with remorse or pity. Instead, a muscle jumped in his jaw.

Then he flipped his cape to the side and reached in a pouch around his waist. She heard the unmistakable sound of coins as he opened his hand and offered them to her without looking at the amount.

When she didn't step forward, he threw them on to the bag at her feet and addressed the youngest one in the group who had walked closer to her. In fact, all the men almost circled her. Their frowns were fierce and she felt a shiver of nervousness.

She didn't know these men despite approaching them this morning. Despite speaking to the man called Nicholas, who suffered from a sword scar across one eye and was larger than any man had the right to be.

The rest had stayed quiet as she'd talked to Nicholas. Some had eyes as cold and unforgiving as any mercenary's eyes, while others appeared merely curious. It was Nicholas who was friendly, though he seemed to have some agenda when he said she could wait for Rhain to arrive. So that's all she did. Wait, while shivering from the mist and trembling from the pain and exhaustion. She waited.

Now these men looked as though they meant to haul her away, so she widened her stance. She waited because there was no other place for her to go. She'd fought those men last night and she would do it again.

Rhain faced them all and pointed to the boy. 'Take those bags and help her return home.'

When he turned to her, she felt his stare, felt the animosity from him. She had meant to insult him with her comment and succeeded. He'd saved her and she'd lumped him in with her would-be rapists. But he still refused to take her.

After his generous coin for her cakes, after he complimented them and her, after he saved her, she thought he was kind. But in the light of morning, she reflected on the other sides to him. The fact he was a mercenary and he kept his hood up, as if hiding his face, like a wanted man. The fact he knocked those men unconscious with deadly accuracy and today she heard the cold hardness in his voice. Then there were his shadows. Always his shadows.

She didn't know this man at all. He fully intended to leave her here even knowing Rudd awaited her. She had no other compensation to offer for her passage, nothing to barter with except his sweet tooth.

'I made the rest of the cakes,' she said in a rush.

Stillness. Unnatural. As if she'd shocked him. No sharp breath, no blinking of his amber eyes. His face, his body as unmoving as stone now covered with heavy mist that was turning to rain falling harder and soaking them.

It darkened his clothes, his countenance. His implacable eyes swirled with more emotions than she could name. More emotions than he'd shown last night when he stopped those men. When he tended her wounds.

'You made twenty-five cakes last night,' he said, enunciating each word until they held a bite.

'And I made twenty-five more this morning,' she added.

He leaned forward as if to strangle her and just held back. Even so, she felt his anger, surprise and displeasure as his eyes raked down her now-drenched form.

She knew she was lacking, knew she was disfigured. But she could cook and bake; she was resourceful. When he left last night, she'd gathered her strength as she thought through her plan of leaving the only home she had. When she'd made up her mind, she left for the kitchens.

It made sense for Rhain to take her. He had to

know her situation. There was no way she could get his money back and consequently she made the rest of the cakes. Even though the kitchen's heat had pained her more than ever and her ribs protested her every move. But it was worth it because she wanted to thank him for last night and for the expected ride today.

She didn't think it would come to this. That she would be bargaining a life for herself over some flour and honey. That she would be using a cake to prove she was worthy of him taking her.

'We have no horse for you,' he said.

The village didn't have any spares. 'I didn't expect a horse.'

Her heart flipped and churned until she was sure he would notice. Something had changed, but she tried not to get her hopes up. He wasn't saying no any more, though nothing he said yet proved otherwise. He merely talked of horses and convenience, but those were obstacles, not refusal. This couldn't truly be about his sweet tooth, but exactly what it was about, she didn't know.

His tightly locked countenance told her nothing. Especially since even though his hood was up, he was almost too precisely beautiful to be real. The only indications that he was real were the slight exasperation of his breath and the fleeting emotions in his amber eyes.

'I'm not a savior,' he said.

She, of all people, knew no one was and that she didn't deserve one. 'I'm not asking you to be.'

He nodded once, scanned his eyes around the men before he said, 'She rides with me.'

Chapter Six

Rhain regretted his action immediately. It wasn't the delay of departing the village, though by the time they strapped Helissent's few possessions to the horses, and sat her atop his own, the rain had begun to fall in earnest.

The sky was darkening in every direction. The storm was coming and soon even a modicum of comfort, of carrying on a conversation, would be denied them.

Even that he could ignore. He couldn't ignore the woman bundled until he shouldn't feel her and yet her trembles became his. He didn't know why she trembled, it could be the cold. It could be fear. Over Rudd and leaving her home? Or did she fear them? If she did fear his band of mercenaries, it wasn't enough to make her stay away.

It didn't matter he and Nicholas came from nobility. Their lineage was in the past. They were no more or less than what they made of themselves now, which were killers for a price.

Yet this woman had begged to travel with them. He didn't need to guess why and anyone who had suffered as she had would have to be stubborn and brave.

But his admiration for her or her stubbornness wasn't why she rode with him, why he felt her trembles. Why he hadn't kept his hood up for her last night.

For he hadn't.

And she hadn't done what every other woman had ever done. He'd expected it, had taken advantage of it at one point of his life. His face had simply been his reality.

She'd stared and then averted her eyes. It had been almost amusing, if not for the disconcerting fact he actually wanted her eyes on him.

He didn't recognize what it was about her, but he had felt it the moment he entered the inn and it raged like an inferno through him when he realized those men meant to harm her.

Then in the quiet of her home, she'd allowed his touch. She had braced herself, hid her gasps, but she still let him close enough to feel her.

He hadn't thought to brace himself as he touched her. He'd been intent only to see if she'd fractured a rib, only wanted to relieve her pain with the ointment. So he hadn't been ready for how his own body reacted.

The soft heat of her skin, the way she smelled. The feel and textures of her underneath his fingertips. All of it should have made him only think of her injuries, but that wasn't what he had felt at first.

First he felt her as a man would a woman and desire recklessly arced through him. He couldn't move, couldn't speak because he had to choke the sounds of need clamoring suddenly inside him.

Unexpected, and all because of her. Only her. His reaction had nothing to do with his lack of female companionship. Over the years more women than he could count had bent over him or abruptly sat in his lap. Trailed their hands and fingers along any part of him they could reach and he'd felt nothing.

All of that dead to him because he had to make it so. Because when he'd learned the truth of his lineage, he could never take matters further with a woman.

So he hadn't been prepared he'd feel anything when he touched her. He shouldn't have felt anything when she was *hurting*.

All of it was made worse when she took his frozen state as revulsion because she spoke those broken words about her scars. Only then did he realize too late what else he felt.

The roughness warring with the softness of her skin underneath his fingers. That was enough to jar him, to remind him she was injured, and he needed to check for broken bones and apply the ointment.

But it didn't stop his desire for her, not when she inspected herself and he'd wished it could be his fingers trailing along the front of her ribcage and the gentle swells hinted there.

Desire, which was all the more torturous when he yanked off his tunic and watched her eyes widen, her lips part.

Felt the echoing of his desire from the air on his bared skin and the tightening of his body. As he stood half-naked in the dark intimate quiet of the room, she was suddenly someone he needed. His mind and body in complete conflict with each other, he'd viciously stripped his tunic and tied the ends.

All to bind her and unerringly tighten his need as he walked slowly around and watched what the tight binding revealed, what the thin chemise did not.

Her slender shape, the curves of her breasts, the indentation of her waist, the breadth of her collarbones, the curve of her jaw. Her long, long legs. Another circle and he knew exactly the height of those legs, the width and shape of her hips, the location of each jutting bone and all her womanly softness.

All of her, every inch of her in proportion to him. Just a few inches shorter, just enough so when he pressed and lifted her against him, she'd fit. They'd fit.

He couldn't leave her home quick enough. To get out into the cool night air. To Nicholas's sharp wit and even sharper watchful eyes.

But not fast enough. He'd heard her thank him and felt the visceral regret, the frustrating anger that his life wasn't different and could never be. Then he'd closed the door and left her behind.

Except she didn't stay behind. He did what he could to separate from her on this journey. Kept his own conflicted counsel, allowed her to find her own way when they stopped to rest. The men, at least, fed her and shared their water.

It did no good, he still felt her trembles and he bundled her as much as he could against the cold. It wasn't her fault he didn't have enough sense to get out of the rain.

The day was ending and Helissent could barely acknowledge her surroundings. Hours like this in the downpour. They didn't even try to stay dry. There was no point. The wind would merely sweep away capes and blankets and hoods.

Maybe it was the rain, but there was no rest.

Allowing everyone to relieve themselves only once, Rhain kept the slow but unrelenting pace.

And the almost brutal silence. It was as if he said what he needed to and then refused to say any more. She thought at first it was the rain, but the others talked though they sputtered and shouted to be heard.

No, it was only for her he kept the quiet. Kept his anger. He had not wanted her on this trip and let her know his displeasure. Which made his reason for making her ride with him all the more confusing.

As did him swiftly pulling his cloak over him and her, and yanking her blanket to cover her. All of it seemed to cushion them from the driving rain, but didn't soften his utter silence. Subsequently, she was left with only her thoughts, only what she could observe. Both were like a downpour on her senses.

She'd left her home. Her village. A place where people knew who she was, who knew what happened to her and allowed her still in their presence.

She hadn't thought of that when she decided to leave. She had only been thinking it wasn't safe any more. But was she any safer outside her village, and from the villagers, who knew her home had burned to the ground with her family in it? Who knew she survived when she shouldn't have, when she tried not to because she failed to save her sister as she had promised?

Her village was her home and her cross to bear, and she had left it.

No. She was forced from it. The pain of the loss, the anger at her attack and what she had to do today was overwhelming. What other choice did she have? None.

She didn't even guess if this was a punishment for her shame and cowardice. She knew it was and would endure it as she had everything else.

But she didn't want to think these thoughts, to break down as she had done a thousand times in the past and pick herself up as she'd done just as often. Not in front of strangers.

These mercenaries were strangers and remained that way all day. Once in a while they'd glance at her or Rhain, but mostly they talked amongst themselves in languages she didn't know. When they stopped they were polite, helped her, but for the most part they left her alone.

Even more so as Rhain's frowns grew fiercer and his eyes held some turbulent light that caused Nicholas's gaze to grow more watchful.

She wondered about their strong friendship. Nicholas, a giant scar-faced man, eloquent with his words, but rough with his actions, and holding himself as proudly as Rhain.

But she didn't know about the other men whose ways with each other were strikingly different than the villagers. It wasn't only their ways that confused her. It was their ease with each other…and with her.

As they rode in the rain and her hair plastered to her side so it no longer hid her scars, she expected eyes that were bright with malicious curiosity or with horror and revulsion. She expected some to either resent or pity her. These were looks she'd received her entire life, from villagers, from other strangers.

Yet, she received none of those reactions. In fact, she didn't receive any reactions except that same curiosity as when she'd approached them that morning. As if all that concerned them was why she rode with them and shared her cakes, not who or what she was.

At least the rain eventually stopped as did the wind, and they could all lower their protection. The sun warmed her, but it did little to dry them. Clothes and leather squished and chaffed. Her journey, her hopes, her hardships mimicked by the weather.

The sun was much lower in the sky by the time the men in front of them slowed. When Rhain stopped their own horse, Helissent's entire body was equally seized and rocking forward.

Her skin was terribly tight. She could do nothing when Rhain set his hands on her hips and dismounted with ease. He kept one hand on her while she clutched the saddle.

'Can you dismount?' he said.

His first words to her since they left and she couldn't seem to answer him with a yes or no. In some part of her she heard him call Nicholas over. Nicholas, who with one eye assessed the situation immediately and walked to the other side of her.

All of which made her nervous. Alarmed. 'What are you doing?'

'What needs to be done.' Nicholas grabbed her ankle and pushed her leg up. While agony arced through her leg, Rhain pulled her towards him and off the horse.

Then he let her legs dangle as tingling, then pain, cut through every one of her bones and every inch of her skin. She glared at Nicholas, but he'd already returned to his own horse. Accordingly, all she had was Rhain, who still hadn't set her down.

Here she'd vowed she would be strong, wouldn't slow him down, and undermined her words by being unable to properly dismount a horse. 'Set me down.'

'Your legs can't take your weight.'

She didn't care. Humiliation was warring with

other emotions inside her. Like him securely holding her. His hands, his body becoming familiar when they shouldn't. She didn't need security, or familiarity. She'd rode with this man, seemed more saturated by him than the rain, and the ache inside her was beginning to hurt more than her legs or body.

She needed to be left alone. 'I can walk.'

He eased his hold, and she slid. Her body shuddered when her feet first pressed against the ground.

'All this for York?' he said, as if he teased, but was frustrated that he did so.

She saw him laugh with his men at the inn, but never any lightness directed towards her and certainly not last night when he'd almost killed those men.

Cold. Merciless, though he'd let them live. Then his anger at her this morning.

She only had to get to York. A large bustling city, where she could get lost on days she remembered the innkeepers, and punish herself when memories of her sister and family became too much to bear.

York would be her inn with people and strangers and regulars. People would need to eat and she'd find her way there somehow.

'There's no other place for me,' she said as he let her go. She would have toppled to the ground except she grabbed on to his horse at the last moment.

A horse he slowly led to the others that were being released of their burdens.

She couldn't let go and gripped the saddle as her legs wobbled in some sort of painful shuffle. But the horse ignored her as did Rhain. As did the rest of the men. Because of that she felt useless, but not foolish.

Again, a reaction she didn't expect. There was no cruel laughter, no pointing out her deficiencies. She had forced herself on this trip and was obviously a weakness to men like them. Not only for her being a woman, but one who could barely stand after a day's ride.

But she merited no more than a passing glance. Even in full sunlight when she knew her scars and the sloping of her eye were all the more hideously visible.

She couldn't make sense of it, subsequently she dismissed it because they were tired, soaked, hungry. Their thoughts were probably on their comfort and food. Already Rhain was talking with the younger man, Allen. Already they were removing the saddles, feeding the horses; it was time she was useful.

Her feet protested every step until she could ignore the pain as she had in the past. Work would help, but that would be difficult. The men bustled around her with purpose and ease. They had a system going, one honed out of years of working together.

Rhain was right. She had no place here. Yet if she could contribute nothing here, what would become of her in York? She truly would be on the streets.

She had nothing else now but herself. And as much shame and regret she had with her family, she wouldn't let the innkeepers down. They had spent time caring for her, and had written about it.

The parchment. She'd recovered it in the mud outside her home. She hadn't had an opportunity to read it. But it was wrapped and hidden in a pouch. A parchment with words from the healer to the innkeepers. About a time when she was a child, where only immense pain encompassed her world. Where she knew only loss. Her erudite French father, her caretaking English mother, her baby sister, who'd put her hand trustingly in hers. All gone. All lost.

She would always carry that shame. Felt it with every glance given her way. Ensured that people did see her scars so she would feel the pain and yet…

Yet, she would never try to end her life again because John and Anne had believed in her.

She hadn't believed Rudd's spiteful words.

That they saved her to become their servant. They did it because they loved her.

So she'd carry on. Carry the shame, carry the love. And a golden man as beautiful as an angel wouldn't deter her. She would get to York; she would find a place for herself.

To do that, she would start here at this camp. Where only a few men spoke English, but they all seemed to know what to do and what would happen next. For however long it would take to get to York, she would find a place for herself.

Like now. Rhain left with some of the men to hunt. He didn't even spare her a glance. But Nicholas did as he approached and said, 'He'll be gone for hours.'

Helissent forced her eyes away from Rhain's retreating back. It didn't and shouldn't matter that he was gone.

Who was he to her? A stranger, as was this man before her. But she was a traveler with them and they gave her their protection. For now, she would pay them back.

'Is there any dried meat left, water or herbs?'

His brow rose. 'We have some meat and enough water. The men wouldn't know a herb from a grass blade.'

She nodded. 'If I can have some of the meat and water, I will gather the sorrel we passed.

It'll be enough to start before they bring the rest of the meat.'

'To start what?'

'I intend to cook for you.'

He shook his head in amusement. Did he think she was asking for their supplies for herself? 'Land's wet; you won't be getting any fire.'

'I brought some kindling in my sack which should be dry enough. With what else we can find high in the trees, the fire won't smoke long before it catches. It'll be strong by the time they return.'

Nicholas smiled then and it lit the darkness of his one eye. But that wasn't why she stared. She realized how his smile softened his fearsome countenance and she could almost see the man he once was.

'It appears Rhain did something right after all,' he said. 'Let's get this kindling and start the fire. I know the Spaniards will be glad for the warmth. This weather is their weakness.'

She darted her eyes to the other men, who were darker in hair, eyes and skin, but not in manners, which were light and fluid as they unloaded the horses and set supplies on boulders and a large fallen tree.

Spanish. That was the language they spoke that she hadn't heard before. But the others that Rhain left with didn't speak the same language.

'Where do the others come from?'

'Flanders.'

A country she never heard of. 'Is it far?'

'It depends, but they are some of the best mercenaries in the world.'

Mercenaries. For a moment she was tempted to ask more questions, but it wouldn't get the work done. So, too, if she asked questions of them, she worried they'd ask questions of her. All she needed now to do was to reach her satchel that was with everyone else's.

Except she'd have to get by them and that would require words or at least to indicate what she needed and it was all foreign. She was used to people ignoring her, not talking with her in almost a friendly manner.

'They don't bite.' Nicholas nodded towards three men sharpening the tools. 'But the men from Flanders probably will.'

She almost smiled and caught herself in time. Knew that her face twisted in those moments and she didn't want these men seeing it.

As she approached, she expected the Spanish men to step away or stare, instead their eyes were merely questioning, almost friendly like Nicholas's.

Then one of them grabbed her scarred hand and said something in rapid Spanish. Startled, she tried to yank it back. But he held it firm until the man next to him said something sharply and he released his hold.

Nicholas approached then. The Spaniard who grabbed her hand pointed to her hand, then streaked his fingers across his unmarred face.

Helissent didn't need to comprehend the language to know she was insulted. She lifted her chin, tilted her face so they'd see the full extent of her scars. She felt that burn of familiar humiliation at her shame. Yes, she was scarred; yes, she'd failed her sister; yes, she'd scorched her soul with her cowardice. But they had enough staring and she had work to do. When she turned, Nicholas stopped her.

'Wait,' he said. 'I can't interpret what they are saying; give me a chance.'

'You haven't had to live with it. I know exactly what they are saying.'

His eyes turned kindly to her. 'Patience.'

Nicholas, whose face was as scarred as her own and who was friends with these men.

The Spaniard merely repeated the same words as he gestured to her hand and then to his arm.

The other Spaniard said something clipped, direct. The one who'd boldly grabbed her hand blushed. When he began to roll up the sleeve to his tunic, and she saw the raw reddened patch of peeling skin, she understood what he'd asked.

She didn't have a lot, but she would share every bit of her salve if it meant she could help these men.

The Flemish left him over an hour ago and Rhain still walked slowly back to camp. A camp he could see in the distance because of a brightly burning fire and the smell of food that shouldn't be cooking.

The food had been scarce, but the Flemish were master trappers, and he used a bow and arrow, stayed downwind and got lucky. In the end, they had enough food to last them for a few days, but expecting a weak fire with lots of smoke, they'd only stripped some of their kills by the stream.

Afterward, he cleaned himself. The water by the village provided little privacy, and here he could take his time. He breathed deeply now, knowing it was only he and his men. And Helissent, whom he had been avoiding.

Only a few more steps and he'd be clear of the trees. A few of his men already heard his approach and glanced his way, but not Helissent, who was bent over the fire that had guided him here.

She had made some sort of soup. The steam wafted from several small clay pots hanging over the fire. Rabbits hung next to them, their skin crackling in such a way to make the paltry meat they carried edible.

Her hair looked not brown as he thought it was, but golden and red in the fire's light and it curled wildly around her face though she had plaited it back at some point.

Which revealed all of her face to him. Though she kept it at an angle so her wounded side was tilted away from the fire's flames. He wondered if the heat hurt her, or if she subconsciously kept it away from flames that had caused the injury.

No. She never did anything subconsciously when it came to her scars. She made sure everyone saw them, so her averted face was because it hurt her. When he saw her wince as she reached over to lift one of the burdened sticks to turn the meat, an irrational concern flooded him.

What were his men, what was Nicholas, doing letting her work? He hurried his steps, but then she abruptly turned her head and stepped away from the fire to address Carlos.

Who shouldn't have been talking to her since he couldn't speak English. Who shouldn't be standing that close to her or turning around or pulling up his tunic as Helissent stepped even closer, as her hand reached out—

He stomped into the clearing and Carlos stepped quickly away, but not quick enough for him.

'I'm hungry,' he said, yanking a stick off the

fire. He didn't know if the meat was fully cooked and didn't care. He also didn't care if Nicholas's brow rose. All he cared about was getting this cursed journey over with. Then he could stick his own neck under Reynold's sword because he deserved it.

Chapter Seven

Stretching his arms behind his back, Rhain watched the men dismount and Helissent walk slowly to the woods to relieve herself.

She moved more slowly than she had yesterday and he knew she was hurting. As he had before, he didn't acknowledge her pain or injuries.

But he couldn't ignore it. He was too aware of her hurting and it pained him. What could he do? He knew what happened the last time he touched her and he wouldn't order the task to someone else. Not after he felt as he did when Carlos stood too close to her.

He might not be able to ignore her, but he could ignore his men's glares as he sat on a boulder and pulled out his mother's necklace from the pouch around his waist.

This necklace had been his focus for five years and would be for what remained of his life. As ever when he saw the silver glinting, everything came flooding back to him. The way his mother was in the last moments of her life, bloodied and in pain.

'Did you have to behave that way with her?'

He didn't raise his head at Nicholas's taunt, nor did he put the necklace away. Nicholas, who only knew he searched for the pendant, but not why, had seen it many times before.

'A few kind words would not go unnoticed by her…or the men.'

He should have known Nicholas wouldn't walk away. The man was relentless, forging in where he didn't belong, where it wasn't safe to go. It lost him an eye once and still he did it.

'She demanded she travel with us and I allowed that.'

'Travel with us, but not to be ordered about. Last night you stormed into the camp and ate like some brute. She made that delicious soup and you didn't even thank her. Instead you pointed to her and demanded her to get on with her own business because she was slowing everyone down.'

He had been rude. Something about the woman chafed him with emotions he hadn't felt in years, if ever. He was no better than his brother had been when he met his wife.

His brother…his *cousin*. Would he never learn or remember? He had no brother. His life wasn't what it once was; he wasn't what he once was. Apparently it didn't matter when the emotions were the same and all of them futile.

She hadn't been slowing them down. With the fire going and the food cooked, they'd readied the horses and themselves far more quickly than they would have on their own. As a result, they left earlier today and were almost to Tickhill Castle.

But all her helpfulness didn't matter when he'd seethed with jealously all evening and might have got even less sleep. All because Carlos had at first backed away from her, only to then step in front of Helissent as if to protect her...from him.

He had burned to confront the man, but instead forced himself to ignore the implied meaning and then watched as Carlos gave Helissent his blanket and shared kind words and his attention.

He shouldn't care. They would soon arrive in Tickhill, which was just as good a place to leave her. They didn't have to travel to York. He'd be rid of her and the complications she represented.

'It may be a fortnight before we reach York,' Nicholas said. 'Even you couldn't be that cruel for that long.'

He couldn't be that cruel now as he searched the woods for her return. His eyes had been drawn to Helissent as she readied for bed last night, too. As she sang a song absent-mindedly under her breath. Quietly, haltingly, he knew she wasn't aware that she sang it.

It was a song he didn't know even though he heard her sing it in such a way at the inn. A song he was certain no one would comprehend simply because Helissent sang the song so abysmally, it would have hurt his ears if she sang it any louder.

The other men noticed as well, but they simply gave her amused looks. He couldn't seem to keep his eyes away from her. The song did something to her features, calmed her in a way that wasn't there before and it only intrigued him.

When Nicholas cleared his throat, he returned his gaze to his friend.

'We should arrive in Tickhill before evening,' he said.

Nicholas's lips thinned. 'So that's the way of it. Does she know?'

'There's no point. Tickhill has what she needs.'

'But certainly not you, or me and what the men need. We already agreed to avoid the castle in case Reynold had spies there.'

'We can't ignore it now since I won't take her to York. She'll have a place to sleep and kitchens to cook in. Everything she could find in York.'

'As well as your benevolence since the King owns it. You'll no doubt assure she's taken…and kept inside.'

'She won't be a prisoner there.'

'No. But Tickhill happens to be the most formidable fortress in this entire region with highly
trained soldiers for protection.'

'She doesn't need protection, or didn't you
take care of those men well enough?'

'I won't rise to that taunt.' Nicholas crossed
his arms. 'If you feel this strongly about dropping her so soon, I wonder why you brought her
in the first place. You didn't even tell her what
you did that night.'

'Tell her what? That I gave the villagers coin
to care for her? Shatter what little pride she has
because people had to be paid to be kind to her?'
It still burned Rhain that he'd had to do it, when
those people should have cared for her regardless of his money. 'Plus, you know that money
gives no guarantee that they could actually protect her. It was merely a…precaution.'

'A precaution that alleviated your guilt for
leaving her.'

'I have no guilt; her travelling with us practically guarantees Reynold will kill her.'

'Consequently, you leave her to Tickhill's care.
She won't agree to it, you know. She said she
wanted York and she doesn't act like a woman
who would settle for something she doesn't
want.'

No, she didn't, but it would be safer for her

in Tickhill. The more time she spent with him and his men meant more time Reynold could discover her.

'She's never seen Tickhill, perhaps it would suit her.'

'It would certainly suit you,' Nicholas said. 'You and I know why your temper's too finely honed, but that woman, who was brave enough to fight those men, and the punishing pace of travelling here, does not.'

'I am no more nor less than I've been.' He forced his hand to stop clenching the necklace. 'And I have no time for your amusements.'

'Ah, but I'm wondering if you intend to lock me up in Tickhill to protect me as well. But until that delightful point, we have a half-a-day's ride full of tension, resentment and anger ahead of us.'

'All the more reason to leave her at Tickhill. And I thank you for the idea of leaving you behind, too.'

'It's not her who will continue this discord, it's you. The men don't like how you treat her.'

'I don't care what they think as long as they obey orders.'

'You know orders don't work with them. It's the only reason they've banded together instead of tearing themselves apart, or setting their sights on tearing apart this country.'

Rhain's gaze returned to the necklace in his hand. The workmanship was exquisite, but he hardly saw it without deathly images. The mercenaries' skills were like the workmanship of the necklace, beautiful and deadly. 'I earned the right to lead them.'

'One on one, yes, and your connections have made the venture most profitable for them. But if you keep your frowns, they may mutiny.'

Rhain wasn't used to Nicholas mincing words. It had always been he who used words for weapons, for prodding. Who pieced them together because he liked the way they flowed. Until that day when all words were yanked out of him and he practically choked on the lie his life was.

When he learned his brother was in fact his cousin and his mother and father weren't Lord and Lady Gwalchdu. When he learned he was a bastard with a terrible secret flowing through his blood.

'Tell me what you want and get it over with.'

'Isn't it obvious?' Nicholas said. 'She is a lone woman, but injured and has suffered greatly in the past. Instead of being afraid of mercenaries, she's tended their wounds and fed their bellies. Hence my counsel to you is stop frowning at her unless you intend to get killed by them instead of Reynold.'

He didn't frown at her any more than anyone else. It was the situation, the outstanding questions of his family that might never be put to rest, that shortened his temper. It wasn't the woman or the attention of his men.

Yet, it still burned in his gut remembering how Carlos looked at her, how she touched his arm to inspect his wound...

Nicholas chuckled. 'I like watching you struggle. It's refreshing.'

Rhain knew he frowned then. 'You think I like her.'

'I know you like her; in fact, I'd wager that it's something else. I don't blame you, she can cook like no one I've ever known. Imagine what her fare would be like if she had a decent kitchen, and money for finer ingredients.'

'You think I like her for her food?'

Her food was exceptional, even when it consisted of only dried meat and water. But it wasn't the food that made him watch her. It was her. After he tasted her soup, he knew why she stayed bent over the flames though it pained her. He could taste it with every bite; she loved cooking.

'So it's some other reason you growl and bite?' Nicholas's expression feigned thought. 'Is it her wounded manner? Or how she carries on even though you know she hurts and yet she's brave and strong and...sweet.'

Rhain clenched the necklace and welcomed the bite of the metal. A part of him seethed at Nicholas's words.

The other part feared Nicholas wanted her for all those reasons he listed. Or even Carlos. Carlos, who didn't have Devil's blood in him, and didn't have a madman after his head. Carlos, who had money and could care for Helissent the way he never could. Why was he thinking he ever could? He deserved no one and would release her to someone else's care at the earliest opportunity in case he forgot...or lost whatever fight was going on inside him.

To do so, he had a simple plan. To praise the benefits of Tickhill until she thought it her own idea to stay.

'Leave me alone in this. You know even if it's true, I can do nothing. We jeopardize her enough as it is without someone overhearing this conversation that could be interpreted in the wrong way.'

'Interpreted by whom? By Reynold and his spies? Are you saying if it wasn't for Reynold, you would be different than you've been for five years? All this time, women have been rubbing against you and you haven't spared them a glance. Yet with her you are. You even listen to that dreadful song she constantly sings.'

'Enough,' he growled. 'I'm a dead man, why bother with these questions?'

'Because you're a dead man and for some reason you're coming alive again.'

Chapter Eight

Helissent's body ached with the continued ride north. Her injuries from the other night barely noticeable in the flame that was her skin's protest, the only relief was Nicholas announcing their arrival at Tickhill. A place she'd heard about, but never seen.

From the distance she saw the castle upon a high motte, ramparts jutting out of the countryside. It was large, far larger than she could ever imagine. The closer she got, its presence became blocked by the winding streets, the closely packed homes and businesses. Blocked by the noise and chaos of the village as children, shepherds, animals and people ran in the muddy streets.

But she knew it was there, could feel it looming and, in wonder, she craned her neck to find it again. Then they turned a corner and a smell caused her to sit roughly back. It was overwhelming, like suddenly being enclosed in an airless privy.

She was used to how her village smelled: a mix of wide open fields, sheep and people. But she wasn't expecting what assaulted her the moment they turned a corner and the countryside's air no longer flowed freely.

'It won't be like this everywhere,' Rhain said in her ear.

He must have taken her sudden startling differently for he speeded up the horse a bit. 'The smell, it bothers you?' he said.

She shook her head. The smell did bother her, but hardly noticeable, not when Rhain talked and his voice didn't hold anger or some seething frustration he harbored since she'd mounted his horse and rode with him.

His voice was pleasant, almost concerned, and that did bother her, but how she didn't know.

'The lower streets always smell, most villages purposefully make it that way,' he said. 'This is where the tanners, the butchers, the blacksmiths are housed, but as we wind our way up there will be the cordwainers, the tailors and so on. The castle won't smell at all.'

Rhain's reassuring words didn't ease her thoughts, but she didn't know why. Taking as few breaths as possible, she watched people throw slop down blocked drainages, and livestock defecate on the slimy narrow streets.

Sights she'd seen before, but the sheer number of people made it worse.

And the sounds. There were sheep where she lived, a few goats. Here was overrun with bleating sheep, restless cattle and cantering horses. So many dogs, she knew they had to be as wild as everything else.

When they turned the corner she could glimpse the castle. The road was also wider, and as Rhain had said the air was fresher.

'See—it's better,' Rhain said. 'Did I ride too fast? Your ribs, do they still hurt?'

'I didn't apply the bandages today. I don't think it matters. It rarely stings now.'

'Then your ribs are merely bruised. Your cheek looks like it's healing.'

It was the salve, always the salve, which had been part of her life since childhood. But now it carried a different memory. One of that night and how this quiet man had touched her as no one had before.

She tried to distract her thoughts with the scenes around her. Many travelers had been to Tickhill, but none of them described it as it truly was. 'Have you been here before?'

'No, it's simply typical for a castle town.'

He was talking and, curious despite herself,

she would take advantage of it. 'You've travelled a lot?'

'Many years, many countries. Castles can be built differently, but maintain most of the same features and layout. I lived in one as well.'

He sounded wary now as if expecting her to ask more questions.

Knowing she had a past to be cautious of as well, she didn't say any more. For now, what he said was enough. His pleasant words didn't ease her, but at least there wasn't animosity lacing them.

They continued on the wider road and the magnificent castle was always in view. When they arrived at the gates, the ramparts, which looked large from a distance, up close were formidable and intimidating. Probably more so because of the guards above looking down over the village. She could feel their eyes on them and she shifted in her seat.

Her scars. In the bright sunlight, they'd see them. As they'd wound through the village, she'd forgotten them. The thought she could forget them, even for a few moments, surprised her. Her skin needed constant care with the kitchens, and with the changing seasons. She never forgot them.

'Do not worry,' Rhain said. 'Their keeping the gates closed is customary, as are the men on the ramparts. The benefit to this castle is that it's strategic and well maintained. A more protective fortress you'd be hard pressed to find.'

The word fortress didn't appeal to her, but Rhain's puzzling attempts at conversation did. He was lauding the benefits of the castle, perhaps to put her at ease, but why?

'It used to be privately owned,' he continued, 'but now it's part of the King's holdings, though he's not in residence.'

He was privy to the whereabouts of the King. 'You know the King?'

'I was fostered under his care.'

The information didn't surprise her since he was a wealthy knight, who once lived in a castle. Of course he'd be familiar with the King, but to be fostered under his care was something else altogether, and another reminder of the vast differences between them. 'So they know we were coming?'

'No, I could hardly announce my whereabouts.' Rhain lifted a cord he wore around his neck. On the end was a ring. 'This is my passage inside. Black Hawk is my family crest. There were only two made. The King's steward will know it.'

He dangled the great thick gold ring like it was merely a rock instead of something so valuable she never could have dreamed of before. It was beautiful in the sunlight and emblazoned with red and black stones.

'It will also ensure you are well attended,' he said.

More than unease at Rhain's remarks skittered up her spine. She was merely a visitor, and didn't need attendance, but before she could address his words the door to the side of the closed gates opened and a lone man stepped through.

Above their heads, the guards had notched their arrows, which now pointed to them. The man was very little, very old and quite sure of himself as he approached the mercenaries at his gate.

The moment Rhain showed the ring, the man waved his thin arm in the air and the gates swung open.

'Welcome, sir, welcome indeed. Your intended stay and care?'

'Two days for me and my men.'

The man nodded and ambled off at considerable speed through the side door.

It was then she realized what should have occurred to her long before now. Rhain hadn't said anything of her. 'Where am I to stay?'

Rhain urged his horse forward and they slowly entered under the gates. Helissent took in the numerous guards. The sharpness of the portcullis, its metal smell in the shade of the ramparts before they emerged in the outer bailey.

She was in an outer bailey for the first time in her life. Though she'd asked questions from patrons, she wasn't prepared for the chaos or industry. She couldn't stop her eyes from taking it all in, but her ears heard Rhain and then heard nothing else.

'I'll find you a room. Only give me today. I've been to castles, but not this one. For your protection I cannot give you free rein. While I can guarantee a roof and food, I cannot guarantee your safety until I am apprised of the men here. There may even be a few I know.'

There was censure in Rhain's voice, but also caution. Too much caution. 'Is there danger here?'

He paused. 'There is always danger and I need to ensure it is safe for you.'

She listened to the creak of the heavy gates shutting behind her. They sounded as final as Rhain's words. But she had to be wrong for he announced they'd be here only two days. Why would he need to ensure it was safe for her when she was surrounded by mercenaries?

Rhain didn't like the way the conversation was going. He hadn't been prepared to explain Helissent's relationship with them. No doubt the castle inhabitants thought her his whore. He had warned her of that, but he could tell she didn't understand. Which only confirmed for him she

118 The Knight's Scarred Maiden

was an innocent, honest, hardworking woman, who sang terribly, but baked like none other.

In all his travels he never met anyone like her. How could the other patrons have left her alone all this time? Because of a few scars? They were fools; all of them.

But the guards and villagers here were worldly. They'd been exposed to the King's court and to nobility for generations. They were used to debauchery and to excess. He hadn't introduced her as an innocent maid and they would think nothing of Helissent as his whore.

While he was here, it would give her some protection, but when he was gone, it would cause her only harm.

Unintentional harm. He hadn't been thinking when he approached the gates. He only thought of the few days they had left together.

As if they would share those days. As soon as she realized what the residents here thought of her, she wouldn't talk to him again. She wouldn't talk to him as soon as he told her he would leave either.

He still had two days to remedy his mistake. Then it didn't matter if she ignored him. He would do what he must. Ensure Tickhill was secure for her and leave.

Except he didn't like it. Foolish perhaps, dangerous most definitely. When the steward came out to greet him and he gave his request for a stay, he noticed the steward's questioning glance to Helissent. He hadn't liked that either.

Rhain dismounted, acutely aware he did it in public, under the scrutiny of men and of her future home. Consequently, he displayed all the manners he had long set aside. Helping her down, attempting to appear courtly, he was assailed by her scent, felt the warmth of her hands clasping his forearms for support. Became aware of her height. Always her height, which only made him think of her legs…and how she would fit him.

When he didn't release her, she looked at him questionably.

'Are your legs hurting?' he said, trying to cover his response.

Rhain wasn't frowning, but she sensed his distracted concentration. Was it concern? She didn't know.

Her legs did pain her, but not like yesterday, yet Rhain held her steady. His hood was on, only she could see his eyes, how they searched hers as if puzzling something and not liking it. It was a look he'd given her before that she couldn't comprehend, because it never had anything to do with her scars. He stilled this way when he looked into her eyes. As he was doing now.

She didn't understand his sudden concern or

attempts at conversation. She didn't understand how his kindness warred with his anger and frustration. Were the shadows him, or the light? Why did her breath hitch in some breathless way when he clasped her elbows more firmly?

'I'll be fine,' she lied. Her body hurt, as did her skin. But the ache inside her was growing. They were here for two days, and this was only part of the journey to York. She should have no ache.

The men had already dismounted and were following servants towards a smaller wall's archway. The steward returned and he and Rhain engaged in conversation.

She still felt his touch as they walked to a smaller courtyard surrounding the keep. A castle, her first, and it was an impressive sight. The curtained wall alone was nothing like she'd ever seen. After taking the stone bridge into the inner bailey, she could see the full grandeur of the giant circular keep that jutted out on top of the hill.

There were many buildings inside the walls, smells and sounds she recognized. Another blacksmith's with several fires blazing and carts of charcoal nearby. Some fletchers were making arrows and dozens of servants and soldiers were busily milling about. Voices surrounded her in dozens of pitches and tones, underneath, the sounds of stables and mews reverberated.

Everything familiar, but grand. Despite how

she arrived here, despite the fact she rode with strangers, with mercenaries, this was what made her realize she was no longer home.

If it wasn't for Rudd, she might have never done this. Would have spent her entire life in her village. She should have been scared, or at least wary, but maybe because she rode with mercenaries she experienced none of that. Instead she wondered at the beauty surrounding her.

And she noticed the stares. Some more polite than others. Brushing her hair aside, she slowed her pace so Rhain didn't block her and everyone could see her.

It was best to get this over with. To let them see her or else she'd be plagued with furtive gazes the two days she was here. The questions would come later, but the stares, the horror and pity, she wanted them out of the way.

Probably because of her pace, Rhain, who was whispering to Allen, looked over his shoulder, his eyes darted over her features and flashed. He grabbed her elbow and moved her hurriedly towards the Hall.

'There is no need for that,' he said low, but heatedly.

'For what?'

'Subjecting yourself to their scrutiny as though you're some…aberration.'

She deserved to be some aberration. 'But I am.

Why do you pretend otherwise? People need to see, and I simply make it easier for them.'

Rhain felt every emotion and none that he should. Such as reason, objectivity. Impassiveness.

He saw her do this with his men when they first arrived at the inn. Watched as she did it for every new traveler. At first he thought it was merely her mannerisms. But now that she slowed, and brushed her hair aside, he couldn't deny she was putting herself on display. He didn't like it.

A foolish idea when she was most likely used to stares and knew how to confront them to make it easier for her. Yet, he knew it didn't make it easier for her. There was a tenseness to her body like she was bracing herself, and he watched the pain travel through her eyes before she nodded as if in satisfaction.

But he wasn't satisfied. He was certain she *hurt* when she did it. Damning the consequences, he pulled her more protectively towards him.

'This way.' The steward pointed to the stairs on the outside of the keep that led to the Hall above. 'I hope you'll find all that you need for your stay.'

They had travelled from London, with all its opulence and amenities. He grew bored there. Tickhill was a fine castle, but in his travels he had been to warmer climes and as much as his home country brought him the greenery, it had stopped being his home somewhere along the way.

No, he knew the exact moment this country had stopped being his home. When he discovered who his mother was and what ran through his veins. Then he knew he belonged nowhere.

Chapter Nine

When they reached the top of the stairs and entered the Great Hall, Helissent suddenly stopped and gasped.

The steward smiled proudly, then continued further into the Hall to direct the servants who were setting the table and bringing in food piled on platters.

Helissent continued to gaze around the Hall when Nicholas passed with an amused look. Rhain shrugged and put his hand to the small of her back, but her feet were firmly planted, her expression in raptures.

Unable to comprehend what held her attention, he tried to look at the Hall through her eyes. As expected the vaulted ceilings and large tables were heavily decorated. This had always been a wealthy man's home and now it was a king's.

The rushes were fresh; the furnishings were

all for the greatest comfort. The amount of sconces anchored in the stone walls provided plenty of light. The ornateness, polish and size of the floor candelabras was immense.

Having come from her village, Helissent would never have seen such a sight before. For a brief burning moment, he wished he could show her some of the homes he had seen. Show his own home of Gwalchdu, which was three times as large and of a newer construction.

He leaned down to whisper, 'Impressed?'

'Very.'

'When the King is in residence, I'm sure it is more opulent than this,' Rhain said.

Helissent's expression turned from raptures to puzzlement as she looked at the tapestries he pointed to.

Then he realized. 'You weren't looking at the room, were you?'

She had been staring fixedly at the tables. The tables that were now heavily laden with meats, cheeses, fruits and nuts. His men were sitting around grabbing anything that they could reach as the servants brought in steaming bowls of soup.

He chuckled and Helissent glanced at him then. 'It's the food that garners your attention, isn't it?'

Helissent gestured in front of her. 'I know your

men are hungry, but how did they suddenly serve all of this? And how do they make the presentation of it look effortless?'

She looked astounded, but also designing, as though she was taking it all in, yet at the same time already making changes on how to improve it. He stood next to her, watching her, watching the men eat until the flustered steward came over and asked if anything was wrong.

'No, it's lovely,' she said.

Then the steward looked to him. 'Will she be eating at the table with you?'

He felt Helissent's stare and cursed himself that he could not address with the steward her position just yet. He'd requested Allen to gather the information on the residents here. But that would take at least a day.

'She'll dine with me.'

The steward glanced at her again before he directed a few servants, who scurried to do his request.

Helissent didn't move. 'I may be from a village, but there's only one reason he needed to ask if I was to dine with you. That is, if I didn't have a rightful place at the table. He thinks I'm your—'

'Wait.' Rhain would have rather had this conversation elsewhere, but at least his men were too busy to overhear. Nicholas would never forgive him if he knew he'd put Helissent in this position. 'I will correct their assumptions when I deem the castle safe. Until then, I can provide you a certain protection.'

She stood staring at him, a myriad of expressions on her face, but he could decipher none of them. Aware they were garnering stares, he said, 'Let's sit at least and I can give my apologies for the next hour.'

Helissent sat at a table with nobility and the residents thought her his whore. She should be outraged, but what she felt was far from that emotion.

She was obviously not cut from the same cloth as the men here. Not only regarding their skill or their reputation. But their clothes and manners were fine. Before they approached the castle, Nicholas and Rhain donned their spurs to indicate their status. She could now see the other men were equally garbed with some finery.

The Flemish mercenaries had metal strappings on their legs that were polished to a high sheen, and they wore curiously long tunics with different symbols. The Spanish wore studded blue vests that were thick and yet looked soft.

Only she stood out in her overly mended clothes with burns along the sleeves. She was much taller than either innkeeper, and their spare clothing was given away. But she wished she'd kept a few of their nicer pieces now.

'How is it even possible?' she whispered.

'Is what possible?' he said.

'That he would think I was your whore?'

'We rode together. I should have had you ride, while I walked beside—'

'No, that's not what I mean.'

Burns on her sleeves, scars on her face. She'd forgotten again in the moments she'd gawked at the food being presented. Forgotten, and she couldn't grasp it. A few hours with these men with their scars, burns, and slices to their skin and she had felt almost normal with them.

But here in the finery of the castle, with the steward's words and Rhain's response, she was again reminded of her hideous visage. The fact she clothed herself in pauper's clothes was of little import. Still she removed her hand from the goblet and placed it in her lap. Ran her hand down her clothes to check for newer stains or something she might be able to repair.

But there was nothing she could do. Stains, tears, frayed threads mocked her. She was no woman to any man, let alone this one of utter perfection.

'Are you saying you believe no man would want you?'

Of course that was what she was saying. She

knew how deeply deformed she was. She also knew her shame, and while this man might not know it, everyone in her village did. Nobody there ever asked for her as a man would a woman.

Except the way Rhain was looking now paid no heed to what she knew was fact. His face had quickly turned from conciliatory to dark.

'Those men at your village were fools. All of them not to have seen the gem they had in their very midst.'

Gem? The warmth of his earlier words now hurt. 'You jest.'

His eyes searched hers and something flashed across his features. 'Forgive me. Would you believe I once was glib of tongue?'

He'd spent most of the time with her in silence.

'No, of course not, but if I could… I would let you know.' He took in every one of her features from her scars to the freckles on her nose until she grew warm from his amber gaze.

'You are a gem, Helissent, and very rare. I've never seen your like before. I could say the color of your hair was brown, but that wouldn't take in the red streaking throughout or the almost golden blond highlighting you like a halo. Your eyes aren't only green, but grey, and the softest of browns. You bake cakes from the crudest of ingredients and they would make angels weep.

You worked hard serving ale, and you are honest. How could any man not want you?'

Every part of her insides frothed and bubbled. The way he talked, the way he looked and touched her. She almost felt like she was the finest of flours, or some rare ingredient she'd never experienced.

Why would he say such words? Not for a moment did she believe he truly thought her a gem. It must have something to do with the castle and the steward's perceptions of her role with the mercenaries. 'That was a nice apology,' she whispered past her heart vigorously kneading in her chest.

'That wasn't an apology, that was—'

'Here we are.' The steward beamed as the servants set down their trenchers, goblets and pewter knives. 'I hope it all meets with your satisfaction.'

Rhain looked at her until his frustrated expression shuttered closed and he abruptly turned his attention to Nicholas on his right.

Leaving her shivering with something she couldn't guess at. Forcing her to do or see something other than the words he laid out before her. She gave her thanks to the steward before he bowed and left.

Her first meeting with a steward. Her first feast. Only a few days north of her home was this castle and whatever expansive kitchens that produced fare at a moment's notice. Granted, the fruit and nuts and latticed bread was already ready. The soup could have been prepared this morning for tonight's meal. The rest was cold cuts of meat and bits of leftover vegetables, but all was artfully arranged. She didn't know that food could be *arranged*.

Her eyes on the food, her thoughts on Rhain's words. Had he meant them? If so, what did they mean coming from a man such as him? His beauty was as unreal now as it was when she first saw him. He rarely smiled, but when he did, it was like looking at the sun too long. He gave them with ease, but they never lasted long. As if he once had smiled freely and now no longer should. He was so full of shadows...

Platters of fish were brought in, the steam wafting the soft scents of fresh herbs. The men ate this food as easily as they ate her dried meat and water soup over a campfire and cheap cuts at the inn. How did they stomach her cooking?

Even Nicholas and Rhain, now deep in conversation, ate the food like it was commonplace. She listened while they discussed the weaponry and what had to be done at the blacksmith's. There was a natural friendship between them she enjoyed listening to. A warmth she didn't often see.

It wasn't that her village was full of Rudds, but

it was small, mostly farming, herding and transient. She hadn't made a friendship like they had. Her chest gave a tiny pang she could do nothing about, so she lifted her cup to take a drink.

It was wine. Wine she'd never tasted before. The scent was heady, the tiny sip she allowed caressed divinely across her tongue. The elaborate fare simply waiting for her to taste as well, though she didn't feel she'd get anything down her restricted throat.

So strange how her life had changed from peril in the fire, to love with the innkeepers. From peril with Rudd to…this.

And *this* after everything was almost more than she could bear. She dined in a castle. Though she could feel the servants stare at her, she didn't sense any hostility, nor could she sense their disapproval.

Then there was the travel with the men, who didn't stare and asked for her help.

And Rhain with his words that she was a gem. The way he looked at her in the lone candlelight with a wary defiance. As if something as broken and undeserving as she challenged him—

'If the food is not to your liking, as the highest noble ranking here, I could simply order a beheading or two,' Rhain whispered.

Something flashed in his eyes. Something piercing before there was only a light-hearted amber reflection she didn't know he was capable of. Over the last few days he'd shown only shadows, now he was showing some other facet of himself. Humor. Teasing, but almost like he couldn't help himself. Like those smiles he felt he shouldn't give.

He said he was once glib of tongue. Had he also once been happy? If so, there were too many shadows for her to make sense of him.

'Are you mocking me?' she said.

'I'm making you smile.'

'I don't understand you.'

The corner of his lips quirked. 'Neither do I. It's the bane of my current existence.'

He was teasing her as he did with Nicholas that time in the inn. Again, she wondered about this man she'd met only a few days before. He might be in shadows, but there was one certainty—he was a rich noble and the world was at his feet. 'You have no banes of your existence.'

'Well, of course I don't and I can't imagine anyone else would want to live with theirs.'

Light and mockery in his eyes. She should laugh and she felt the curve to her lips. But there was always something she felt he was telling her, something underneath the words.

'You're staring at me again,' he said.

She closed her eyes briefly in embarrassment. She wasn't used to being talked to this way. Usually conversations were brief between serving ale and food. Sometimes she gathered the courage to ask questions. Mostly travelers liked to tell their tales and they never asked questions of her.

But that's what she felt with Rhain and his puzzling looks. With his silence and mockery, like his meanings underneath his words, it felt as though he was asking questions of her.

'I meant what I said,' he whispered. 'Though I shouldn't say a word and I have no right. Every one of them was true.'

He was too perceptive, in such a brief period of time how could he know her this way? She didn't delude herself that the awareness she felt for him he somehow mirrored. That would be something to laugh about.

Except he said those words about her hair and her eyes. He told her he meant them. How could he?

She was scarred, disfigured and ugly on the inside with her shame.

Years of love and care from John and Anne, and never did she forgot her scars, nor did they. Even when she had to lift John because he'd become so frail and couldn't relieve himself, he asked how her skin fared with his extra weight. No, she never forgot; she didn't deserve to forget.

Over the years, travelers and children mimicked her walk when her leg tightened, or pulled down one corner of their eye and mouth and giggled. Now this man spoke words, with a tone of sincerity that hurt her worse than the cruelest jibe she'd ever received.

'That I'm a gem? I'm more like the coarsest of flours.' She couldn't hide the hurt lacing the words. 'Unmilled, even, hacked wheat from the shaft. I know no man would want me. No man staring at me would forget. And this…' she waved from her face down her arm '…isn't the worst of it.'

Her face was scarred, but at least she could feel the wind and sun. Along her torso and her right upper thigh she couldn't feel anything at all. There the skin didn't look like skin on any human, but grooves like streams of flat ale in rye flour.

'You may have briefly felt my skin, but you cannot comprehend what is under this gown, Mercenary, and no doubt a husband wouldn't either. Certainly no one in my village forgot.'

Nor would they let her forget. As she intended.

Brows drawn tight, Rhain's expression became all shadow. 'I do not presume to appreciate or comprehend what occurred to you, Helissent, but I'd listen if you'd ever honor me with the telling. However, just as I cannot know what is underneath that gown, you cannot know or question the veracity of my words. I meant it when I said I should not tell you things I have no right to.'

Kindness again. Compassion, though she'd hurt him somehow by rejecting his opinion of her. How could she forget he was shadows and light?

He carried them both. Utter beauty and wealth, and she realized with some pain lacing his words, he wasn't impervious to Fate's cruel whims.

He said he would not presume what made her her. But she had presumed with him. Worse, she'd heaped her anguish on to him and he had done nothing except rescue her. How to set things right, when she had never been glib of tongue?

Then she remembered when they last had an understanding.

'You could be right, though.' She lifted a shoulder and tried to appear as nonchalant as he had when he teased.

His eyes trailed to her shoulder, then back to her lips and up to her eyes.

'About the suitors for me,' she continued, trying to keep her tone light. 'I suppose I should let you know I'm waiting for the man who will equal my cakes.'

His brows raised; his eyes lighting with the tone in her voice. 'Then you'll be waiting a very long time,' he said. 'In fact, I don't think you'll find a man to equal your cakes.'

She pretended to muse about the comment. 'That's true, he'd have to be sweet.'

Rhain's lips curved in a true smile then. She had surprised him and for some reason it felt as good as an apology.

'Oh, yes, most certainly sweet,' he said. 'But also light, rich…delicious.'

Images of the mercenaries the first day she saw them. Rough and unclean from a long journey. How some patrons hacked phlegm to the floorboards that she skirted to avoid. How others, too drunk for manners, filled the inn with their belches and blurting gas from overfilled bellies, until she sought sanctuary outside if only for a moment. Images of Rudd with his blackened fingernails scratching his protuberant hairy belly, then sinking those fingers into a freshly baked roll.

Men as something that could be rich, light and delicious? The first laugh escaped her before she meant it, then she couldn't stop and she covered her mouth with her hand until tears formed in her eyes, but her laughter only increased. Rhain handed her a goblet when it seemed she would choke.

Trying to control the images in her mind and her laughing, she glanced around at the other men, certain they would be grimacing at her since her scars were worse when she laughed.

Or at least outraged at her lack of decorum, but they were looking at Rhain, not at her. Their dark countenances were gaping, which made her laugh again, her hand clapping on to the goblet he still held. Out of everyone around the table Rhain looked the most shocked.

Over the rim, she giggled. 'Rich, sweet, I'll grant you that, but in what circumstances could men ever be delicious?'

Absolute silence, while she watched both of Rhain's brows raise.

Nicholas's chair thwacked forward. The clang echoed off the stone walls. His body flopped like he lost his famed balance and use of his limbs.

In almost unison, the mercenaries bellowed, slapping their backs, spilling their wine, flinging food and the dogs yipped from the sudden treats and noise.

When her eyes returned to Rhain's there was a different look to his eyes than the men's. Different than his surprise from before.

There was…heat there. His brows had lowered, his chin dipped, his amber eyes, deeper, just a bit darker. His lips held a curve that had nothing to do with mere friendship. The flush across his cheeks had nothing to do with shared laughter.

'Did I say something?'

The men around her were talking animatedly,

keeping the laughter going, causing new guffaws to echo in the Great Hall.

'I said something, didn't I?' Then she thought, it hadn't been her, it'd been him. He said it; she had simply repeated it. 'You said it first.'

'I did.' A brighter smile, almost sharp with intent. 'But I didn't expect the...result.'

Nicholas's laugh bellowed out over everyone's. 'It's the women who don't expect the results!'

Rhain's grin flashed again, but it couldn't survive the heat in his eyes, or the way his mouth softened and his eyes couldn't stay away from hers.

All her life she'd been surrounded by drunk travelers and jesting patrons. From the knowing suggestive expressions around her, Helissent knew she said something bawdy.

Times like this she wished she could blush, or pretend some sort of modesty when she knew that was the correct response. Instead, Rhain's expression made her curious.

'You're not laughing like the rest of them. Why?'

There was humor in Rhain's eyes, in the cant of his head, in the sensual curve of his lips. Certainly, his eyes flashed with great mirth at Nicholas's comment, but there was something more to Rhain's expression. Some knowing look that sent a flash of heat through her.

'I don't think I'm capable of it.'

His words were slow, deep and deliberate. Each syllable sinking into her. Until by the end of the simple sentence, the easy delivery of the words, the Grand Hall, the sumptuous fare, the raucous laughter and revelry of the men disappeared and there seemed to be only Rhain, and his words.

She was not so naive not to know what went on between a man and a woman. She lived and worked in an inn. She was more than aware of desire and lust.

The villagers were circumspect, but those who travelled through from London to York had no such qualms. Well dressed, courtly even, but the more ale she served, the more heated glances and suggestive touching occurred. They didn't care at all what they flaunted, or what they said.

But never, in all those years, had any such flirting or flaunting been directed towards her. She wasn't even sure it was happening now, except the way her body heated while he stared at her. Her body felt as though he was flirting with her.

No, not flirting. There was nothing light in the way he looked at her now, his amber eyes darkening, his lids heavier, his mouth softening as he glanced at her lips, then back to her eyes.

'No, not capable at all,' he whispered low.

Words only for himself, only for her.

A frown, an adjustment in his seat as if he was suddenly uncomfortable. As if he realized what he'd said and it was too much.

She felt as though it was too much. 'I don't understand you.'

'I hardly understand myself right now.'

They kept repeating the same words to each other, but she felt no closer to the truth. 'The others laughed.'

'The others aren't imagining what I am, what I shouldn't be. What I haven't for years now. Not even a temptation.'

He made her sound like she was a honeycomb just out of reach. 'And you are now?'

'Yes.' He grabbed his goblet and his fingers flitted around the stem as they did with the dagger at his waist.

If possible, those slight caresses wound her tighter to this moment with him. The fact she knew, somehow, he was aware of her, as a man is of a woman.

It was an absurd thought, but there was something behind Rhain's eyes as he then retrieved her goblet and set it down.

Rhain, who seemed incapable of taking his eyes off her lips until she was sure she'd left wine there and darted her tongue to lick it.

His chest expanded and he turned his attention to the table. His eyes darted as if looking for answers until they fixed on her empty trencher. 'Should we eat?' he said. 'You've done nothing but eye the food. You're torturing me with the wait. Don't you wish to taste it?'

She was certain she couldn't get food past the constriction in her throat. She couldn't even breathe properly now. 'It's almost too beautiful to destroy.'

His eyes slid to hers, wary again before some tension eased and he said, 'But I can tell you already want to make changes.'

She did. She would be beyond fortunate to have the budget and kitchens that Tickhill seemed to possess. All she hoped for, was that wherever she landed in York, it would have better supplies than Rudd's. If so, it would be prudent to take her experience here and add it to her cooking.

For now, however, that thought was overwhelming. She was seated in a great hall of a king's castle and realized she didn't even know in what order to serve the food. She'd been too busy staring at Rhain. So she stalled.

'Is it always like this? With servants pouring your wine and food too beautiful to eat?'

His lips quirked at that. 'Are you worried it'll taste better than yours? Try the soup, Helissent.'

She knew a challenge had been made, but it was the coaxing sound of his voice that held power over her, for she did try it and it was better than the wine.

Then she didn't care about the increased quirk to his lips, or that he might not be as interested in food as she was.

She dunked her spoon in again and she simply had to know.

'What's in it? I know it's chicken and mint, but what's that other flavor?'

The flavor was a revelation. She didn't know food could taste like this.

'Cinnamon? Clove?' His eyes were lit like she amused him. But he scooped up a fillet of fish, sliced cheese, forked goat that fell apart and beef so thinly sliced she swore she could see through it and laid it all down on her trencher.

She didn't care if she amused him. She took another sip, greedy for more. 'This is the best soup I've ever tasted.'

'Aren't you curious about the rest?'

Without thinking of manners or in what order to eat, she bit into the fish and closed her eyes to fully relish the sharp bite of herbs against the soft textures.

'Good as well?' he asked, his voice holding a husky tone.

She nodded. 'I never had enough sorrel to make my sauces taste like this. They must have gardens here.'

'All castles do; we had them at Gwalchdu.'

'Gwalchdu?'

'Roughly translated as Black Hawk.'

'That was your home in Wales?

He gave a dismissive nod and suddenly turned more fully to her. His actions were attentive, but his expression too quickly shuttered. When she looked over his shoulder, she noticed the serving women staring avidly at him.

How long had they been standing there, and why had Rhain adjusted in his seat until he could no longer see the women?

She recognized his actions immediately because she had done it many times herself.

'Can you tell me about the gardens in your home?' she said.

The relief in his eyes confirmed that he wanted to ignore the staring women, though she was curious why he did so. In truth, she was curious about the gardens as well. She dreamed of having proper ones, but lacked knowledge of what they contained.

'When I was a child, I spent—' He stopped, shook his head.

'What is it?'

'I have not thought of the gardens in a long time.'

And by doing so, he became reflective. 'I'm sorry, I didn't mean to offend.'

'No, it's not that. They were happy times.'

She felt as if they were talking about more than mere gardens. With the inn, she'd ask questions and people would stumble over their words to tell her their tales, but Rhain never did. With him, she realized with a pang, she wanted to know.

Life had taught her never to be greedy; she didn't deserve to have everything she wanted. So she took a drink and thought how to change the subject.

'When I wasn't home,' he began like there wasn't a pause, 'it was the scent of lavender that drew me to the gardens in the spring. Rosemary in the summer. Or better, like this time of the year now, when both bloom. As I grew older, I don't know if I sought out the gardens because I was constantly hungry or if it reminded me of my mother.'

'Your mother…the healer,' she said.

His eyes darted over her shoulder. 'I told you of her, didn't I? She was always in the gardens. She carefully tended the seedlings when they were growing. I often teased her that she gave more care to the herbs than the people, but once plucked, she was ruthless with them. As a consequence, I was grateful her attention was on the plants rather than me.'

'Did you get away with much?'

'Only when she was busy crushing herbs.'

'She must have been very good.' Helissent tore some bread.

He raised a brow. 'Why do you say that?'

'You have much pride in your voice.'

His brow furrowed. 'I do…don't I?' He plucked the goblet off the table and took a drink. 'There's a market tomorrow, you should have Nicholas take you.'

When Rhain engaged Nicholas in conversation, Helissent knew she had been dismissed. Rhain was all light and shadow, but this time, he was nothing but darkness.

Chapter Ten

The noise woke her in the morning. At first, it was faint and jostled against her sleep. Soon she was aware of the noise's origins and actively listened to the cacophony: bleating animals, greeting calls and shouts from one vendor to another, hammering against wood and metal. She went to her window certain the market was just underneath, but the stalls were outside the castle walls.

The market that Rhain mentioned last night at supper. Rhain, who'd avoided her after he turned to Nicholas. She was shown her room, given water to clean up, freshly laundered clothes and her ointment that she slathered on her sore leg and torso. It didn't take long for sleep to claim her.

When there was a knock at the door, she opened it and knew from her brief disappointment she had foolishly expected Rhain, but she schooled her features when she greeted Nicholas.

It didn't seem to make a difference because Nicholas replied, 'He's already at the market.'

She didn't know where her disappointment came from. Rhain ignored her on the journey from the village. Last night, though he gave her some attention, he quickly dismissed her and said Nicholas should show her the markets. Clearly he was back to shadows and his kindness wasn't to continue.

She was used to being dismissed and ignored, so it shouldn't sting. She was used to standing on her own two feet and would have to do so in York. But she wanted more for herself than to merely stand on her own. She wanted to truly excel and she wouldn't get that by observing food served, she needed to go to the source.

When Nicholas asked whether she wanted to go, she requested only that they see the kitchens first.

Nicholas didn't question it, but she did. Yes, she needed more skills if she was to find work in competitive York. But another thought lingered as well—if Rhain was at the market, she wanted to be somewhere else.

Rhain shook the man's hand and waited for the next contender. He woke this morning only thinking to partake of the market, but was too restless for strolling through crowds. It didn't take much to gather some of his men and a crowd to train instead.

He wished Mathys was here. He was almost as large as Nicholas and would recognize that Rhain simply wanted to thrash someone until he was worn out.

But Mathys and a few others were gone per his orders. They left Tickhill last night to ride north. To see if the roads were clear between here and York. Rhain accepted that he was a dead man, but he wouldn't risk his men and the trip north would be precarious.

Still he was fortunate since there were trained soldiers here to add to his sport. There was only one unspoken caveat with his men. They could never show their true weaknesses or strengths to others.

He knew he was about to break that pact when he spotted Carlos walking towards his ring. Then he realized he was fortunate that Nicholas was out with Helissent because his friend would never approve of what he was about to do.

Of course, Rhain suspected his temper was short, his need for blood even more pronounced, precisely because Nicholas was out with Helissent this morning.

What had happened between them approaching the gates and dining last night? Too much. He needed to make Tickhill attractive to Helissent; he didn't need to engage her further. Yet he couldn't stop his curiosity. To see her in raptures over simple food…to take those greedy spoonsful of soup. Or that first delicate sip of wine. He wasn't even supposed to be looking, but he saw how she rolled the warming liquid over her tongue and he'd almost groaned with unspoken need.

Once he heard her laughter, he was lost. Her laughter, which was nothing like her singing. If there was any more musical sound in the world, he'd never heard it.

She'd covered her mouth and it broke something inside him to see her do it. He wished he had the right to take her hand and lower it. To see the joy flow from her, as he kept holding her hand.

To see how the joy would change to desire as he raised her hand to press a kiss upon her inner wrist. To whisper and show her how skin could be delicious. How he knew she would be delicious.

He'd never been this close to a knife's edge with a woman before. Never wanted the way he wanted her.

Carlos entered the ring and Rhain tossed his sword from one hand to the other. When he struck Carlos exactly at his weak point, Carlos's eyes gleamed. Challenge accepted, Rhain felt satisfaction for the first time in days.

Her mind buzzing with all that the kitchens had offered and with the orderliness and efficiency of each room, the market's chaos was an affront on Helissent's senses.

Luckily, she could take it all in since Nicholas was more taciturn than Rhain. At first he attempted to be polite and asked her questions on her castle experience, but all attempts at conversation died.

Her heart wasn't in it. She liked Tickhill well enough, but she was overwhelmed by the market stalls and they dodged the many people vying for their attention to sell their wares.

Her village had been too small for a market. The villagers had to travel to sell their foodstuffs. Upon their return, Helissent was always happy to hear the news as she helped the innkeepers feed everyone.

From their descriptions, she thought she had a grasp of the industry, but experiencing an actual market was something else. The smells of fresh fish, of bleeding-out pig, of hot metal. The last day had been dry and dust and flies billowed and swarmed.

Nicholas dragged her away from the food

stalls and down the lanes showing gentler wares. None of which grabbed her attention like the confections and twisted bread she saw, but it was here she spotted Rhain at the end of the lane. He wore a fine linen tunic and leather breeches. His hair looked dark, wet. His back was to them as he held a small needlework in one hand and a silver necklace in the other.

Delicate, beautiful. They were hardly items for a mercenary, or even a knight. They were a woman's things.

Pretending to look at pottery, she watched as the vendor took the items from Rhain and slowly inspected each item.

'Do you want that piece?' Nicholas said.

Helissent almost dropped the vase in her hand. She'd been pretending to inspect it and could see that both Nicholas and the vendor expected her to purchase it.

'No, I'm sorry.' She turned and smiled at the vendor, who winced before taking his ware from her hands.

When she looked back up, Rhain was standing at the next market stall.

'Do you want to return to the food stalls?' Nicholas said, his voice wavering as he swallowed.

She shook her head, though she wanted to tease him. Nicholas hadn't liked the food section of the market at all. Instead for now, she wanted to stay and watch what Rhain was doing. He wasn't purchasing, for it was him showing the needlework and necklace to the next vendor, while the first vendor was waving his hands and talking.

'You should leave him be,' Nicholas said evenly. He looked kindly, but also determined.

'How long have you been friends with him?'

'We fostered together at King Edward's court. I'd lay down my life for him and have on several occasions…like now.'

Helissent's neck hurt from craning to look at Nicholas, but she could read nothing from his expression. She thought she heard the emotion in his voice, though, and something within her lightened.

'I'm glad he has a friend like you,' she said. 'He has too many shadows.'

Nicholas's expression at once turned to regret.

When she realized how personal her words sounded, she tried to correct her mistake. 'I only meant—'

There was no fixing her words that wouldn't make it worse. Thus, she turned her back on Rhain and his business, as well as Nicholas's too-watchful eyes and secret agenda and quickly walked towards the food stalls, which she easily found.

The market was large, but now that she'd walked the entirety of it, she knew it wasn't large enough. Especially when Nicholas quickly caught up with her. 'Please let me talk.'

Reluctantly, she slowed her pace, but didn't glance his way.

'All women like him. At least with you, your admiration has merit past his pretty face. You're the only one he's ever saved and granted privileges no woman has had in the many years I've travelled with him.'

For some reason the thought warmed her even if it was futile. Rhain could never return any feelings for her...even if she had any towards him. Which she didn't. Couldn't.

'Be assured he's safe from the likes of me.' She waved to her face. 'I can't even smile without making a toothless vendor wince.'

Nicholas raised one brow. 'You think no man would find you attractive?'

The words were too close to what Rhain had said to her last night before he'd dismissed her and shown how false his kind words were. She stopped walking and didn't care about her neck pain as she glared at him. 'Did you talk to him last night?'

When Nicholas actually flushed, which made him look very unmercenary-like, her embarrassment turned to anger.

Nicholas, with his deep scar across his face and lost eye, with a mountain for a body instead of a normal man's, was mocking her.

'I know what kind of men find me attractive, as do you. You met them, remember?'

Nicholas's eye darkened. 'I should have killed them. Especially if it's left you continuing these foolish thoughts. You are no young maid; you have to know Rhain wants you.'

Oh. She couldn't look at him then, but not because she believed him. Because there could be no truth to it, even if, for the first time, she hoped there was. 'Maybe he's the foolish one, then.'

'I think Rhain's sane for the first time in his life, but now I have to wonder how sane you are.'

Not very if she was even considering Nicholas's words as true. 'It's not true, and even if so, it'll pass.'

'Definitely should have killed them,' he muttered.

But because Nicholas's words had been a bit kinder, she said, 'I wouldn't want you to scald your soul.'

'Scald?'

She lifted a shoulder. 'As when milk burns to the bottom of the cauldron. It ruins the pan and the food.'

'Ah, cooking terms I know nothing about, but

men like that I do. It's better that they were dead than them praying on those less fortunate.'

She hadn't thought of that. 'Will those men try again?'

'No—' he smiled cruelly '—and they're no longer men.'

That must mean… She didn't want to think what that meant, but she did want to know about the other things he said. 'Why was it a privilege for me to travel with you? I know about travelers and the women who go with them, but aren't there exceptions?'

Nicholas resumed walking. 'Are you asking why there aren't other women? Are you setting your sights on someone else though I told you Rhain wants you?'

'As though I'm the finest of pastries?'

'More baking terms?' He paused to think. 'No, you're more like a pastry displayed in some shop that Rhain can never afford.'

He made her sound like something rare, when she was far more common than that. Rhain had said similar words, and she no more believed Nicholas now, than she did Rhain.

Even if she did, she had no experience with it. She had never been spoken to this way before. Teased and flirted with as if she could ever have suitors. She didn't know how to respond. 'What of…what of the other men?'

'We're all stray dogs. I haven't been home since—' Nicholas's eye darted to the side and he cleared his throat. 'The other men we've met along the way of our journeys in Spain and down south. Subsequently, they haven't been with us that long, but we stop often enough; thus, there's been no discord about women travelling with us.'

And there was his protective tone again. 'You think I'll conflict with other flavors?'

He raised a brow, all serious now. Or puzzling her terms, but she didn't know how else to phrase it. The subject was too painful and filling her with a longing she didn't know she even had.

When he shook his head and shrugged one shoulder, she said, 'I'll cause discord by travelling with you?'

A knowing look in his eye like he was pleased with the direction of the conversation. 'You already do.'

She wasn't pleased; her heart sunk. She hadn't meant to cause discord, hadn't even realized she had. The men were quiet and she'd seen no arguments, but what did she know of mercenaries?

'I'd like to apologize to the men for making Rhain take me.'

Nicholas almost smiled then. 'I'd talk to Carlos; if anything, he'd understand.'

* * *

Nothing. Yet again. Rhain fought his bitter frustration as he wound his way through the market stalls to return to the keep.

Tickhill wasn't large, but some of the stalls were decent enough to show the needlework and necklace. To ask a few pertinent questions.

The answers were the same. Polite remarks on the needlework's workmanship; gasps of greed and sometimes envy as they regarded the necklace's beauty. But never any indication of who might have made or sold the necklace in the past. Never any recollections of the pendant's whereabouts.

This time, he felt the loss and knew it came because Reynold was coming for him. Tomorrow or the next day, they'd leave for York and he wondered if he had enough time for the markets there. York was very large. There was still a chance to find the answers on who his father was, on why he'd abandoned his mother.

He felt loss, but he was beginning to wonder if he felt another loss now. One that didn't make any sense since it was fragile…only a beginning. How could someone lose a beginning? Yet, that was the other emotion he fought. How he was soon to lose Helissent.

She didn't know his past, or the ugliness that flowed through his veins. He'd shared with her stories of his mother, his true mother. He'd never done that. Not once. If his mother came to conversation, he'd talk of Lady Gwalchdu, who died during his childbirth. Lady Gwalchdu, whom he thought was his mother until five years ago.

No, the woman who was truly his mother was Sister Ffion, whom he thought to be his aunt. A healer most of her life, it was she whom he followed in the gardens.

It was she who he told Helissent was his mother. What was it about Helissent that compelled him to tell the truth? Not even his cousin, his brother, knew the whole story, and he told Nicholas none of it.

He trusted Helissent as he had trusted very few and, last night in the hall, he had hurt her. He'd probably hurt her again today. But there was no remedy for any of it, not if he intended to keep her safe.

Rhain stopped short of reaching the keep. To his right, unmistakable in the soft light of the afternoon, was Helissent wandering the gardens with Carlos, alone.

He watched as Helissent lifted a sprig of rosemary to Carlos, who tilted his head to smell the fragrant herb.

A pleasant exchange, Carlos attentive as he walked a respectable distance on Helissent's scarred side. To anyone it would appear they were merely exchanging friendly conversation, but when Carlos's eyes lingered on Helissent's lips, no doubt to interpret the terminology he wouldn't understand, Rhain didn't care.

Chapter Eleven

Helissent heard the steps before she saw the source, but knew it was Rhain when Carlos scowled and stepped away.

Rhain said a few words in Spanish. Carlos said words back, stronger, very curt before he bowed to her and took his leave.

Rhain's eyes stayed with him, as did his fierce expression, then he turned his amber gaze to her.

Fierce. Troubled. She didn't expect, nor should she have expected, Rhain's attention today. Not after being dismissed by him yesterday.

And yet, with his studying gaze roving her features as if starved for the sight of her, a tiny bit of herself lifted inside.

Had Rhain meant those words from yesterday? She could almost believe it. Right now it looked like he was still trying to decipher the color of her hair and eyes. But she didn't know.

Didn't know the way of any of this because he'd thoroughly dismissed her yesterday and ignored her today.

'Do you like these gardens?' he asked.

He wished to talk of plants? She was certain she didn't understand. After her strange conversation with Nicholas, and then with Carlos, who was more than attentive, gardening was the last subject she expected to talk of.

He waved his hand around them. 'Are they vast enough for you?'

The gardens were magnificent, but his question was far from what she thought he'd say. 'Why are you asking me?'

He leaned down and brushed his hand against a lavender plant. 'After yesterday's feast, I expected you here before now.'

He hadn't been ignoring her, had known where she was. 'I've been at the market...like you.'

He nodded as if she answered his suspicions.

'Why did you show them that needlework and necklace?' she asked, though she'd been hardly aware she wanted to know.

He gave a small smile. 'Why am I always talking about her with you?'

Her... Last night, he'd dismissed her after they talked of his mother. 'I didn't know I was. I—'

'No, don't apologize. It's... I have not talked

of my mother with anyone for a very long time and yet with you it's as if I cannot stop.'

Why not talk of his mother? A noble woman, who also knew gardening and healing. She sounded remarkable. Then she realized what she should have before. 'She's gone, isn't she?'

'Five years now.'

She had lost family, too. Maybe this was why he seemed familiar to her. Though in truth, nothing about him and his gaze seemed real to her, let alone familiar. Especially not in the soft glow of afternoon with the heady scent of sage and rosemary.

Not when the very cut and color of his clothes differentiated them. The fine leather of his breeches, the thickness of his belt, the weave of his dark-green tunic, all of it a marked contrast to her torn and poorly patched brown gown.

And yet they strolled through the same gardens, they shared moments of their past together. They were sharing this moment.

'The necklace and needlework were hers,' Rhain said. 'She left them to me. The necklace is missing a pendant that's depicted in the needlework. I'd like to find it, hence when there are markets, I make enquiries.'

When he cleared his throat, and averted his eyes she knew he wanted to find it very much.

She knew how she felt about the parchment.

The one she'd opened finally, but still couldn't fully comprehend. A few letters looked familiar. Her father had taught her how to read with a stick in the dirt. It had been many years since then and she'd forgotten most of it.

There wasn't much written down on the tiny piece, hardly anything, but she longed to understand it.

Was this how Rhain felt? She didn't think it was possible to understand another human being, let alone this man who looked as though the world fell at his feet. Yet, they both felt loss and longing. For one bright moment, she thought of showing him the parchment.

Perhaps her longing to know the contents of the parchment were like his longing to find answers about the necklace. But what if the parchment had no answers? At least with him, he would have other markets, other opportunities. Once the parchment was read, she would have no more hope. Would be left with only…longing.

'What do you think about the castle?'

He changed the subject again, but it was easier to talk of castles instead of connections.

She waved towards the soaring structures to her right. 'I know I am to be impressed by the ramparts and the gatehouse, but the kitchens would have to be my favorite.'

Rhain's hand went to the hilt of his dagger

before he clasped his hands behind his back. 'I hoped you would get a chance to see them.'

'Oh, yes, and the cellars. I dragged Nicholas there before we went to the market,' she said.

'Were they everything you expected?'

She could never expect the abundance she saw. 'So many duties, rooms and supplies! Everybody had a position and all worked together. It was mesmerizing to see.' She almost smiled and just stopped herself.

They walked in silence until they turned the corner where the garden wasn't as private.

Three women stopped their animated conversation to stare in their direction. At first, she turned her head so they could see her disfigurement. But they weren't looking at her.

Rhain turned his head away, but one of the women giggled and it was apparent they wouldn't hide their gazes until they caught his eye.

He'd forgotten to put his hood up. She thought he used it because he was a mercenary, but it was for this. He must have been plagued with stares all his life. How could he not?

He was god-like. Perfect. From his golden hair, to the arch of his darker brows, to the almost blackness of his long lashes framing eyes that rivalled warmed honey. Days she'd watched him and now travelled with him. Of course, she noticed the looks he garnered.

His face too beautiful, his body lean and predatory. Her father had told her of wild beasts in other lands. Of lions displayed on the King's arms. When she couldn't imagine them, he'd drawn one in the sandy dirt. He was always drawing and explaining when they should have been tilling the field. She remembered the lion's great mane, the paws the size of a man's head that held claws as big as daggers.

Her father was too analytical to exaggerate, and yet, she didn't believe him when he said the lion would rest and wait for his prey, then attack before the prey realized the lion was there. How could no animal notice such a fantastical creature?

Rhain was like that. A lion. A golden beast, who lived in the golden sands and sun of some far-off land.

But she imagined the lion proud of his strength and of his dominion over those lesser. Rhain acted as though he hated it.

What man hated the attention of women? At the market that morning, she'd watched as Rhain crossed a different section than her and Nicholas. Constantly he was given free tastes of food, and handed small trinkets. A little girl had given him a handful of perfectly round pebbles. Almost like offerings to a god or a lion.

Attention. Honour. Respect. All because of

the way he looked, his obvious wealth and the spurs announcing his station. He lived a life exceedingly opposite of hers, but never more than in this. His beauty against her beastliness.

Rhain didn't spare the women a glance and she almost felt sorry for them. She understood. Days in his company didn't lesson his beauty. The sunlight or moonlight only revealed other facets as if he was a gem.

Though they no longer faced the women, Rhain's scowl did not ease, and his fingers flitted around the dagger at his waist. Was he tempted to throw it at them?

'They cannot help it,' she said. She knew that when it came to her own face.

He didn't pretend to misunderstand. 'They need to.'

'Is this why you wear the hood? Shouldn't you be used to their stares?'

He arched his brow. 'Like you?'

He had thrown the dagger; a verbal one, and it hit close to her heart.

'I've seen you do it,' he said. 'Like now, your hair off to the side, perfectly covering the left side of your face and revealing all of your scars.'

He was turning that verbal dagger and she wanted to increase her pace, but that would be too telling. 'You're being ridiculous. This is but one—'

He shook his head. 'No, it's been everywhere. I've watched you do it. What I can't appreciate is why?'

'Are you saying I should hide under a hood like you?'

Rhain lowered his eyes. When he raised his golden head again, there was a determination in his steady gaze. 'No, never. But maybe it would be better if you did.'

She had never, not once, been truly insulted by him. He had been so at ease with her. Now he revealed he knew the same horror everyone else felt when they saw her scars.

'You need to let me pass.'

He grabbed her scarred wrist, held her lightly, but firmly. 'No, you misunderstand. I don't want you to hide, but for some reason I don't want you to show your scars to others.'

She wouldn't believe him. 'You're ashamed of me.'

'*Never.* Only tell me why do you do it?'

For a moment she wanted to spill her pain to him, but in the next held back. He could never understand.

The women still stared and she knew they were making a scene or at least a prelude to a scene. But it didn't feel that way with Rhain's fingers sliding across hers…like a caress.

'Let go of my wrist.'

His amber eyes snapped to their hands, which were all but holding like they were lovers, and he released her slowly, reluctantly.

He caressed her wrist. He talked to her, but avoided other women. He'd known loss as did she. Something about the way he looked bothered him; her own appearance only gave her pain. Yet, now he dismissed her, was short with her, as he had been with Carlos.

'What did you say to Carlos?' she asked.

He walked in the direction they'd come and she allowed him the reprieve as he roughly brushed his hand against the lavender. When some flowers broke away, he rubbed them until their scent released into the air.

'I always loved the scent of lavender.'

'What did you say?' she repeated.

'I wanted to give you something, Helissent,' he said. 'He needed to go.'

Shadows. He was all shadows now. They hadn't finished talking of his mother, she almost mentioned the parchment, and now it felt like all was lost.

Because of those women, because he was displeased she showed her scars. Why did he want to know why she did it?

Did he feel the same, wanting to know more about her, the way she did about him?

He wanted her to believe Carlos needed to go

so he could give her a present. But she was learning. Carlos needed to go because Rhain didn't want him there and it had nothing to do with presents.

'I don't need anything,' she said. 'Tell me about Carlos.'

'You need this.' He gave a light teasing smile that didn't reach his eyes. 'It has to do with my mother again.'

This wasn't the same as knowing more of him. She knew it wasn't the same, but resigned, she gave a quick nod.

'She kept journals of her gardening, and her healing,' he continued. 'I can't tell you how many times my men and I used the different healing properties with other healers along our trails.'

'You must have had some fierce arguments with those healers.'

A curve to his lips. 'I had no idea such things could be up for such debate.'

'There were two healers in the town where I… stayed. I think I was their pride and their experiment to see what salves worked on me.'

He stilled and she realized she had confessed something about herself. Something she hadn't shared with anyone.

'Did their care hurt?' he said.

'Sometimes, but everything hurt then. I've had a great admiration for healers ever since.

Always wished I had learned something before I returned to the inn.'

'I want you to have them,' he said in a rush.

'No.' She shook her head. 'I couldn't possibly, you said how useful they were. You aren't quitting being a mercenary?'

'Have you ever known a mercenary to quit?' He wasn't truly asking a question.

'Other than you and the men, I know none at all, but I do know you get hurt. I won't have them.'

'Tender care, Helissent? I'll have you know it's wasted on me.'

She'd blush if she could. She certainly felt embarrassment. But Rhain didn't avert his eyes and they were as sincere as she ever saw them. 'You mean it.'

She couldn't accept such a gift. She had nothing of her mother's, only vague recollections of warmth and discipline. The smell of sunshine on laundry reminded her of that fateful day, but also better days. She knew how she wished for some trinket or spoon that her mother touched. But what Rhain was giving her was more than a spoon.

Precious writing from his mother in her own handwriting. More than that, the journal contained medicinal healing subscriptions. He needed the journals.

'You'll treat them well,' he said. 'You said you always wanted to learn.'

This wasn't right. She knew it from his voice, from his stance. He expected her to disagree. 'Why are you doing this?'

'Do you like Tickhill?' he asked.

It all came together then. Why he asked how she liked the gardens. Nicholas giving her a tour of the kitchens. The fact Rhain started talking to her when they reached the village.

'You're leaving me here.'

His eyes were completely shuttered, his jaw like stone. 'Yes.'

'I want to go to York.'

'Tickhill has kitchens, gardens, markets,' he said. 'It's a castle. I know the men here; you would be guaranteed a position. You'd most likely teach the cook a few tricks. You could bake for royalty.'

'So I wouldn't be a whore here,' she bit out.

He shifted his stance. 'I remedied that impression this morning before I visited the markets. Allen had gathered some information for me and I talked to the steward and ensured our... relationship.'

They had no relationship especially since he intended for her to stay behind. 'All you wanted was to repair my reputation so that I stayed here.'

* * *

He didn't deny it. Rhain knew he'd hurt Helissent, though she deservedly cut him with her words.

He'd take more words if it meant she'd stay, but her chin was lifted, her eyes narrowed on his. She wouldn't accept the journals or Tickhill and he feared he didn't have the strength to make her. Nicholas was right when it came to her.

This woman, with her unaccountable hair and hazel eyes intrigued him in a way that he had no control over. She was making him come alive and it was too late. He couldn't have her around him any more, or he might forget. Like now.

All he wanted to do was take her in his arms and kiss her until any such arguments were forgotten. Lacking that, he was left with her looking at him fiercely and standing toe to toe.

She wouldn't be bought off and with her past she deserved to know the truth…though he was fool to reveal his weakness.

'You have to,' he said. 'It isn't safe to travel with me or my men.'

She stepped back and gave a frustrated sound. 'I already gathered that. I may not know mercenaries, but I'm not naive. I only intend to stay until York.'

'It's not that I'm only a mercenary. Someone wants me dead.'

She frowned; she didn't understand.

Why would she? He was a mercenary, of course someone would want him dead. 'The man in question is powerful and he'll stop at nothing. Anyone I'm around can, and most likely will, be killed as well.'

She looked away at that. 'Nicholas.'

He told her her life was threatened and she thought of his friend. 'Yes, him as well.'

'But the men…your skills and connections.'

'Are all naught against this particular man.'

'You speak as if you're already dead.'

'I'd be a fool not to. I have a man from one of the most influential and corrupted families in the country after me with a rightful claim to my head.'

She looked at him sharply for that. 'What did you do?'

'It was personal. Which is why when he kills me, it will be personal. Hence, it's safer for you to be here. Perhaps I should have warned you before you came, but I couldn't leave you in that village either.'

'No.'

It wasn't an option. 'I intend to leave you here. You shouldn't, nor will you be able to, travel with us again.'

'I need to get to York. There isn't anyone else who would take me. It has to be you.'

'It's safe here, Helissent. There are walls, and guards here to protect you if it comes to that.'

'Why do you care about protecting me?'

'There's a chance just in the brief time we've been acquaintances he would know of you. You could be a target.'

Disquiet folded and stirred in her stomach, but it wasn't enough. 'We're just strangers.'

He held that studying gaze. His warm amber eyes, so like honey. As a child she used to hold it to the sunlight or a candle and stare at it between her fingers. Always it shone a different way depending on the light. His eyes were like that, showing her a different way and one she never knew she could take. Or one that she deserved.

'We're not strangers, Helissent. I don't think we've ever been.'

Was he saying she was familiar to him? No, his gaze was too warm for that. He spoke of desire, of want and need. It was undeniable that she desired him. It had been there, underneath all her musings and wondering about him while he sat at the inn with his hood up.

Even hidden, she noticed him. It was worse because her attraction wasn't simple like those women on the other side of the gardens. She wondered and was curious about *him*.

She'd never felt this way before, not once for

any traveler. Only him. But that didn't change anything. Not when she was flawed on the outside, and even more on the inside.

'You recognize this, don't you?' He took a step closer to her. 'I do. Too much. The longer we spend together, will only make me forget why I need to stay away.'

Desire, but she was still unwanted.

She averted her eyes.

'I'm giving you warnings,' he said. 'With an enemy or without, I'm not safe with you.' He touched a finger to her chin, to return her gaze to his. 'Ah, it's my other words you do not believe.'

Nicholas had said something of Rhain's desires. She had years of evidence to the contrary. 'This isn't true; none of this could possibly be true.'

'Why? Because of your scars?'

'Yes,' she said. But it was more, because she didn't deserve someone liking her that way.

'I watched you those days, as you watched me. How kind you were to strangers even though most weren't to you, and you weren't kind to yourself.'

He brushed her scarred cheek with the back of his finger. 'Are these the reason you aren't kind with yourself, Helissent?'

She jerked her face away from his simple touch. They stood in the gardens where anyone could see them.

No, they somehow stood in the part of the garden that was private. Great yew shrubbery and rose bushes surrounded them. No one would see them; her modesty was safe.

But she didn't step back for modesty, she did it because of how it felt. How his simple touch across her cheek prickled and tightened her skin, her blood, her body. All with…want. She wanted Rhain of Gwalchdu. As a woman does a man, and he was leaving her.

'You don't deserve an answer to that question,' she said.

'I know that more than anyone, and yet…' He cupped her jaw between both his hands and stroked his thumb across her bottom lip. Then he dipped his head. His breath still; hers caught.

The smell of lavender, sage, leather and steel. The smell of *him*. The heat from his skin; the pressure of air between them. Drawing his brows in, he dipped his chin lower so that his lips hovered over hers. Once, twice, her heart beat like this. Then a soft exhale of air and the tension around them released.

'Stay, Helissent, be safe,' he whispered against her lips. 'I am no savior.'

She stood as still as the lavender bushes and just as inconsequential when he walked past her and out of the garden.

Chapter Twelve

'This is not happening again,' Nicholas said, trying to sound aggrieved, but he was laughing all the same.

Rhain wanted to gut him, would have, too, but he wanted to strangle Helissent more. It was early in the morning, he'd gotten no sleep and was exhausted. There wasn't any rain this time, but she stood as stubbornly with his men as before.

Helissent, who was again dressed in everything she owned except there were no bags at her feet. From the look on Carlos's face, he was the one who tied her bags to his horse. He would address Carlos's assumptions another day.

Today, it seemed his attention would be taken by a woman he never wanted to forget…and who appeared as though she wouldn't let him.

'I'll need help getting on the horse,' she said.

Aware of his men's eyes on him, he said, 'I thought you were intending to stay.'

'No. I'd like to travel to York.'

He couldn't outright deny her. Only Nicholas knew of Reynold, but she didn't know that, and still she stood here defying him.

He was too soft with her, but he was always too soft with her. The man he was before had been free, forgave easily and was curious. He thought that man was killed upon his mother's death, upon learning the truth of his past.

One glimpse of Helissent in the inn and he learned that was a lie. He wasn't dead, only wished he was.

'Do you have any cakes?' he said.

She pulled a tiny scroll from her belt. 'No, but I have a parchment I thought you could read for me?'

He took it from her outstretched hand, twirled it in his fingers as he noted the darkened places where the mud had clung to it when Rudd threw it to the ground.

Then he handed it back to her and hoisted her on his horse.

They rode for hours, but Helissent didn't speak and neither did Rhain.

He wasn't angry this time. She knew what that felt like when she forced herself on the first trip.

No, Rhain's silence was more powerful than his anger, with a *frisson* of something like anticipation.

It was more acute than the garden when he'd cupped her jaw, and leaned until his lips were close to hers. He hadn't kissed her yesterday, but she'd wanted him to. His breath, his lips soft almost a zephyr against hers. Unerringly in that moment, she had intricately folded him into every bit of her like the most substantial of recipes.

She knew she could never extricate herself from him. He'd got too close and she had let him.

Riding with him didn't help. The way he breathed, slow and steady, each inhale moving her own body until her breaths matched his and she had to force her lungs at a different pace.

But that didn't separate him from her, not when he'd turn and she'd feel his warm breath against the curve of her ear, or feel the subtle pressure of his legs against the horse to urge it in some direction that somehow urged her, too.

His arms were worse. For though the intention was to cradle her on the horse, the result was they cradled her to him as well.

She hadn't been held this much, or this close to another person for years, if ever. It had to be that that caused the ache inside her.

He was silent, with emotions she could only

guess vibrating between them. The silence would continue if she didn't break it. If she felt like this now, she didn't know how much further she could ride…how much further he would let her.

He told her she would not be leaving with them today and she gave him no choice. She owed him an explanation for her demands.

But simply arguing that she needed to go to York wouldn't be enough. She owed him much more than that. Except she didn't feel like she had all the answers. She hoped the tiny scroll could help her.

'Can you read the parchment if I take the reins?' she said.

'Of course,' he said, releasing his entwined fingers from the leather straps and wrapping them around hers. Looser, but she felt the well-worn warmth of the reins, and wanted to hold them that bit closer. Slowly, he unrolled the tiny piece of paper to read the contents.

She barely glanced at it. After staring at it for hours and days, she had it memorized. It was all lines crisscrossed. There were letters next to numbers. Some she understood, most she did not.

Rhain's thumb systematically brushed across and down the lines. While he spent a lengthy time looking at the small scrap of paper, she waited until the back of her neck prickled and her shoulders tightened with discomfort. Then she held out her hand. 'I'm sorry, you can give it back, I just thought—'

'I know how to read, Helissent,' he interrupted, his tone wry. 'I'm simply atrocious at reading ledgers.'

'Ledgers?'

'This is accounting, plain and simple. Some letters indicating goods, which I can't decipher because they don't amount to words, and numbers next to them indicating price. This number here is zero, which means the account was good. Whatever was bartered, it was paid for in full. Nothing was owed in the end.'

The prickling on the back of her neck rushed down her back to her feet. Like a wave of ice water in a cauldron that swamped the contents in the bottom. She felt like those drowning contents.

A ledger. No indication of how she fared as a child, alone and in pain. She knew Agnes was formal and brisk. But she'd expected, wished, for some inkling of caring from John and Anne.

'This is an accounting of you, isn't it? It's what Rudd had that night?'

'Yes, it's between Agnes, the healer, and John and Anne from the inn. I…suppose it's what they paid, or bartered to pay, for her care of me.'

He carefully rolled the parchment and put it

away. She didn't bother with noticing where because it didn't matter.

It was just more of nothing to her. She shouldn't be disappointed and yet she couldn't help it. She was no better or worse than before. It just felt like it.

Gently, he took the reins from her, and she tucked her now-cold hands into her skirts.

'Well, some of the handwriting on there is theirs at least.'

She almost cried then. Not because her hopes were nothing more than dregs, but because Rhain guessed why she wanted it to be read.

The ledger's writing all looked the same to her, but it was kind for him to offer her something. He was a good man and owed much more than the trouble she layered on him.

She didn't have any goods to barter with to make their account zero, but she had one thing she'd never given before.

'I don't remember much of my parents,' she said. 'I was but eight when the fire happened. My sister was four. My mother and I were hanging laundry. My father and sister were resting. My father was older than my mother. He was tall, lanky. Educated. He had an accent different than my mother's English; I think he may have been French, but I don't remember very well.'

Nothing in the way he moved the horse, or

the way he breathed, told her he was listening. But she saw his right hand flit along the rein and knew his focus was on her words. It was enough for her to continue.

'My mother was stern, and constantly waving her spoon around. I was terrified of that spoon. My sister, Aimee, would giggle. Father wasn't much of a sheep farmer. He had a book. Small, but wrapped in the finest of cloths and positioned on a shelf. No matter how many times he took it down and read us a few of the words, we all held still to listen.'

'Why are you telling me this?'

'Because....'

Something in the way he asked let her know she didn't have to begin her tale this way. Even if she only told him the end, he wouldn't care. He didn't need to know everything, but for some reason she wanted him to.

For him to understand not like the villagers or innkeepers, who were there that day. They knew the facts. She wanted to tell Rhain her story because he had known what that parchment meant to her.

'Because I owe you. You told me to stay and I'm here again.'

'So since you have no cakes, you'll pay me back with an entertaining tale of your horrific childhood.'

Mocking words indicating he didn't truly think that. Derision in his voice belying that a part of him did.

'No! You told me of the danger against you.'

'Ah, a consolation prize for me because I'm a dead man.'

This conversation wasn't going as she intended. Not that she had specific expectations. After all she never expected to tell the tale at all. Ever. But he had told her he fully expected to die from some powerful man's sword. Then there was the way he looked for his mother's pendant.

He told her to stay to protect her. She wanted him to know she listened, but she had her own powerful reasons to go.

'Please.' It was all she could say.

Rhain's right hand clenched, released. Then he gave a sharp whistle that Nicholas turned around for. Whatever was communicated, Rhain slowed their horse and Nicholas kept pace so that soon there was distance between them.

'You don't have to,' he whispered. 'I'm taking you to York.'

'I know.'

'I'm a curious man. I may ask questions I have no right to ask.'

She thought she understood that as well. Except for the part when he said he had no right to hear her story.

In truth, she expected him to ask questions. At the same time, she expected this conversation to cause her pain. But there was another factor, one that she didn't expect, and it felt like gratefulness. Because this man cared enough to be curious about her.

'You have questions already?' she said.

She sensed his quick smile. 'Yes. Already.'

'Then ask,' she said, bracing herself.

'Why do you not know more of your father?' he said. 'Did no one in the town talk to you about your parents?'

That wasn't the question she expected, but she was thankful for the ease of it nonetheless.

'No one. I think they thought it was best forgotten. John and Anne told me a little, but they, too, didn't want to approach it. I don't know how much they even knew. They were older than my parents. They had three sons and all of them were gone by the time I lived with them. They couldn't have been close to my family because I don't remember them from before the fire at all.'

'But the village must have rallied to help you—'

'Oh, no. There wasn't a healer in our village. I was sent away.' She adjusted in her seat. 'I don't remember much after the fire. The pain was excruciating. For weeks, I could only sense someone wrapped and gave me salves. When I could remember, there was a hut attached to caves. A brisk woman, Agnes, with gnarled hands. I remember honey. The taste of it on my lips. Day after day of honey. You'd think I'd be sick of it, but I think my craving for it only increased. It was almost a year later when I returned to the village.

'John and Anne came for me. At that time, I was wrapped from head to toe in bandages I could change myself and pots of honey with herbs in it were in my sacks.'

Rhain remained quiet now though he'd warned her he'd ask questions. She didn't know if his silence made it easier or harder to tell what she had to next. But it wasn't her place to make further demands on him. To request he talk to make things easier for her.

She knew more than most that there was hardship in the world and hers was merely one tale.

'John and Anne immediately took me to where my old home was,' she continued. 'I didn't ask them; I think it was for me to comprehend that I would be living with them; that my family was truly gone and they would be my family. They were strangers and I hadn't fully comprehended what they had done for me, what they would become to me. I had thought Agnes was my future. They waited patiently while I searched for trinkets. I may have been searching for hours. I didn't expect to see my father's book, but a burnt spoon handle would have done. I wasn't looking for anything of worth. I thought… I thought everything useful had been used to pay the healer. Until Rudd told me otherwise.

'Rudd had told me—'

'I heard Rudd that night,' he said. 'I shouldn't have let him live.'

Nicholas had said the same.

When Rhain didn't elaborate, she rushed on. 'Well, between the innkeepers and…his arrival, my life was good. They were old and I was happy helping them. I learned to bake.'

'You learned to bake very well,' Rhain said.

It was a question as much as anything else. 'I scrounged up any spare ingredients I could find. Sometimes my cakes were tiny and they made barely a bite. But it was enough to keep going.'

'No one helped you?'

'John and Anne could cook, but they exchanged food or goods for bread, and I saw a way I could help them.'

'You spent a lot of time in the kitchen…in the fires.'

'You're asking how I could stand it.' She thought the conversation was going to be easier. 'At first I couldn't.'

It wasn't only the lack of ingredients that

caused the cakes to remain small, but also the amount of time she could stay within the kitchens while the fire blazed. She still braced herself before she faced the oven directly to retrieve a loaf. She'd burned herself more times than not, but the innkeepers had saved her and she'd do anything for them.

'At first, the fires were too much. Yet sometimes there are people we know that are worth the pain,' she said.

He exhaled a quick breath.

'Do you know about that?' she asked.

'Very much.'

They rode in silence again, but this time, Helissent could feel Rhain's turbulent thoughts. She had some of her own. Her tale wasn't done yet. Though she wasn't prepared to tell him all of the end, that part was between her soul and God, she wanted to tell him most. She wanted to bare part of her shame, if not her cowardice.

'My mother saw the fire before it consumed the house.'

He made some vital sound and she stopped. Waited, but he stayed in silence, and so did she.

The only sound between them was the horse's hooves beneath them. Its occasional snort as it pulled on the reins to catch up with the others. The men's voices wafted around them, but they were far ahead, and she couldn't follow their words. She and Rhain were alone as much as they'd ever been.

'It's enough,' he said after a while. 'What you said before. I don't need to hear any more.'

'I know.'

'Do you…need to tell me?'

'I've told no one this before. The villagers and the innkeepers knew the facts.'

'But travelers, did they never enquire?'

He was curious, he was asking questions. She was glad for them. 'When I was a child they asked many times,' she said. 'I never stayed around to listen.'

'You wish to tell me otherwise?'

He'd wanted her to stay at Tickhill to protect her. He'd almost kissed her. He had been familiar to her from the beginning, but now it was more. Maybe that something more was what prompted her to say, 'Very much.'

He did something startling then, he combined the reins in one hand and took one of hers and held it. She hadn't realized she'd been trembling until he secured her own disfigured hand in his. She didn't realize she needed that touch until that moment.

Her eyes focused on her hand in his, she said, 'The fire didn't look like much from a distance. If my father and sister were resting, then there was still a chance to get them. When they weren't outside, we ran into the house. There we had to force our way in because the fire was worse inside.

'My sister was in the main room, mere feet away from the door. My father was nowhere in sight. My mother shouted for me to take my sister out while she went to the back to get my father. I...' she breathed a shaky breath '...never saw my mother again. I grabbed my sister's hand. Her eyes were big, scared. So relieved to see me. There was a lot of billowing smoke. It burned to breathe; to see. I tripped on something, I don't know what. I didn't let go of my sister's hand and she fell with me. We were scrambling up when part of the ceiling caved in. It pinned us down.

'I was able to break free, but she was stuck. I knew my mother and father were already dead. The bedroom where my mother fled to was a wall of flames. I was holding my sister's hand when the smoke overtook me.'

She couldn't tell him the rest. Not when tears ran down her face and Rhain engulfed both her hands in his.

Rhain struggled to breath. The weight of her words, the weight of her pain was crushing him. How had she picked herself up afterward; how could she bake cakes? He knew before he asked the question, yet still he asked, 'Why me, why now?'

She took a shaky breath. 'Tickhill is wonderful, but it is too efficient. I couldn't get lost there. I couldn't find my way. I don't know if you understand, but I need to be... I don't know how to explain it.'

He did understand, pain, loneliness, an orphan. Tickhill was a king's property. Rich, well supplied and prepared. Incompetence and inefficiency wouldn't be accepted, and it had been running that way for years.

Whereas for the innkeepers, she learned to face the fires, to bake and cook. When they fell ill, she fed and cared for them. They truly needed her and she needed them just as much.

There was another part of her tale he understood as well. How her scars were outside and his were in. But scars were scars as were needs.

And he had them now. Every bit of her tale demanded he protect her, revere her. The halo of blond around her face, the delicate lines of her neck, the wave of her hand. The way she felt in his arms as they rode on and on... All of that was something else indeed. Desire. Lust. Need. All for her.

This brave, beautiful woman he found at this time of his life and he couldn't give her an answer of why he understood her. For to answer her would be making some acknowledgment of her importance. She couldn't be important to him.

'It'll take us days to reach York.' His voice sounded hollow over the roaring in his ears. 'You may live to regret it.'

He already did. More days in her company when his desire for her was undeniable.

More chances for Reynold to discover her, use her...kill her. So strong, brave, more than he could ever guess, but she stood no chance against Reynold's sword or wrath.

'I know you wished to protect me from this man after you, but I couldn't stay at Tickhill.'

How could she still not understand the full truth of why he wanted her to remain at the castle? 'I didn't make arrangements for you to stay at Tickhill only to protect you from my enemy. I did it to protect you from me.'

Chapter Thirteen

'Should we send out two more?' Nicholas asked. Though he knew Nicholas was circumspect, Rhain looked around from where they sat. They'd stopped the horses to rest and stretch, and most of the men were throwing daggers at targets. Helissent had left for the woods and would soon return.

'We send any more men, they'll be noticed. York is merely days away. We'll meet halfway before we run into any trouble.'

'You think there will be trouble?'

Rhain took out his mother's necklace and let the silver strands slide from one hand down to the other. Back and forth until in the afternoon light it looked like water.

'Reynold shouldn't know we're anywhere near this part of England, but York is large and there are many places to hide if he lies in wait for me.'

'But not for me?' Nicholas said blithely. 'The way you cut me out of the discussion, I could get my feelings hurt.'

'Who cares for your feelings when it'll save your head?' Because he could, Rhain gazed pointedly downward until Nicholas and he laughed.

And it felt good.

'We haven't talked like this since…' Nicholas stopped, shook his head.

Rhain's laughter left him. 'Are you going to mention her again?'

'No, it changes your mood of late. You're growing surly on me.'

Surly was a mild word for the raging of emotions clashing inside him. He'd begun training again if only to release some of the tension. It didn't help when Helissent watched.

'Perhaps some of that mead will help. Do we have any of it left?'

'From Tickhill?' Rhain lifted a shoulder. 'I doubt we've drunk it all in the half a day since we left.'

'I don't trust the men from Flanders. They keep leaving to hunt food. Who knows what they're pilfering?'

'We're eating their food, and you think they have time to steal?'

'Then we could have a celebration of sorts.'

'A celebration when there's a madman after us and you and I will soon be dead?'

'Yes, precisely for that reason. Danger's always a good reason to drink.' Nicholas exhaled roughly. 'I could use some mead now.'

Rhain recognized that tone. 'You *are* talking of her.'

'You did take her again.'

He owed Nicholas an explanation though he didn't know what the explanation would be. 'You were there this morning—you think I had a choice?'

'There is always a choice. You thought to leave her at Tickhill, and then you didn't.'

'How do I not know that Reynold is riding mere days behind us? I couldn't leave her undefended.'

'You used that argument when you sent riders *ahead* of us to watch for Reynold. Come, you used to be more quick of tongue and mind. Surely you can conjure a stronger argument than that.'

Rhain stilled his hands. 'We're not working with a logical man, why should my moves be logical?'

'Well, at least you admit to being illogical.' Nicholas paused as they watched Helissent emerge from the woods only to bend down around the trees.

At this angle, Rhain could see none of her scars, only the beauty she was born with and she had copious amounts. From her tall slender form to the delicate upturn of her nose and the stubborn tilt of her chin. Now that he knew her story, he knew her true beauty was revealed by her scarred side. Her true worth was somewhere in the very heart of her.

He'd wanted to taste her lips, to steal a kiss. He'd made his want all the worse when he agreed to listen to her story.

Nicholas's eyes tracked Helissent's progress with the herbs. 'Though I still can't perceive why you've refused the other women, at least with her, I appreciate why you won't let her go.'

Was he so transparent? His interest in her kept increasing, from that moment he opened the inn's door and tasted her cakes. Then that last night in the village. While rage still seethed through his veins from Rudd, desire coursed through his very marrow as he tended her injuries and watched her eyes darken in candlelight.

Fascination. Desire. More than he'd felt in years, more than he'd felt ever. Still, because of Reynold, because of who he was, he should have walked away.

Except now she'd told him how she rushed into her flaming home to rescue her sister. It only took a few words for his resolve to weaken.

His fascination and desire turning to need. He struggled not to find excuses to be alone with her. He failed every attempt to not track her with his eyes.

'I'll let her go, just as I have the others.' Though to let her go now would be equivalent to him stopping his own breath.

The irony was not lost on him. He was a dead man anyway. At least by letting her go, she might live.

Nicholas's watchful gaze was both warning and triumphant. 'So sure of that?'

Rhain clenched the necklace in his hands. He'd handled it more now than he ever had in five years and knew he did it to remind himself.

He might need Helissent now, but he was not worthy of her. His very blood would taint her. 'York will be her new home, but it won't be ours.'

It was only the end of the first day away from Tickhill, and the air was laden with Rhain's remarks, his studying amber gaze and his shadows.

Carlos was still attentive, but more reserved. His eyes darted to Rhain every time she asked about the burn on his arm. Which made her contemplate more on the words they exchanged that day in the garden.

It had sounded like a warning, something territorial. It felt territorial to her now once she combined his remarks with Carlos's politeness and Nicholas's secretive behavior.

Nicholas who equally smirked and watched her as carefully as she had her cakes when she first began baking.

But all of it, even as busy as she was gathering kindling, cooking, through it all, she watched Rhain.

Alone outside Tickhill, he didn't bother with the hood. She should be getting used to the graceful litheness of his body, the angle of his jaw, the warm hue of his skin, but it wasn't possible. It was like getting used to a combination of ingredients that should have been ordinary: a nose, lips and shoulders. But somehow with him, combined, he was something sublime. Like when he walked or simply ate, or when he touched the hilt of his dagger at his waist.

The grace and competence of it fascinated her. It wasn't a nervous gesture, nor one that seemed to reassure him, but something born of habit, a part of him.

He was acutely effective at it and it compelled her to watch.

How he separated his fingers so that each one felt the length of the three leather-ribbed strips circling the hilt.

Then his hand would still and his forefinger would arc to the hilt and caress the well-worn metal pommel. Around, around, around.

Always three times as if to inspect the rounded hilt and sides. All the while the rest of his hand would stroke upwards and his fingers would meet again. Before he'd finish, he'd cup his hand along the top and rub like a ritual.

Sometimes that same hand would do nothing at all, just rest on the edge of a chair arm. Most days he'd simply use it to tear his bread or throw his cloak over his shoulder.

His ritual was never over for her. Hours afterward the caress thrummed and vibrated through her. At night she only needed to remember and a wave of heat would arc through her.

She knew she'd never feel such a caress from him. Though something was different when it came to him. There was enough silence in the day for her to wonder about it. Perhaps it was how he and the other mercenaries treated her.

For the first time in her life, and on several occasions now, she'd forgotten she was scarred and full of shame. It was a revelation to her, but it didn't change the facts. She did have scars, she did carry shame.

And she didn't deserve to forget no matter how much she was beginning wonder, or long for caresses. As soon as they reached York and other people cringed from her, she'd be brutally reminded of who, and what, she was.

Chapter Fourteen

She heard the tromping of heavy feet and knew her time laying in the sun was over. Though he'd never had heavy feet since the moment she met him, she knew Rhain was beyond the tree line and the shrubbery that bordered the small stream where she had just swum.

It was early morning, all of the men except Nicholas, had gone hunting. It seemed like an opportune time to take advantage of the small stream nearby and wash away the campfire's ash.

She had divested herself of her gown, hose and shoes close to the camp, intending only to remain nearby, but the coolness of the water stung her skin and she swam further downstream until it eased.

Rhain should have been nowhere near here and she scrambled to stand in her dripping wet chemise to address him.

'I noticed you didn't bring a towel,' he called out beyond the low shrubbery, 'and thought you could use one.'

She watched his strong arm vault a large piece of cloth over the bush.

'You came all this way to give me a towel?'

'Along with your clothing and a new chemise.' Those he laid out on the shrubbery, but she still couldn't see him.

'I thought you were hunting.'

'Nicholas found me and told me what you'd done.'

'So he thought I should have an escort?'

'It's dangerous. You know this, though you swam away versus staying around the camp where Nicholas could hear you.'

'Wouldn't it have been simpler to stop me himself?'

'He knew better than to stop you himself.'

That comment was cryptic, but warmed her none the less. Was this because he wanted no one to see her in her chemise?

'What do you expect me to do with the clothing?'

'Change. Walk back with me.'

And be naked in front of him with her scars. She couldn't see him, but that didn't mean he couldn't see her. 'Do I have a choice?'

'I wasn't planning on giving you any.'

She didn't think so, but she could be quick. When she snatched the towel and clothing, she didn't see him in sight.

Not until she had stripped off her wet chemise and grabbed the towel.

Then she heard his voice very close indeed. When she looked up, he was there, a pot of ointment in his hand.

'I almost forget to give you this...' he said, his voice trailing.

She stood stunned. It wasn't because he suddenly stood in front of her. It was his expression. It was his locked stillness, as if something she did, stunned *him*.

Then he breathed raggedly, his eyes dipped and roved, and fixated on her. His hands clenched around the pot like such a tiny thing could provide support. Trying to smile, she offered her hand to accept it.

'I do need the salve. Thank you for remembering.'

It would help her skin which was beginning to sting again now that the coldness of the water wasn't there to alleviate it.

But as he stood there and continued to caress and clutch the pot, she realized her skin wasn't stinging. It felt like it was tightening. Becoming all too aware of the warmth of the sun against her shoulders, the cool wind that brushed across the tips of her breasts.

In other parts of her body, she felt heavier, her belly, her legs languid. Gooseflesh prickled along her arms and the back of her neck.

She watched changes to Rhain as he stood there, the unevenness of his breaths, the mottled flush to his cheeks, the slight parting of his lips.

Rhain's amber eyes returned to hers, but they were darker now. As if they were in the deepest part of the ovens where it should be bright with fire, but instead was black with heat.

She felt as though she was in the deepest part of the ovens...and he had put her there.

She lowered her outstretched hand and he avidly watched that movement, as if something fascinated him.

'You were changing,' he said, his voice tight.

'You said to; you brought me clothes, which is kind because the water was cold and I don't think my other chemise would dry.'

'Cold,' he repeated, rubbing his hand across his mouth, holding out the salve and dropping it when she tentatively offered again to take it.

He took a step abruptly back.

She bent to apply the salve to her, then froze. She remembered she was naked. Before Rhain. Exposing him to all her scars, the very worst of them.

Her hand still clutched the towel and she wound it abruptly around her. 'You came around the shrubbery!'

He blinked, released his eyes from where she clenched the towel. 'Only to hand you the salve. I—'

'You could have just told me about the salve, and set it down.' She burned to feel a blush. Burned with embarrassment that he saw her scars and her disfigurement.

Why didn't she have any modesty or at least the ability to feign it? If she did, she would have covered herself the moment he appeared.

'I could have.' His lips curved. Teasing. When he did this, he was all light with no shadows fleeting in the amber depths of his eyes. 'Would it help to know I thought you still covered?'

No, not when he hinted another reason why he came around the shrubbery. To catch a glimpse of her. What she couldn't understand, even with his words of yesterday, was why. Why would he want to see the horror that was her? 'I think you're mocking me again.'

'I believe I'm mocking myself.'

'How am I to believe that while I stand in front of you half…half-naked?'

'Easily.' His head tilted as if he wanted to see her from another angle. But he kept his eyes with hers and never once did he lower them, which was at least some courtesy, but he didn't walk away.

She kept the cloth wrapped around her. 'You're a strange man, staying and carrying on a conversation like we are in some Great Hall, when you caught me bathing and I'm struggling to cover myself.'

'I see nothing strange with what I do. All I see is how I'm failing every resolve I've ever made with you.'

'Is it possible at all for you to give me privacy?'

'I don't think so. Not the way you are now.' He adjusted his stance. 'You've accomplished covering your scars, Helissent, I can only see the few on your neck, along your cheek, but hardly any others.'

She meant to cover her scars, she didn't mean for him, for anyone, to see them in the bright light of the dawning day. Her scars were paler now than they were after the fire. She was used to them, but she knew others wouldn't be. He couldn't possibly be.

'Do you need help applying the salve?'

She did, but the way he looked in her eyes, she didn't think she could stand him applying any to her back. She shook her head.

'No? I'm here to apply it.'

'You are mocking me!' She tightened the towel even more.

Rhain let out a hiss and closed his eyes. 'Then please, Helissent, if I can't use words to alleviate this…between you and me. You need to dress. Quickly, I think.'

'Are there others coming?'

Opening his eyes, he let out a pained laugh. 'You're torturing me. There's only me. But I am a man like any other and I'm trying to remain honorable.'

She understood what was wrong before, but now she held the towel. Now she feigned modesty at least. 'What's wrong?'

He sighed raggedly like he was in great pain. 'Your scars are hidden from my eyes and most of the bounty of your chest since you clutch that towel. But the towel is not that generous.'

Gasping, she stepped back and scanned her body. Her breasts and her entire burned right side were covered, but by clutching the towel, she exposed all of her legs and the juncture between her thighs.

She couldn't even feign modesty correctly.

Uncaring if there were eyes behind her she unfurled the towel to her front. 'Go hide behind the trees!' She might not care that he saw her, but he didn't need further glances at her scars and she didn't need to hear his mocking words.

Words that warmed her, that filled her with

more longing. They hurt since she didn't deserve it.

'Nicholas was right,' he said. 'I don't think I'm capable of staying away.'

It was the pained tone to his voice that suddenly riveted her. No mockery and a rasp to his voice that made her shiver.

It was the way his chest stilled as if he held his breath, then inhaled like he was trying to catch it again.

It was the way his amber eyes heated and his lids lowered as his lips parted. A softness that she wanted to call slumber, but felt much, much heavier.

The longer she stared right back, the heavier it felt to her until she couldn't deny it. Didn't want to.

Not when he stepped forward again. Close enough to feel the heat of him, to catch the scent of leather, of warmed sunshine, the scent that was uniquely his.

All of it reminding her of them together in the darkness of her home. When he'd leaned over her as she clutched her chemise to her chest. There, she hadn't shown him her scars. Here, he saw almost all of them. She searched his eyes, trying to find the difference and seeing none. Could it be he wasn't mocking her?

'What are your thoughts?' he whispered.

'This is like then, isn't it? After Rudd when you—' she said.

His eyes dimmed as he stepped back. 'After you were hurt, you mean. This is different than then. I could hurt you far worse than those men.' He pointed behind him. 'I'll be beyond the trees. Let me know when you're clothed.'

He turned to go.

'Rhain,' she said.

He looked over his shoulder, a curve to his lips, a brittle glint of light to his gaze. 'Do you want me to look, Helissent? I would be more than happy to look.'

This was mockery, an edge to his teasing. It hurt.

She turned her back to him and hastily applied the salve before pulling on the dry fine chemise that wasn't her own, but fit all the same. He wasn't going to look to see and she couldn't comprehend why she suddenly felt like showing him. She was damaged. Scarred.

She had barely got her gown over her head, when he reappeared.

'I thought I was to call you when I was done.'

'And I knew you were done enough.'

Heat suffused her body, but none to the surface of her skin. The only way he could have known she was dressed was if he'd watched her.

'Your expression, Helissent. Wonder and pique. I wonder which is the truth.'

Finished tying her gown, she said, 'What do you think?'

'I think too many thoughts. When it comes to you, my curiosity burns bright. Like now, I wonder why I can't make you blush.' His eyes roved over her. 'You make me blush.'

She wished she could, then the heat suffusing her body would surface to her skin. Instead, it roiled inside her.

'You've seen me and you wish to talk of my lack of blushing?'

'No,' he said, 'there's other matters we could be talking about, other actions that require no words at all.'

Teasing again, but his voice was laced with something deeper. She quickly tied her hose and pulled on her boots.

After wringing her hair, she picked up her worn chemise. It was damp, but dry enough to carry.

Rhain strode closer, watching Helissent's wonder and pique increase. But it was the other flickering emotions that beckoned and tempted him.

For days he'd been plagued with awareness, days he'd wondered how it would feel to touch her again, to truly kiss her. Days wondering if she felt the same. Now it was all confirmed.

He shouldn't have looked. A knight wouldn't, a nobleman certainly not. His coming around the shrubbery was an accident, but he was also a dead man and maybe he was allowed some hedonistic pleasures...like her cakes dripping in honey and a glimpse of a body he'd wondered about since he wrapped her in his torn tunic.

She was as beautiful as he suspected. Long lines, the curve of her breasts, the sharp indent of her waist accentuating the feminine curves of her hips.

Her skin was pearlescent and feathered in places with light pink scars. Except along her torso. There, the scars were grooves of dark red, like claws had ravaged her.

The fact she carried them made him want her all the more. His first and only instinct was to pull her into his arms and kiss her by the bank. She was covered now and it didn't matter at all. He'd seen her.

Then to make it all worse...she didn't flush, didn't look embarrassed. Her eyes held steady with his and it called to his curiosity. 'I'm trying to guess why you're not shy.'

She tilted her chin up. 'The flames took more than my appearance from me. They also took my modesty.'

She truly didn't see her scars the way he did. His curiosity, his need to know her, now acute.

His need to hold her almost unfathomable. Instead, he said, 'Tell me.'

She shook her skirts out. 'It's simple. I couldn't wear clothes. Then when I could, it took the healer months of encouraging me to get in the habit of wearing them even when winter came.'

'Were you as stubborn then as you are now?'

'More so.'

'Did you not go outside?'

'Not for a year.' She lifted a shoulder. 'It wasn't all dire. Agnes's home was in the woods, away from the village and against some small caves. They were not extensive, but they allowed me room to grow when my skin was too sensitive in the sun.'

But all in the dark. He remembered his own childhood out in the gardens with his mother, then the lists in Edward's court. He could not remember a time without sun and yet this woman had lived without it for almost a year.

How much pain she must have suffered to remain inside for a year. He wanted to ask many more questions. No, he wanted to ask only one. How did she find the strength to go from the dark to the fire again? Instead, they quietly walked along the banks of the stream towards the camp.

It wasn't the inconvenience of the approaching camp and his men stifling his questions and curiosity. He was concerned how much more he could withstand. What if she told him more of her childhood and of her trials at the inn?

His desire only increased the more he knew. The tightening of his body when he was near her was almost incessant now. Her tale of her childhood made him want to snarl and snap and comfort. He battled from knowing about her to wanting to know her in the Biblical sense of the word.

Aware that they walked in a silence too laden to bear, he forced his conversation to something lighter.

'You intrigue me, Helissent of nowhere. I still could not describe the color of your hair, or your eyes. You lived in darkness most of your life, yet you are not scared of the light. What do you want when you get to York?'

She dreamed of how her food and cakes would be revered. How she could make enough money to have an inn of her own. 'I just need to find some work and a place to live.'

Helissent didn't know if it was easier to tell of dreams or of her past. All she knew was, though she didn't know where this conversation was going, it was changing something inside her. She was dreaming now. That, somehow, he was changing her with his kind words and studying gaze.

He was like no one she had ever met and he treated her like she was a favored spice instead of some hideous beast.

The innkeepers had been kind, but always protective. Always aware she was damaged. Even travelers, those that didn't back away in horror, treated her this way.

When she first returned to the village the regulars stopped touching her. She was young, but there were no more comforting hugs, or pats on the arm. Fearful they would hurt her, they kept their distance. It hurt.

Only the innkeepers' love had kept her strong. Yet with Rhain and his kindness, nothing hurt. She was *forgetting* her scars. 'They don't bother you. My scars, they don't…affect you.'

She was just starting to realize and didn't think it was possible. She had to be wrong.

But the mercenaries didn't act the way the people at the inn did either. Her demands to travel with them didn't raise a brow.

Was it because they were mercenaries and the less questions they had for her the less she would have for them?

That had certainly been part of her reasoning when she decided to travel with them from her village. After all, she never thought of requesting passage from other travelers.

But she now thought it could be something

else. Maybe she decided to travel with them because they had scars and burns from previous battles and fights, and hers were no more or less.

From their perspective, she was beginning to see the fire this way: as a past battle or fight she had survived.

Not from everything, there was too much the fire had taken from her, too much she gave to it when she'd remained with her sister. But this, even if she was accepted for her appearance, this thought felt like relief...or freedom.

'It's true, isn't it?' she said, stronger this time.

He started to walk away as if to escape, but she wouldn't let him. She felt a clamouring inside her that was difficult to maintain. Maybe she didn't have any modesty and didn't know how to be embarrassed when it came to her body. But right now, she'd use that to her advantage. Because this advantage felt something like happiness.

'Please,' she said and he stopped.

He was beautiful. Everything about him powerful and golden like the purest of oven fires. Everything about him wholly opposite of her, but though she didn't quite believe she deserved him, Rhain looked at her like she did. He looked like he was incapable of looking away.

'They bother me—' his smile uneven '—but not in the way you mean and not in any way I should tell you.'

'Why shouldn't you? Because of some enemy?'

'A man who will soon kill me should never be disregarded and I'd rather talk of more pleasant matters. Like your childhood.'

No teasing or mockery, but he again was trying to change the subject. This time, she let him. 'That's pleasant?'

'Fair enough. How about something happy then.'

She didn't know why her scars bothered him in a way she hadn't meant, but she wouldn't get an answer from him now. She tried to think of other facets of her childhood, but it all came back to the scars. Instead she said, 'Do you have any happy memories?'

His jaw tightened before he answered, 'I had the gardens. I had forgotten that until you reminded me.'

'Nothing else?'

'Nothing that was remarkable for anyone in my station. My brother is a Marcher Lord in Wales; I grew up with privileges. When it came time, I squired at King Edward's court, then I returned to Wales.'

But something had happened between the time he'd returned to Gwalchdu in Wales and now; he'd changed. She knew it was then when he shrouded himself in shadows.

'How did you go from Gwalchdu to now?'

His mouth quirked. 'You mean how did I go from being the second son of a Marcher Lord to a mercenary? Someone who roams instead of living off the fat of the land?'

They continued to meander, far from the camp and the place she swam. But she didn't care. She wanted this time with him. Wanted to watch the graceful way he weaved around the trees.

He was deep in thought now. Remembering, maybe. Most likely contemplating how to edit the telling of his life. But her disappointment was softened while watching him because as he thought, he again caressed his dagger's hilt.

It had the same effect on her. The familiar heat that started with the brush of his hand along his pommel only increased until it flared throughout her body.

This time, in the seclusion of the woods, away from any distractions, it felt faster, deeper...

This time, he caught her watching. She had slowed her pace and perhaps in concern he turned around. Whatever he saw in her expression made him raise one brow. Defiant again.

She didn't know what she looked like. Too stunned, too affected and breathless to move. Too naive to cover what must be embarrassment in the twitch to her mouth or the blinking of her eyes.

Though why she was embarrassed she didn't

know. He couldn't see the heat that was flaring through her body, or the prickling across her skin.

But she couldn't hide her breath coming in a little too shakily. How it worsened when his gaze locked with hers and more so when his eyes lowered a bit and held before they swung away to the trees again.

Her breath stopped at that moment; everything in her stopped when he looked at her lips. Looked at them as if he studied them as intently as he did her eyes. As if the answer to whatever was puzzling him was entwined between her eyes and lips.

He continued to walk, his hands seemingly restless now. *He* seemed restless. Then he cleared his throat. 'Despite how it sounds, it's actually been quite beneficial for me.' His voice was low, husky, the only manifestation of whatever had occurred between them.

'For the last five years as a mercenary, I've travelled to Spain, France, Belgium. It's how I met the men you know today, or rather they met me. I also felt sun much warmer than the clime here and tasted foods much spicier.'

He spoke of a life she could only dream of. Travelling and eating different foods. But she was curious about the friendships he'd formed as well.

'How do mercenaries work?'

He shrugged one shoulder. 'Not like ours. Most troops are hastily and poorly formed. Some are gathered from dungeons where the men don't have a choice between one kind of death or another. Other times it's villagers too poor to appreciate that farmers can't compete against trained warriors.'

She swallowed, not sure she wanted to know all the ways Rhain risked his life. 'And yours?'

'All trained, all highly selective. Sometimes it only takes our arrival to end a border dispute or an unjust siege. We're paid handsomely all the same.'

'So you haven't always fought,' she said.

'There's more to it than riding the horses and protecting borders.' His voice warmed to his subject. 'I've heard interesting things along the way. Corruption where there should only be innocence, betrayal where there should only be love. And treasures—no, legends—I thought were only childish games, but that actually may be true…' He paused. 'I always meant to follow up with that one.

'That's it for the most part.' He shrugged. 'And for you?'

'For me?'

His lips quirked. 'This is how conversations are to go. I say a little, then you.'

'I don't know what else to say.' She'd told him the worst and he knew about Rudd.

'You must have other memories?'

She did, but they weren't about castles and knighthoods and legends. They were ordinary. *She* was ordinary, completely unremarkable that she didn't know how to carry on a conversation. Yet, he had told her a little about himself. Couldn't she be brave enough to do the same?

'I suppose my happiest memories were with John and Anne, and those buckets of honey. I went home with them and they showed me a bed. Linens hanging from the ceiling for privacy. It felt like home and for the first time I cried.'

'This is a happy memory?'

Helissent almost laughed and raised her hand to her mouth to cover her scars. 'It is. I cried for days, tears and wails of sound. I was a mess. Bandages still needed changing, honey salve still needed applying. I was old enough to help, but clumsy with it, too. I found I enjoyed the honey, dipping my hands in it, watching the color of it change the color of my skin.'

Sometimes they had thickly applied it until the scars underneath disappeared. When the pain was not excruciating, she pretended they didn't exist.

'All through my crying that would never stop,

Anne was there singing this song. She sang every note over and over while she dabbed at my tears and runny nose. While she wound and unwound the bandages, and applied honey where I couldn't reach. It was beautiful; I wish you could have heard it.'

'I have.'

'You have what?'

'From you. You sing this song constantly. It's hers, isn't it?'

'I *sing*?'

He nodded his head. 'Terribly. I didn't have the heart to tell you. Shouldn't tell you now that I know what it means.'

Embarrassed, she blurted, 'I'll stop.'

'Not if it makes you happy.'

She didn't know what to say to that, or to the warmth in his amber eyes.

'I haven't cried since, not even when they died. They'd given me an abundance of care and love.' She shrugged one shoulder. 'Then Rudd showed up.'

Rhain's expression darkened and she didn't know if it was at the mention of Rudd or because they came across the camp and there would be no meandering now.

She couldn't hide her disappointment at seeing the fire or at hearing the other men's voices. She didn't have many happy memories. Her mother's spoon, her father's book, Anne's song, her first perfect honey cake.

She didn't have many memories, but she'd shared them all with this man and, by doing so, might have just created another. She didn't want it to end.

Then she felt his hand on her wrist. He held it lightly, but it was enough to stop her progress. Enough to stop her heart as heat entered his eyes and he whispered in her ear, 'No more frowns, Helissent. I won't allow it. Not now that I know how unsurpassed your legs are. In all my days I've never seen finer.'

She released her wrist from his hold, and wanted to frown at him for mocking anything about this time together. But his eyes were all light and she realized he did it to make her smile. And she almost did. 'You weren't looking at my legs.'

'No, I wasn't.' Flashing a grin, he walked into the camp.

His face grim, his scar pronounced, Nicholas stopped him almost immediately.

'What's happened?' Rhain said.

Nicholas glanced at Helissent and lowered his voice. 'Mathys has returned.'

Chapter Fifteen

'What'll we do?' Nicholas asked after they talked to the men.

Rhain rubbed his eyes. The conversation was short, brief. Precise as a knife and just as deadly.

Mathys had no trouble riding to York. It was on his return that he and his party were stopped.

Supposedly it was a friendly conversation. At first, the other riders enquired about the weather and the roads. Nothing personal, not even names or where they hailed from, was exchanged.

Then as they turned to leave, the leader had said this, 'Tell him she has safe passage into York.'

Rhain had compensated Mathys for his time. Now the mercenaries ate and circled Helissent to protect her. Though no explanations had been said, Mathys was no fool. He knew a warning when he heard it.

It was enough protection so that he and Nicholas left the camp. What they had to say and plan wasn't for anyone's ears.

'It appears we don't have to do a thing,' he said. 'Reynold has found me.'

'Us,' Nicholas added. 'And he knows of Helissent.'

'Which means we're surrounded.' No going back to Tickhill, which obviously had spies reporting to Reynold.

Mathys gave a good description of the man in York, but he could be one out of a thousand men. Further, he had met Mathys outside the city's gates, which meant they were all along the roads.

Had they seen her swim, watched him talk to her like some suitor? He heard nothing, saw nothing. Though he accompanied her to keep her safe, simply standing next to her probably sealed her fate.

'All that's left is to ride to York.'

'Then we confront Reynold?'

'We'll need to stay and determine if he's there, or nearby. We may be there for days, if not weeks.'

'The men will get restless.'

'The men will have to be told.'

Nicholas raised his eyebrow. 'About Guy?'

Rhain nodded. 'Everything. Until we know more, Helissent is at risk. They're already protecting her; they should know why.'

'Carlos will be pleased for more of her company.'

'She won't know the men are following her.'

Nicholas whistled low. 'By doing so you're declaring your intentions towards her. Seems dangerous when Reynold is spying on you.'

Rhain let out a breath in irritation. 'I have no intentions when it comes to her. She didn't ask for a death sentence on her head when she requested to travel with us.'

'No, she didn't, but you rescued her anyway and went into her home for a long, long time. Came out without your tunic—'

'Enough,' he growled.

Nicholas shook his head. 'You didn't leave her in that tiny village, where she'd be a hell of a lot safer than with us. Now you're laughing again. You haven't done that for five years.'

'That man you knew is no more.'

'I thought so, too, but since we picked her up, you're changing. It's because of her.'

Never. That Rhain, that carefree life, was gone. He had been without a care because his brother had taken on a terrible burden. It should have been him carrying their dark secret. At least he carried it now and would until his death. He was nothing like the man he was and resented being reminded of him.

'If you were anyone else…' he warned.

'They wouldn't be able to warn you away from her as I can,' Nicholas replied.

'From what?' Rhain's thoughts darkened and his hands clenched into fists. 'If this has to do with her appearance—'

Stepping back, Nicholas swept his hands in front of him. 'What do you take me or any of the men here for? Any man worth his soul would know that woman is far too good for the likes of us.'

Rhain reined in his temper. 'What do you warn me from then?'

'I told you she's better than any of us here and that includes you. Not only for what we do, but for the danger we represent and that was before your obsession and your...misstep in London.'

Misstep in London. He had a nobleman, with power and wealth and vengeance, crying for his head. It could be described as a bit of careless-ness on his part, but he knew it was a monstrous transgression that Helissent couldn't be anywhere near.

'We travel to York and, after we evaluate the city for a few days or weeks, I'll leave her there. Maybe Reynold will leave her alone.'

'Abandon her without any protection?'

'What would you have me do?'

'You could let Carlos close to her. He maintains a manor in Spain and could give her a position and his protection.'

'Never.'

'And you prove my point.' Nicholas gave a mirthless laugh. 'After all these years of chasing after the pendant for that necklace, you think I can't recognize your obsessions?'

Helissent could barely keep her eyes open as they approached the outskirts of York's great walls. Over the last two days, Rhain and his men, all with hoods up, rode as if their lives depended on it. With no discussion, she now shared riding amongst them.

Rhain's countenance was always dark, his expression dim. Her shadow man had returned and he ignored her.

Except at night, before they went to bed. For two nights now, Rhain would look around the camp as if for distraction.

At those times she couldn't look away from him and, almost against his will, his eyes clashed with hers. Never for long, never enough. But in those brief times, she saw a wild bleakness…a sort of hopeless regret. Shadows, so many shadows, and he seemed more alone than ever. Now they'd reached York.

This was where they would part. She wouldn't know what plagued Rhain or the men, or what

Mathys had said when he returned to their camp. These men were on an assignment, and it did not include her.

'Mathys secured us accommodations,' Rhain said. 'You'll be in bed soon.'

A bed, somewhere to sleep properly, take care of her skin and the harshness of the days in the sun. But they'd reached York and their agreement wasn't on anything further.

'I can find my own.'

'You'll stay where we put you.'

Determination. She'd get no leniency with him now. 'For tonight…' she whispered, too tired to argue. Tomorrow would come soon enough.

Chapter Sixteen

She woke in a spare small room, no more than a cupboard and almost as dark. But there was room for a pallet and some linen. There was privacy with a roof and a door. It was more than she ever had before and she felt even more grateful for it as she laid listening to the sounds echoing outside.

It had to be late in the day—she couldn't remember ever sleeping late. When she was younger, her pain never allowed it, when she learned to bake, it forced her to wake early. Then Rudd had come, and she worked to appease and to stay away from him. Now she had none of those worries as unfamiliar sounds surrounded her.

She had fallen asleep almost immediately last night. Rhain and Nicholas caring for her as they made sure her accommodations were acceptable. Nothing untoward, all solicitous. The innkeeper and his wife kind, courteous. Whatever Rhain paid for her room, he'd paid well.

She would need to find work to repay him.

With a resolve she hadn't felt in a long time, she dressed and went out the door ready to explore her new home.

Hours spent with her feet throbbing from the unforgiving cobblestones, and her skin stinging from the lack of rest and little salve she had left, Helissent was exhausted. Her right leg dragged a bit behind her, but she didn't mind the increased pain. Not after the victories of the day.

It was already late afternoon, but she'd walked the entirety of York. Keeping mostly to the magnificent walls and soaring gatehouses, she gaped at the sights around her.

Atop the hill, the Cathedral was always in sight, stunning, beckoning. Soon she would go to give thanks for being here.

York was a city she could truly get lost in. An over-abundance of people and animals and children. She gathered some looks, a few stares, but everyone was different. Too busy to be cruel. Too self-absorbed to notice another stranger among many.

And the industry, the market stalls, the vendors and shops! The wares and the astounding choices. Carvings and craftsmanship she had never seen before, parcels of pastries, each bite made to melt in the mouth, swathes of fabrics that glimmered, intricate patterns in quilts that would make her blind to sew. Fruits and vegetables of any kind she'd want and most she never knew she wanted. Slabs of meat just hanging, enough to feed her village for weeks.

Anything she could ever dream of was here and her imagination was rampant. What would it be like to mix that particular flour with that suet? Would those currants taste better when they were soaked in that sweet wine?

The colors, the smells, the sounds were different than her own village, where people bartered the same goods day after day.

She had left her village in fear, in anger, in resignation. Because of Rudd, she was forced to leave the only home she'd ever known.

Yet, long before that night, she knew she had to go. Since his return to the inn, it had no longer been her home. He'd snapped towels against her burned side; purposefully thrust out his foot until she tripped—never to spill his ale, but always her own cooking.

In all the months since Rudd's return, not one of the villagers had offered her the safety of their home, or exchanged threatening words with her tormentor. As the weeks passed, Rudd had only grown more confident with his jibes and cruelty.

It was just how to leave and then where to go. From years of travellers' tales, she knew York was near and that it would suit her. But she hadn't expected the abundance of possibilities that it provided.

She also didn't expect to find employment, but she'd done that, too. Early in the day before leaving the inn, she'd enquired with the kind innkeepers if they needed help.

A husband and wife, with five young children. They'd inherited the inn, but it was too large and busy for them to run alone and they'd been losing money. The woman looked grateful that she was willing to help for nothing more than room and board until profits could be made for wages.

Helissent agreed to watch tonight's preparations, so she could see how she could help. They'd even given her a bit of coin for exploring today. While it wasn't enough to try every pastry she wanted, she was able to taste a few and even the bad pastries inspired her.

Now the day had turned to late afternoon. A time of day that would have most of her village's residents readying for bed.

York behaved like the day was just beginning. There were still sounds of carts against cobblestones, shutters slamming, calls out in greeting and anger. But all of it didn't distract her from what she could no longer deny.

That part of her happiness was caused by Rhain and his men, who gave her this opportunity. Rhain and his men, and in particular, Nicholas, who had been following her most of the day.

At first she thought she spied the mercenaries because they were exploring York as she was. But Nicholas didn't like the food stalls around Tickhill and York's were more visceral. For a large man, he had a sensitive stomach. He was there because she was.

It didn't take much to surprise him, not when she stood in the butchery section for a protracted time and he had to duck out to the nearby open courtyard.

When he still looked green after great gulps of air, she felt a little guilty, but not much.

'Why?' she said. She would get an answer.

Nicholas didn't start at her approach, nor was he surprised by such a question. Irritated at being followed, she was relieved to know he hadn't thought her a simpleton to not notice a giant man following her.

'Did you truly expect us to just leave you like that?' he said. 'To get you through the gates, find you a place to sleep and then go?'

She had when she began this journey, especially when Rhain made it clear how reluctantly he took her. But then Tickhill happened, as did the walk along the stream.

Then Mathys returned, and the men became grim and forbidding. Passing her like a flagon of ale amongst them. Rhain's expression darker and more tortured than the rest. Last night, she was tired and she took their courtesy because she couldn't have survived on her own.

'York was all I asked for; you don't bear responsibility for me any more.'

Nicholas gave her a slight smile. 'Since you joined our band of men, you should know your room is paid for the month.'

'I can't afford to repay such a debt!'

'We take care of our own. You're not thinking of abandoning us, are you?'

Teasing. Unexpected, though things had been changing between her and the mercenaries. Still she was wary; she alone knew her cowardice. That a part of her was undeserving of their seeming acceptance, their generosity. But he was teasing and she could, too. 'Well, it's true, I don't know how you survived without my cooking.'

He laughed. He was a handsome man and, though he looked like a fierce giant of a mercenary and no doubt was, he was kind. How often did she notice his jagged scar across his eye? Rarely.

She only ever saw the kindness in him. She looked around the market. They were in the open where people were visiting and eating.

No one paid any more attention to this man with his brutal scar across his face than they did her with her scars sloping her right eye.

When she first left her room, she'd raised her chin to show others her scars, but as the day progressed she noticed something she'd never seen before.

There were other people with disfigurements. Some were treated cruelly, but mostly there was acceptance.

She didn't know how she felt about it. Too much had been taken from her when Rudd returned, but this she didn't know if she could accept. Finding her shame by others looking at her was an integral part of her. She didn't know who she was to be if others didn't see her shame the way she did. She didn't know what to do if she was…accepted. Maybe others received their injuries by accidents. Hers was from a broken promise. She shouldn't deserve acceptance, yet, because of these mercenaries and all they'd shown her, she could feel a change within herself.

'Is it always like this in larger towns? Are we to simply go unnoticed?'

He looked over her shoulder, his eye dimming with memories, and she wondered on Nicholas's past, and his home he hadn't returned to.

'I haven't been everywhere,' he said, 'and I

expect there are exceptions, but it's like this in most places.'

She exhaled, breathed in deep, but it didn't stop her heart from expanding. And that wouldn't do. Life had taught her that she didn't deserve kindness or acceptance. Still, she was here. York was all she'd hoped for and possibly more. She would be grateful for it.

Just as she was for the men who followed her around today, but eventually she knew they'd go. They needed to work and so did she. She also needed to say goodbye, and give her thanks.

'Where is he?' she asked.

Nicholas's eye dimmed. 'Busy, most likely.'

Rhain was responsible for their group. He was most likely procuring business for them, or maybe had friends here to visit or was preparing for an upcoming trip. But she wouldn't let him go without thanking him.

'I just want to see him for a moment. I've seen most of you today, but not him.'

Nicholas frowned. 'You should leave him alone.'

Something of his tone stopped her. 'What's happened? Is he in danger?'

'Worried for him?'

She fluttered her hand in front of her. 'It's just…we've been running the last few days and the men have been on double watch at night since

Mathys returned. Now you're telling me to stay away from him.'

Nicholas looked away. 'He told you of the trouble we're in?'

Rhain had told her only vague facts, but she wouldn't confess that to his friend. Not if it would reveal a bit more. 'What trouble is he in?'

She could almost answer her own questions. Rhain must be in great danger. She hadn't seen him all day though he would have needed to find food and eat.

With or without Nicholas's help, she would find him.

She moved to go past Nicholas, who stepped in front of her and put both hands out as if placating her. 'It's not that you're…he's safe. It's the other matter.'

'What other matter?'

Nicholas's sudden discomfiture was obvious on his giant shoulders. 'I'll let him say.' He shook his head like he'd said too much, but then he continued, 'It's only… Though I don't know why, he's always like this after a few days in the market, and now that time is running out, it's worse.'

She didn't understand half of Nicholas's words, but he had said, 'like this', and whatever that was made Nicholas protective of his friend.

Maybe Rhain wasn't in danger, but he had

done a kindness for her and maybe she could do one for him. 'Tell me now. Please.'

At Nicholas's expression, she added, 'If you don't tell me, I'll simply walk the entirety of York again. Wouldn't it be best to point me in the correct direction than searching for me all night when I get lost?'

He sighed, but there was a curve to his mouth like he was secretly pleased. 'He's in the gardens by the Cathedral.'

If Rhain was in the gardens then he wasn't in immediate danger, but still her heart wouldn't stop thumping heavily in her chest as if something was wrong.

'He's that way.' Nicholas pointed in the direction behind her. 'I hope you know what you're doing.'

She didn't. But she did need to thank Rhain for bringing her here; she would have the courage to do that.

Chapter Seventeen

She found Rhain on a bench near the wall. She stayed quiet, though if he wanted to be alone, he would have been elsewhere. The gardens here were nothing like Tickhill's where there was a modicum of privacy.

Here it was as bustling as the rest of the city. She welcomed the din that masked her footsteps when she approached him and stopped so she could observe him without his noticing.

His hood was up, but she would notice him anywhere now. Despite that he wasn't moving, or touching the hilt of his dagger. It was his abject stillness. How alone he looked even in the midst of bustling York.

He sat, his elbows resting on his knees, his hands clasped before him, his head bowed. As if he was praying. He hadn't stopped at the chapel in her village, nor the beautiful private one built by Eleanor of Aquitaine at Tickhill. Just behind him was a cathedral thousands made pilgrimages to and he was avoiding it.

He had, in fact, avoided all churches; given wide berth to the monks at Tickhill. He even dismissed her request to attend mass when she asked whether he was going.

Yet he was praying now, but his tranquility felt dangerous. Like a warning. Maybe this was what Nicholas spoke of.

'How long did Nicholas last against your demands to tell my whereabouts?' he said, his voice resonating.

Rhain hadn't changed his posture, his eyes still closed, his hands clasped.

'How did you know it was me?'

The corner of his mouth curved and he looked up. His hood should have shielded the color of his eyes and the expression of his face. But the soft afternoon light inveigled itself underneath and glowed against the stubble of his jaw, reflected in the goldenness of his eyes. They shone like the brightest of lights. Was it only the light making them glimmer like that, or his troubled thoughts?

She swallowed. 'I may have said please.'

'Well, that's practically begging coming from you.'

'I never beg.'

'No, but you give a man no choice either.'

His words cut. She hadn't given him a choice to say no at the village or at Tickhill. Nicholas had warned her not to come here, but she demanded that, too.

Why? To help? He was praying for that, and she had intruded. But she did have some words she needed to say.

'I wanted to thank you for bringing me here and for paying for my room.'

He pressed his hands on his knees and straightened. 'Did you find what you wanted here?'

She was needed in the innkeeper's kitchens. The wife had grabbed her hands when thanking her, and she had felt a lightness she hadn't felt in years.

She didn't now. It was Rhain and how alone he looked. But he wasn't a cake she could fix, wasn't a recipe she could change. He had danger after him, but he was a knight, a mercenary, and could take care of himself.

Even if he was troubled, what could she do for him? She had broken her promise to her mother and her sister had died. She wasn't good at helping anyone.

'I found work,' she said. 'I'm to help them tonight and begin early tomorrow morning.' Rhain sat unblinking as he listened to her paltry words. She gave a light shrug, unsure what to do with her hands or feet. Unsure what to do with herself. 'I will leave you now.'

He nodded once, his head at an angle, and his hood almost hid his eyes. When she turned, she saw it.

On the other side of him rested the little bit of needlework and the necklace. They were not religious and he didn't need those for prayer.

He noticed her stare and looked to his side and winced enough to push back his hood. When he faced her he looked...wary.

She didn't know why she'd come here, but she felt a little closer to the truth then. As she recognized what might be the reason Rhain was praying in a garden and it had something to do with his mother.

'Or, perhaps, I could stay?' She pointed to the space next to him.

He grabbed the needlework and necklace and slid over so she sat where he had. She watched him rub his thumb along the necklace and needlework, his fingers flitting in that smooth instinctual way when he stroked the hilt of his dagger.

She wondered again if he knew he did that. If he knew it vibrated something inside her even as it soothed him. But she kept silent on that, as well as everything else as she sat next to him. Her need to help him seemed insurmountable now. It was the almost-quiet of the garden in this spot where he sat, the fact he made it sacred with his prayer.

It was him carrying that necklace and needle-work all this time and how he handled them both like rosary beads. She knew they belonged to his mother, who was dead. She knew they held senti-mental value and significance when he'd showed them to the vendors in Tickhill.

Yet she was unprepared for the overwhelm-ing awareness that those items held for him. Be-cause as she sat in the silence with him and felt him consider words he hadn't said, she felt the weight of something descend upon her.

His mother had died; so had hers. But there was something else she experienced with that death. Something that with certain terrifying clarity she knew he felt, too: Guilt. Shame.

Rhain's mother had died and something about her death brought him regret. It was so clear for one startling moment she wondered what flaw she held that prevented her from recognizing it before now. Was she so broken from her own hurt that she couldn't sense it in others? In *him*?

Shame had shaped her scars, cowardice haunted her days and nightmares at night. Her family's death was folded in every fiber of her being. She deserved it, earned it with her failure. All this time, she felt unworthy of being near

Rhain, knowing she carried such scorched blackness within her. She justified it only because she knew their acquaintance would be brief.

And yet…and yet. The emotions rolling off him were unmistakable.

Nicholas had said Rhain needed his privacy when he was 'like this'. Did Nicholas know the source of Rhain's regret?

She came here to thank him for his kindness for bringing her to York. But she couldn't help him with this; she'd never been able to help herself.

Rhain shifted his feet and she watched the fineness of his boots become dustier. Still, they were new, thick, with a quality she could only guess at.

She had to be mistaken about Rhain's feelings. Rhain was noble born and he had charm and looks. His friends were loyal to him. How could he have regrets?

Rhain returned his concentration to the ground while Helissent, her eyes lowered, grew frustratingly silent.

Even so, something within him finally eased. For over an hour he'd been in the garden, surrounded by the smell of the lavender and sage and dirt.

Some quiet, a moment of prayer was usually all he needed to find the resolve that had carried him for the past five years. He didn't even know if he prayed to God any more. As the years went on, as the trail to find his father became less likely, his prayers became more abstract. Finding his resolve afterward that much more difficult.

Yet, always he found it. All he needed to do was remind himself there was the next town, the next market stall.

However, today, it was all final. There were no other towns for him, no other moments because if it was true what Nicholas reported, he should be dead within the week.

Devastation crushed him when he realized he would never know the truth of his mother and his father. She'd died horribly for something he couldn't fully comprehend. Fervent in her wishes for a pure Welsh ruler of Gwalchdu, her illness overwhelming her, she threatened the lives of his brother and wife.

In the end, she'd been mad, but once she'd been happy and danced. Once she had been loved and he was the result. He thought he could find answers. To know who and what she was, so he could fully understand what ran through his veins, but he'd run out of time.

Only a couple more days in York to locate Reynold or his spies, then he and his men would go. He'd either make it north to Edward's camp or not. Either way, he had to find the means and strength to hide his pain regarding his mother. Weighted with thoughts like this, his men could ask questions. He didn't want questions any more.

Just some way to calm his chaotic thoughts. That's all he meant to do now, but he hadn't quite succeeded when Helissent approached.

He'd sensed when she entered the garden and could have hid what he did, but he didn't. It was almost like he wanted her to see his loss, wanted to share it with her. That was something he didn't do even with his family, with his brother, now cousin.

Except he didn't know how to share within Helissent's tumultuous silence; he didn't know how to begin. He lifted the needlework depicting the lost pendant and wrapped the necklace in it. As he placed it in the pouch he wondered whether he'd ever take them out again.

Then he saw what he had forgotten. 'I have something for you,' he said.

Helissent watched Rhain extract from his pouch a small, tightly wrapped, cylinder-shaped object.

'What is this?'

'Open it,' he said, placing it in her hands.

Almost shaking, Helissent laid the package in her lap and untied it. Inside was a tiny cylinder sparkling in the afternoon light. It was rough and she could see it was made of tiny granules. Some had clung to the fabric wrapping.

'You gave me salt?' she asked. Although the cylinder was darker in color than salt, it had the same look about it.

It was a strange gift, but welcomed. She had no money for such things and she loved cooking.

He gave a small smile, his eyes alight. In this light, she saw little flecks in the amber around the darkness of his pupil. Like when honey was unfiltered, which for her gave it the richer flavor.

'No,' he whispered. His voice was warm and coaxing like honey.

She lifted the cylinder to her nose. It didn't smell like salt.

'You're torturing me,' he said.

'You say that a lot.'

'I'm a mercenary. Torture is our only fear.'

She couldn't imagine him fearing anything.

'And you're quite adept at it,' he continued. 'Especially with making me wait. Taste it, Hellisent.'

'It's food?'

At his nod, she licked her finger and scraped it across the loose grains on the linen. Acutely aware of his eyes on her, she turned her head aside and placed the grains on her tongue.

She heard his rough exhale, but she didn't look as something incredibly sweet filled her mouth.

Immediately she swiped her finger against the fabric again. This time she turned to him. 'It's not honey,' she said around the finger in her mouth.

His expression was one of almost triumph. 'It's not honey. It's called sweet-salt.'

She wanted to devour the entire tiny cylinder at the same time bury it like some lost treasure.

'I've never heard of it before; I've never seen it. Where did you get it?' How could she get more?

'It's rare. The Church is powerful and they can afford such wares. Hence the markets here tend to have goods such as these if you know what to look for or who to ask.'

So it was rare and expensive. 'I'm not making you a cake with this.'

He laughed low. 'That's all for you. It keeps, as long as you don't get it wet.'

She carefully wrapped the sweet-salt. 'Why?'

'I wanted it for you.'

He looked at her eyes, then back to her lips. She felt as if maybe she had sweet-salt lingering there before he looked away.

When she licked her lips, he pursed his.

She looked at the tiny cone and felt her eyes brim. This was a treasure, but that wasn't what brought the tears to her eyes. It was that this was something very personal. Significant.

There was more going on here than she knew. He'd paid for her room and gave her a gift. They'd raced from Tickhill to York like they were pursued. Now, he provided a hidden escort for her.

'He's here, isn't he? That man who is after you?'

He glanced at her. 'I should never have told you of him.'

He hadn't. Not really. She didn't even know his name. 'It's not that I gave you a choice. You were trying to warn me off travelling with you.'

'Do you think that's the only reason I told you? To frighten you?' He shook his head as if he couldn't believe that's what she thought. 'You were almost irreparably harmed, Helissent, and still you were strong and stubborn enough to make cakes, and brave enough to demand from mercenaries a passage to York. I don't think my vaguely mentioning a man after me would have frightened you to stay away, to stay safe. Although I hoped.'

This felt monumental. 'Then why did you tell me?'

'Because when it comes to you, I can't seem to stop myself from sharing. Though it isn't safe, it isn't wise and nothing can come from it.'

That's how she felt with him. Despite all else, all logic, they…shared. 'Tell me then.'

'There's a chance if I tell you nothing you won't be harmed.'

'He knows about me,' she pointed out.

'The message conveyed he'd give you safe passage to York, which could mean he merely spotted you. Nothing more.'

Even so they'd rode hard here and he'd procured her a place to stay. A safe place. She could see that now. Small room, no windows, plenty of people about for security.

But Rhain was troubled regarding this man. What hope did she have for remaining safe regardless of the precautions he took?

'Tell me,' she said.

'You must appreciate that this man is no one to trifle with. Many have tried to kill him. I've heard he's been stabbed and sliced and burned. He's been betrayed by others and his own family, but he survives…and becomes more powerful. When I say I am a dead man, I mean it.'

'Who is he?'

He gave a humorless laugh. 'You see how little choice you give with your demands? The man who is after me is Reynold of Warstone, and the man I killed was his brother, Guy.'

She didn't know the family, but from the way Rhain said it, he expected her to know.

'Why did you kill him? Was he...did someone pay you?'

He adjusted in his seat, his only indication he was uneasy with the conversation. 'Reynold is not fictional. He could be here now. Any one of these people in this garden could be his spy watching us converse.'

He was trying to distract her. 'Did someone pay you to kill him?'

He looked around, sighed. 'No, it was a reckless, heated moment.'

Rhain's answer surprised her. She never saw him do anything that wasn't methodical or carefully planned. He mocked things, which made people laugh, but he wasn't reckless. Everything he did was towards providing for and protecting his friends. She'd never seen him behave recklessly except the night with her, when Rudd...

'You were protecting someone, weren't you?'

He rested his elbows on his legs again. 'No protection at all. She died.'

Pain sliced down her middle. There was a 'she' who'd died. Rhain tried to protect a woman, someone he cared for very much if his reflective expression was anything to go by.

She had no right to her own sudden discomfort, but in these days with him, there had been no reference to a woman before. But of course there had to be a woman in his past. Rhain was wealthy, unmarried, and women coveted him.

Maybe he didn't like them looking because he mourned and longed for this woman he failed to protect.

If that were true, she knew how that felt; she had failed to save her sister. 'Tell me about her,' she said.

His brow furrowed. 'Not much to tell. A man killed her and the babies stood no chance.'

She gripped his wrist. She couldn't stand it. 'Rhain, tell me what happened.' No pain for her any more. All for him. All the pain for him.

This was why he'd banished himself; why he was so alone. Children…dead. If she could, she would have killed this man, too. She wanted to kill Reynold simply for threatening Rhain.

'My God, you're crying,' Rhain said.

'You told me that babies died, how could I not?'

He cupped her chin and rubbed his thumb along her cheek to catch her tears. His expression was full of wonder. 'All of these for me? I don't deserve them, Helissent.'

She cried harder then. So much pain for him. So simple to shed tears. 'I can't seem to help it.' She wanted to gather him to her, to…hold him. 'What was her name?' she asked instead.

'I don't think she had a name, not one that

I ever heard.' He dropped his hand. 'Oh, you should see your expression. Anger now, pity before. Do you recognize it's another gift you give me with your emotions? I'm in the mercenary business; no one tells the truth let alone displays it on their faces. But why are you—?'

'Rhain, how could you not know her name? This woman who died, who had your children!'

He chuckled, but there was an encompassing warmth in his eyes. 'I didn't know her name because she was a dog.'

'A dog?' She knew she displayed every emotion she felt. She didn't care if she looked the fool. She felt his pain from before, felt it now.

Rhain nodded. 'Simply a dog. No one claimed her as their own, but she and a pack of others were always begging for food. I must have fed her the choicest pieces because she followed me around the most.'

'So the babies were puppies?'

He nodded and turned away from her. His elbows on his knees again, his hands clasped as if in prayer.

Not a wife or a child, but he still hurt. She felt it. 'Oh, Rhain, I'm so sorry.'

'Because I was a fool? I was kind to her; it was why she was beside me when she gave birth and that's when Guy found me. He wanted to do business right then and I told him no. I knew what kind of man he was, that he didn't desire fortress protection or to correct border disputes. He wanted murderers. I knew the caliber of man he was and had no intention to agree to his terms.

'But the dog had just given birth and my true thoughts were on her. Instead of courtesy or formality, I gave Guy of Warstone a blunt no and didn't raise my eyes to him.'

She'd dealt with cruel unreasonable customers before. She could somewhat appreciate the kind of man he'd refused.

Rhain shook his head like he was the unreasonable one. 'I've been a mercenary for five years, a knight before that. I've been doing this a long time because I'm one of the best.

'I know how to negotiate, to interact with men like him,' he continued. 'Never take your eyes from them. Always stand on higher terrain. Never kneel. Never show interest in anything that could be used against you.

'When Guy stepped into my tent, I was kneeling by that dog's side, helping her with the birth. The babies had just started suckling...'

He pulled in a breath and pressed his hands against his knees. It looked as if he was bracing himself for what he was telling her. She wished she could brace herself, too.

'He stomped on her belly, then ground his heel

on her head before I could stand. Before I could take my sword and gut him.'

Helissent shivered and wrapped her arms around herself.

'Nicholas immediately killed Guy's two guards while I gathered the puppies and we fled. We had spare horses then, but they were getting shod and we had to leave them. My men fled with me. Except Nicholas, no one knew what happened. I compensated the men. Some were… indisposed. We were to be there another week of rest that they deserved. I put them on the road again.'

Pain in the telling. Incredulousness as if all his reasoning fled him. She had felt like that before. When she entered her home to save her sister. Nothing is rational in the heat of the moment. It doesn't make it less real.

'So for this dog's death, and Guy's,' she said, 'you have the Warstone family, Reynold, after you?'

'Reckless. Ancestors would laugh if they knew.'

How to make him understand? 'She wasn't only a dog,' Helissent said. 'She was your friend and she knew you were hers because she trusted you when she was most vulnerable.'

He put his face in his hands. 'I couldn't save her. The puppies…they're all dead. Fleeing, we couldn't find another nursing female. I tried to feed them other kinds of milk, but they wouldn't take. I thought one would, but then...'

He lifted his head, his hand clenching. 'You're crying again? You've a soft heart.'

She wiped her tears. A soft heart, but only when it came to him. 'I haven't cried like this since the innkeepers came for me.'

'Too many gifts you give me.' His eyes searched hers, dropped lower and lingered on her lips. 'Too many gifts I still want.'

She watched how his expression changed, how his brows drew in. How a muscle ticked in his jaw when he tilted his head and faced her more fully.

'Like what?' she whispered.

He cupped her jaw, his thumb caressing just under her lower lip. 'I want to know, though I don't deserve it...'

His hand was warm against her cheek. His thumb was roughened by callouses. But his touch was soft against her lower lip.

His eyes lingered; his thumb pressed. Her lips felt swollen from the need for kisses he hadn't yet given. Dry from air she couldn't seem to breathe. She parted her lips, inhaled the smell of the garden, of him. Took another quick breath, greedy for more.

Taking in all of her responses, his eyes flared

before his lids grew heavy. 'Though I can't do anything about it as a knight, as a man should…'

She was aware of the silence in the garden, of the zephyr through the fruit trees. She was aware of the slight sound she made as she wetted her lips and the almost helpless tone he used as he said, 'You are, aren't you?'

'I am?' she said, feeling the soft air across her tongue.

'As sweet as your cakes.' He dipped his head, lifted her chin with the barest of pressure.

The heat inside her flared like the fires in an oven that she'd just fed, then he brought her lips to his. Warm. Firm. A hint of ale, of sage. Of *him*.

Better than cakes, better than melting honey, and all too brief. Rhain lifted his head.

Her taste was more than he'd dreamed of. He wanted only to give her a kiss, to sip from her lips. She was so soft, so tenderly giving as she sat next to him and shed her tears.

Except the kiss didn't feel simple when Helissent's eyes darkened and wonder lit her face.

Not simple at all, when he pulled away, rubbed his thumb against her lips and she let out the slightest bit of sound…of need.

That was his undoing in this. Already unraveled with the telling of London, of the danger to him. Now desire was filling him. Her hands clenched in her lap, her body turning towards his. Wanting more.

Rhain, branded by her taste, wanted more. His thumb pressed harder and her lips parted. A sound. His? He tunneled his fingers through her hair, and lifted her chin.

To press his lips, to catch her hitched breath. To deepen his kiss. Soft, wet, heat. To claim—

A sound of horses clattering outside the garden walls.

He pulled away. Exhaling roughly from the temptation she made, from the questions entering her eyes, Rhain looked away, scanned the empty garden. Two kisses too many. Two kisses even more dangerous than telling her about Guy and Reynold.

With a breath, a stab to his own heart, he stood and offered her his hand. 'We should leave; get some sleep.'

'Why did you do that?' She took his hand.

'Sleeping at night? It's a habit I've picked up.'

Helissent wasn't letting go of his hand, and he knew he was in trouble. More because he wasn't letting go either.

There was a warmth in her eyes like she was amused at his attempt at humor, but there was heat there as well.

'You kissed me,' she said.

Her eyes searched his no doubt for answers he

didn't have. He didn't know why she was different. In the past, he had found and gave pleasure, but it had always been light-hearted.

Since learning the truth of his birth, whenever he was tempted by women, it had been easy to walk away. All he had to do was remember that frozen moment of reading his mother's books, of knowing the truth, to remember he could never spill his seed with a woman. That any future, of a family with children, was denied him since he was born.

But he couldn't seem to remember that with Helissent. They had shared themselves with each other. His need for her went beyond lust and temptation. Though he felt them both keenly now.

'I can't seem to stop,' he answered.

'Do it again.'

A twist of need he just held back. 'Helissent, you don't know what you're asking.'

'I do. I just never thought myself brave enough to ask.'

He cupped her chin in his hand, felt the slight tremble and tightening of her fingers entwining with his in the other. He saw no hesitation in her eyes, no worries. Only want.

He wanted to be the man to feed that want, but he couldn't. Two kisses too many.

'You're a maiden. You deserve a man who will

stay to marry you, to have children of your own. I'm not that man.'

He saw the want in her eyes dim, the bravery fade. Even before she stepped away and released her hand he felt the loss.

Rhain's words cut jaggedly through Helissent's heart. So suddenly, she startled with the sting of tears she just blinked back. Rejected. Unwanted.

What made her ask for a kiss? She should have known this would be the response. She *deserved* this response. Still, she asked, 'Is it because of my scars?'

Rhain closed his eyes and cursed. When he opened them, the amber of his eyes was darker than she'd ever seen them before.

'You're torturing me,' he whispered. 'I'm wanting to do what is right by you.'

Despite his words or his actions, and her own beliefs of acceptance, it *was* because of her scars. What else could it be?

She yanked up her skirts and ran.

Chapter Eighteen

It was after the evening meal when Rhain found her in the cellars of the inn. He should have looked here first when she ran off, but he hadn't known what to say, or what to do.

Then as he searched for her, Allen and Nicholas intercepted him to report Reynold's whereabouts.

Reynold was either within York's walls or at least nearby. He'd been seen. Nearby enough that Rhain shouldn't be pursuing a woman, or worrying about her tears and anguish.

Certainly he shouldn't be standing next to her in public gardens, or searching for her in her rooms where Reynold's men could easily note his actions.

But dinner had come and gone, and Helissent never returned to her room. Though he needed to be circumspect, he wouldn't leave things as they did in the garden. He could be dead by tonight.

At least for now, it was private in the cellar. Helissent hadn't noticed when he opened the door. He could gather his thoughts and words. The correct words he should have said before.

Yet, he still didn't know what to say; couldn't grasp why she ran. So he watched her walking with her hand trailing along the ale barrels like she was counting them. Then lifting her nose to scent the drying herbs. Another step, her hand slowing so that she was almost embracing the rounds of cheese.

She should have been reveling in the supplies here and the opportunity to continue her baking.

But he knew she wasn't taking inventory, wasn't thinking about all she could cook or serve with such bounty. When she did that, she hummed that song and was boundless in energy.

Now she almost shuffled, lost in thought; she didn't turn when the door closed behind him. Didn't realize the light in the cellar had brightened, then dimmed.

He noticed the light revealing her features, the darkness shadowing them. So like the inn. The left side of her face illuminated to show her exquisite beauty; he'd soon see her other side that weakened him. But that wasn't what made him stop.

It was the tear tracks down her face. He knew

he should turn away then, that he had no right to be here, had told her he wasn't the man for her.

But there was nothing that could tear him away now. Not until he knew she was happy. Tell her she could sell the sweet-salt he gave her and use the coins he'd hidden amongst her things. Tell her she could have another life altogether. Just…not with him.

'There were more supplies in Tickhill's cellars, no?' he said.

Helissent whirled around, almost stumbled into a barrel before righting herself. Standing tall, she shook from the sudden jump through her body at Rhain's voice. Rhain who stood inside the doorway.

'You scared me.'

'If you expected to be left alone, you shouldn't have come to an empty cellar at the end of the night.'

Rhain shoved the hood off his head until the lit torches cast him in shadows and light.

Her shadow man, who said something mocking, but his tone meant something else.

She quickly brushed her cheeks, though it was most likely too late. He was too keen not to notice details like her crying. Maudlin. Pity. She, who had no right to any of it, and yet, something inside her couldn't seem to stop. It was him, the mercenaries, the exposure to York. It had changed her somehow, showed her how life could be different. Or she thought it could. Until the garden and Rhain's rejection.

Which was why she was in the wine cellar avoiding everyone. 'Do you need something? I thought I left the others well versed.'

Rhain took the few stairs down to her level. His head brushed the top of the ceiling until he stepped past the eaves.

'Everything was brought to the tables. Piled high and more beautiful than at Tickhill.'

'But it doesn't taste good. Something was wrong with the fried apples?'

He shook his head. 'Not if Mathys licking his fingers was any indication.'

He took another step closer. There was nowhere she could go. The barrels and shelves lined both walls under the arched ceiling. It was a small path down the center. Just enough to walk to the end and back again. She couldn't walk past him. He took up too much space.

'Then why are you here? Why aren't you eating?'

'You're not there dining with me.'

She didn't understand this man at all. They'd agreed he'd take her to York. He'd done that. Then he'd said all that about wanting to kiss her, but stopped because of her scars. There was no reason he was here.

She wanted York because she wanted to get lost here. Rhain and the mercenaries weren't letting her get lost.

She should be happy, surrounded by supplies, by food and the chance to try some of the recipes from Tickhill.

Instead she had come here to the cellars. To the cold and dark that was the closest she could find to the caves. To escape and soothe the sudden sense of inexplicable loss as she peered through the doors and spotted the mercenaries eating her food.

It was reasonable for them to eat where they wanted to, but knowing they were leaving, she wasn't prepared to see them again. Especially not after Rhain's rejection.

Why wasn't Rhain leaving her alone?

'I'm trying to make a life here. That means I'm serving food, not dining with the customers.'

His brows drew in. 'Why the tears?'

'Dust.'

'It is…dusty here.'

He didn't need to believe her. 'This is my home now. I'll have to get used to it.'

'So this inn is where you intend to stay?'

'They are kind and willing to give me a chance.'

She wished she could turn then, to pause and

absorb her sudden thoughts. Instead, she hoped the flickering light from the torch hid some of her quickly boiling emotions.

'I just realized I should thank you for the inn-keepers giving me a chance,' she said.

'What do you mean?'

Maybe it wasn't strange she saw all the mercenaries eating at this particular establishment. Rhain probably said something to the innkeepers and paid them to take her. He'd wanted her to stay at Tickhill, but she hadn't. Maybe he was concerned she'd wouldn't stay in York.

'Did you say something to them? Pay them to take me? Of course you did.' She waved and her hand bumped a barrel. 'All of this wouldn't be possible without you.' He hadn't just given her a safe journey, he'd provided a means for her to be taken in, to provide for herself.

She thought she had proven herself today. Now she was beginning to realize it was too easy. It shouldn't have been that effortless with her scars. Nothing was effortless with her shame.

She'd never wanted pity from him. She wanted respect. He was so cutting to her that day in the village when she requested to go with them. She thought she'd earned the right to be with them, by making those cakes, by cooking their food, by helping.

Then behind her back, Rhain paid for a room and forced the innkeeper to give her work.

It wasn't only the underhanded part of it, though that stung. It was a direct insult to the only skill she had, to the only aspect of her that wasn't simmered in shame: her cooking, her honey cakes.

Those were hers despite the scars, her failure and cowardice. She had thought she'd earned a little bit of something out of this life she had been saved to live in. But here was Rhain, telling her—

'I paid for your room, but I didn't pay them for your job, but God knows I do owe you.'

She did take a step back then as if she could escape him, as if there was somewhere she could go. 'Is all of this…is this because you feel *sorry* for me?'

His eyes widened. 'No.'

'Then what did you mean, you owe me?' Her tears threatened again and the burden of holding them back was as heavy as a filled cauldron. She shook under their weight.

'You wouldn't have been there that night, if I hadn't asked you for the cakes. You wouldn't have been in the dark heading home from the kitchens when those men…when Rudd—'

'This is pity!'

'Where are my words!' His hand swiped by

the dagger at his waist. 'Helissent, I don't pity you. Despite what I just said, that's not the reason I agreed to your travelling with us, why I gave you the sweet-salt. It's not the reason why I'm here.'

She couldn't feel relief at his words. 'Then why?'

'Isn't it apparent? For you. Just you, not your cakes or your food, not for any reason other than you ran from me in the garden and I had to find you.'

Her heart battering against the sides of her chest whipped and bloomed. 'What are you saying?'

'What I should have said in the garden. What I never should say to you.' He stepped closer. 'You ran because you thought I didn't want to kiss you. That I don't want *more* of you.'

His heated eyes raked over her body, feasted on her lips, her cheeks. She felt every movement like a caress. 'But that's the furthest from the truth. I want to kiss you, so much. It is hard to be around you and not want you.'

'Even with—'

'Are you talking about your scars?' he interrupted. 'Your scars make it all the worse. Your scars weaken me.'

Ice slid down her spine. 'Like those men?'

'*Never* like that.' He released his breath. 'For

years, I haven't wanted to kiss a woman. With you I don't want to stop. Your scars, the way they occurred. How you acquired them. How could you not know? My God, Helissent, I am in awe of you.'

In the garden, he had stopped kissing her. She had thought it was because of her scars. If not that, then because he knew of her shame. Now he was telling her it was for something else.

But his words made no sense. He was perfect; she was not. She'd told him of her failure to save her sister, yet he said he was in awe. Tears brimmed again and this time she couldn't carry their burden and let them fall.

He cupped the left side of her face, tenderly stroked his calloused thumb against the softness of her skin, and brushed away the tears.

'Nature gave this to you. Your pale coloring with just a hint of pink underneath. The curl of your lashes, the color of your eyes and hair that change with the light.

'But this side of you,' he continued as he released her jaw and ran the back of his fingers along her right cheek. 'This side you gave to yourself.'

Her scars. Because she failed to save her sister from the flames. Her cowardice because she wanted the flames to take her as well until John and Anne saved her. 'For my stupidity.'

'Because of your bravery.' His eyes skittered across her features, as if he couldn't take in every flaw, every imperfection fast enough.

'How could you not realize it? Your scars are your most beautiful side,' he whispered. In the flickering torchlight, she knew he could see every broken vein, every purple, burned ridge.

'It is the right side of your face that brings me to my knees. Your scars remind me how little I deserve you, but are also a beacon. A temptation I am failing to withstand.'

She didn't understand. She knew she didn't understand because he was telling her she lived a different life than the one she knew.

No, not only telling her, but showing her. Ever since they left the village the mercenaries had treated her like she was one of them. Here in York she was treated like everyone else. It was stunning that she could be accepted for her outward appearance.

But if so, if so... Rhain had stepped back from kissing her. He had rejected her. If it wasn't for her appearance, then it had to be for her shame. But he was somehow telling her that, too, wasn't the reason.

She shook her head. 'Why? How?'

He dipped his head, looked straight into her eyes; she was helpless against the amber light flaring in them.

'You ran into a burning building to save your family,' he whispered. 'You risked your own life to save those whom you loved. Your scars are what you earned with your courage. Your courage—'

Her shame. His touch, his words were undoing her. He found her beautiful because he thought her courageous. 'I was terrified.'

'Of course you were, but you went anyway.'

He held so much beauty. The torch's light made a halo of his blond hair, like a golden angel. 'They...died. I almost died.'

But she'd lived even when she shouldn't have. Because when she tripped and trapped her sister, she broke her promise to her mother. Because when she realized what she'd done, she stayed in the flames. Rhain's acceptance of her appearance, of her failure to rescue her sister, was too much to believe.

Sudden. As though she was in an oven slowly burning and someone was dousing the flames. *He* was dousing the flames that she'd been living in most of her life.

She hadn't known any other way to be, yet she was beginning to believe there could be another way. She was the same ingredients, but Rhain was showing her a different way of making herself.

'You don't believe me.' He palmed the sides of

her neck, his thumbs stroking her jawline, lifting her eyes to his. 'Is that why you ran?'

She shakily nodded her head. Partly. Partly. He claimed she had courage, but she couldn't quite tell him the rest of that day, which was another indication of her cowardice.

'Never run from me.'

It felt like his palms encased her, enfolded her, protected her. She closed her eyes then. 'Please don't.'

But her words had no strength to them. No structure. Not enough to support her old beliefs.

'I'll show you. I'll make you believe,' he said, stroking her jaw with his thumbs, leaning down until his forehead touched hers. 'Though it is I who doesn't deserve you. To touch you like this; to be this close to you.'

It wasn't true. How could it be true when he looked the way he did, and came from where he did, and gave her protection and kindness? But this close, she felt those words against her skin, saw that he believed them in his own eyes.

And to make sure she understood, he kept saying them until she felt as though they stirred and sunk under her skin, down to her heart, into her soul.

'How could you not know your worth?' he said. 'How could you not know the truth of my words?'

He lifted his head, his palms now moving along her collarbones to her shoulders and back up.

'You're torturing me. I'm shaking, trembling because of who you are, because of how you look here, now. Because I'm all too aware that we're alone and that no one will interrupt us.'

She knew he could see her doubts. She couldn't hide them. Not with his words whipping against her insides, not with the flared intent of his amber eyes in the torchlight. Like heat and honey. Like warmth and wonder.

'I want to kiss you, Helissent, and I'm within a breath of showing you.'

Trailing his fingers along her scarred and puckered jaw line, his fingers skimmed as they did his dagger's hilt. As though he was caressing something precious, as though she was a delicacy that would melt.

'Soft, so soft.'

Was she? She'd never thought of herself this way. From his expression, from his words, she was beginning to believe. His eyes followed the path of his fingers as he reached her chin and stilled his hand.

Held her firm as the roughened tip of his thumb rubbed on her lower lip. Just as it did in the gardens, her lip grew sensitive. Parched until she ran the tip of her tongue to moisten it. His eyes sharpened to that point, his hand stilled.

Then his thumb played with her lip again, rougher this time, more intent, as if he demanded her to do it again.

So she did.

This time when her tongue came out he pushed his thumb into its path so it wasn't her lips she wetted or tasted, but him.

Quickly she closed her lips and he made a disappointed sound.

'Do you know what you're showing me?'

She only knew how she felt. Anticipation, a giddy freedom, a heavy need and want. Ingredients stirring and folding within her.

'I'm going to kiss you. I've warned you.'

'You've already kissed me.'

His lips curved. 'Not as I want to; not as I'm going to. If you want to stop, you need to leave, now.'

She was incapable of moving. He smelled of warmed leather, the acrid bite of steel. But it was the lavender and sage from the gardens that enticed her more. The fact she knew he'd eaten her fried apples from the taste lingering on his thumb.

His thumb continued to stroke both her lips and anticipation heated her like coals to ovens already burning with fire.

She felt like fire, only greedy for more. After one taste of him, after seeing the surprise and feeling the hitch in his breath, she wanted to do it again.

This time, she wasn't tentative about it. She wanted to taste the flavors and the textures of what he offered.

When he caressed, she swiped her tongue against his thumb.

And it was delicious.

With a choked sound, he yanked his hand away and grasped the nape of her neck.

The movement pulled her towards him, her hands rested on his chest.

His gaze heated need. That studying gaze she was familiar with and one she was just now recognizing.

'Do you feel that?' he said.

She felt too much.

'My heart is beating faster.'

Her fingers curved against the soft weave of his fine blue tunic. Underneath her hands were the planes of muscles and the heat of his skin. His caught breath expanding his lungs and pushing against her. The thump of his heart hard, insistent. Like his amber gaze.

'That's for you. That's what you do to me.' Against his chest, he cradled her hands in one of his. 'You wanted more in the garden. I couldn't go further. It had nothing to do with your scars and all to do with what I want with you.'

She glanced up, held his eyes briefly before returning her gaze to their hands and his heart that changed beat at that moment.

This want couldn't be right. She was just now accepting her appearance, but she still carried her shame. Shame of broken promises she'd told him about, and a cowardice she didn't. 'The flames. My scars.'

'Hadn't I explained to you enough in the garden how I shouldn't be the man to kiss you? That I don't deserve you?'

He was stunning, perfect. Strong jaw, hard cheekbones, perfectly sculpted lips. It was she who didn't deserve him.

'No, I can see you can't. Even in your silence, you demand and give a man no choice.'

His stance was wide, strong, like he could stand for hours, but it was also strung with some tension. An imperceptible movement almost like a shiver or shudder she felt flowing through his body.

She recognized it only because of the way her own body felt, both suddenly strong and yet somehow weak. A tension that heated its way just under her skin until she wanted to rub her hands against her arms to ease the prickling, to stop her own shivers.

'Though it may damn me, I'll show you.' His lips curved to a tease. A mockery, but also a truth. 'Maybe we can do this if we pretend, can you do that?'

She shook her head. Any play in her had been consumed in the flames.

'You can, you must. You've already taken us here, at least try for the rest, Helissent. I must go just a bit further than this for your sake, for mine. Time, Fate, my flawed birth won't allow me to prove anything else to you. What you deserve to know, what you should know by now. How could you not know? So for now no more words that we don't deserve. Let's pretend we do.'

'That we deser—?'

His lips pressed on to her opened ones, warm, firm, brief, silencing the denial she intended to say.

Then he lifted up, his gaze taking in her response. She felt her response. Wide eyes. Parted lips. Surprise.

'Are we—?'

This kiss at the corner of her mouth, lingering. A taste of him, his scent. The way he held his breath before he pulled away to gage her response.

'Are you—?' she started to ask.

He kissed those words away, too. Another corner kiss, but now with a slick slide of his tongue along her lower lip before giving the opposite corner a kiss.

When he pulled away, this time she focused

on his reactions. The gleam in his eyes not coming from the amber, but from the black depths in the center. His golden skin flushed, his eyes heavy lidded.

Was he waiting for her to speak again? Or was he waiting for her not to, so they could pretend?

'I...'

Another soft firm press. This time in the center, a coaxing heat to his lips, a bit harder, a flick of tongue. Then he pulled away.

Pretending, but she wanted another game. If he wanted to kiss away her words, she would just keep talking.

'Think—'

Another press, one she expected, so she pressed back.

A sound of approval from him. 'We—'

Releasing her hands trapped by him and curving them to his shoulders, she molded her body against his.

Shadows from his eyelashes fanned as he looked to her lips, then to her eyes.

She only had one word now. 'Should.'

Another swoop of his lips, longer, coaxing hers open until she did, until his tongue tangled with hers.

She gasped and he took advantage of it. More heated kisses as she kissed him back. Her hands moving restlessly along his shoulders.

His grip at the base of her nape grew hot, damp, but never did he touch her elsewhere. Just his lips, which grew greedy as they pressed more, tasted more, felt more.

Still he didn't move, didn't get closer. She felt the need for closer.

Instead he pulled away, his eyes sweeping over every feature. 'So sweet, God, you're so sweet.'

When he moved to step away, to end the kiss, she gripped his tunic.

His body shot with tension. Wary. His brows drawn, his body defiant.

'More?' he rasped before kissing along her jaw, down her throat, his hands hovering over her hips as her restless hands roamed his shoulders, his nape. Tunnelled through his hair when he gave quick flicks of his tongue.

She gasped. He released an answering sound, half-tortured, half-deprecating laugh. All need.

She was on fire, as though she pressed herself into the flames of her ovens. His smell, the reckless heated amber color in his eyes, his hair mashed by her fingers.

More kisses along the other side of her neck up along her jaw, his direction towards her mouth.

'More,' she said.

He jerked away. Startled, she released her hands.

His eyes searched hers, a crease between his brows as if in pain.

Underneath their breaths, she heard the creak of the inn settling for the night, the dimming of voices and heavy boots against the floorboards. Smelled the drying herbs, the saltiness of cheese, the soaked wood of ale barrels.

His face was taut, his lips full and shone like he drank of that ale. Her own mouth grew dry, thirstier for more of his kisses.

When her eyes finally reached his, she was aware of nothing except him, him, *him*. Just heat, hot flowing, swirling in gold.

'You should be in your room,' he said. 'Where it's safe.'

It felt safe in the cellars with him holding her. It felt right.

'I should go,' he said. 'I shouldn't be here.'

He didn't move, and neither did she.

It wasn't his words she listened to, but the tone of them. His low, and rough, as if they were scraped out of him. As if he shouldn't be saying them.

Desire and need battered against her insides as she listened only to the persuasive hunger behind his words. 'Why? We're pretending.'

'We've shared enough kisses.'

'I want more.'

He shook his head. 'I can't pretend any more

or I may just believe. You need to be kept safe. If I go further, it'll be all for naught. Everything for naught.'

Everything felt for naught. Everything except her emotions that poured out of her and seemed to be spilling on him, too.

He seemed undone, like her. Held by something only he understood. But she didn't.

He wanted her. Despite her scars—no, he said because of them. He knew her family died, while she lived, and still he kissed her.

Yet he said he wanted them to pretend, that he didn't deserve her. He wasn't rejecting her, he was holding back. Excitement rushed up her spine. Uncertainty dousing it, but not enough to stop her hope for more.

Whatever was between them was like a scale, precariously balanced. She knew of scales, how a pinch too much of one ingredient could irrevocably ruin a dish.

But whatever was between them felt substantial and heavy. His kisses tipped her more to one side than the other. They were off balance and she wanted more.

She stepped away, pulled off the leather tie holding her hair until it fell loose about her.

He closed his eyes. 'You know now, don't you? It's why you're—'

She only knew her body felt tight like it had by the stream. Now with his kisses, she wanted to relieve it. She had to balance the scale. She unlaced the first lace of her gown. 'Know what?'

'You believe me now, when I say how much I desire you.'

That's how this began, but if she did admit to believing, he would stop, and this recipe needed more ingredients.

'Not enough. I need more,' she said.

His eyes shot open and took in her determination. 'No,' he said. 'We can't.'

'We're not.' She reached the lower laces and began to pull them apart. 'This is merely pretending.'

His eyes lowered, took in her clumsy fingers. She watched his throat move as he swallowed.

Gone was the mockery and the assurance. There was only heated vulnerability and a moment suspended.

'I can't pretend any more,' he said.

'Just a little more.' Tip the scale, a couple of grains, a couple of kisses. Dollops of honey, and she wanted his touch. The laces undone, she let go of the gown and it fell to her feet. She stood in her chemise. The fabric fine, but not sheer. She was still fully clothed, but didn't feel it as Rhain took in her loose hair and bared feet.

Trepidation shook her body as anticipation

beat her heart. Underneath the chemise were the worst of her scars.

He looked wildly around the room. 'Here, Helissent? Here you want me to see you, to touch you?'

She could think of no better spot. The cellar, brimming with life-giving food, with combinations of ingredients she'd never tasted before, with recipes just waiting for her to discover. 'Yes, here. *Yes.*'

A low rumble deep in his chest. Then suddenly, his elegant hands were on her arms, the press of his body against her own, a step back, for balance.

She found none. Only the security of the wall behind her back and the certainty that Rhain was holding her up.

Holding, a moment's pause as if he, too, was surprised he was suddenly there, then he groaned and his lips slammed on to hers.

No more teasing kisses. Only his taste, his smell. Acutely aware of hands rubbing along her arms, of the press of his chest, the strength of thighs against hers. Of his mouth, his tongue, his kisses demanding more, devouring, wanting, longing.

Her hands going between them, feeling the thumping of his heart, the hitching rise of breath in his lungs. She felt…she felt… How could she feel so much?

* * *

Craving more of her kisses, more of the feel of her in his arms, Rhain undid his belt and threw it aside and toed off his boots.

Helissent stood trembling before him. Her unbound hair cascaded over one shoulder, an errant lock across her right cheek. The torch's light couldn't capture the colors. But he could see enough of the tumultuous waves and his fingers ached to know how each strand felt. Her eyes were wide, uncertain, but dark with desire and determination.

She was so beautiful to him and held still as he carefully lifted the chemise off her body and laid it on the ground.

Bared, her shoulders arched back, her chin jutting out. As if despite his words, he might reject her.

He could never reject her. He wanted to fall down on his knees and worship her. The grace and strength of each limb, the full curve of her breasts, the tips rosy and waiting for his touch, for his kisses.

Her entire skin was wrapped in jagged ribbons of scars, some white, a few very dark and deep. All testament to her true worth and beauty.

But now, here, he wanted only to feel her skin, to taste every inch of her. Explore and bring her pleasure. Nothing was about the past and he'd never needed a woman more.

'You humble me,' he said through the tightening in his voice.

Every limb shook, every nerve inside her quivered. Her hair from her scalp to down her arms and legs felt as though they were all trying to escape.

In some way, despite his actions, a part of her still expected pity or horror. She got none of that.

Instead Rhain's eyes darted as if he couldn't take in her features fast enough.

As if he wanted her. Truly wanted her. It was staggering.

'Do you believe me now? How I can't pretend. Look, Helissent, look how I desire you.' He lowered his eyes to his breeches and hers followed his. Followed to what he could not hide. His need, his desire for her, blatant not only in the tension and hardness of his body, but in the flush across his cheeks, the heaviness of his lids, the softness to his lips.

She felt the flush of sweat at the small of her back and around her hairline. He was showing her more than acceptance. Could she believe this? 'I don't understand how you could want me.'

He opened his eyes. Shuddered. 'You're not sweet, Helissent, not at all. You torture a man with your demands. I have no reserves when it comes to you. I've done all I can to show you, now you tell me it isn't enough. Since you give me no choice, I'll make you feel it.'

'How, when I look like this? How, when I thought no one else would?'

'I could not want a woman more. No, I could not want *you* more.'

'But what side of me?'

He padded her gowns, lifted and laid her down. 'There are no sides to you. Is that all you see when you look at yourself? If so, you could do the same things with me... Find parts unpleasing.'

He laid on his side beside her. There could be no parts unpleasing about him. He was perfect. Everything about him was perfect.

'I have scars and bruises,' he said, splaying his fingers and, pushing up the sleeves of his tunic.

Nicks, cuts, healed over by golden skin. 'But they aren't...you.'

'Are your scars you?'

He didn't know of her cowardice. 'Mine are deep. Sometimes I feel as though they've gouged my soul.'

His breath escaped. 'Your soul is pure, Helissent. So pure, my blackened deeds and tainted heart shouldn't be here. But your words demand I show you, that I touch you more.' Sitting up, he shucked off his tunic. Not an ounce of hair covering him like she'd seen with others. Just more of that golden skin and lean muscles. Each line so symmetrically formed, she could level cakes with them.

'You laugh?' he said.

Was she laughing? 'I was thinking of baking.'

'Baking.' His voice was deadpan.

She knew she had to explain. 'I often think of baking when I look at you.'

He glanced down at his bare chest. 'I should be insulted if you think I look like a cake. If Nicholas ever knew, I'd never hear the end of it.'

She did laugh then. 'It's your coloring. I can't help it. Your hair is the color of lavender honey in spring. Your eyes the color of a winter's batch carved from the beeswax.'

His body eased beside her, his head resting on his hand, his eyes warm. 'Coming from you, these are compliments. Anything else inspire you?'

She wished she could blush then. 'The texture of your hair.' She could still feel it between her fingers.

'What of it?'

'It's like the coarsest of rye flours sifted with the richest of butters. And your skin...' she swallowed '...it's golden like—'

'Your honey cakes?' His lips twitched. 'If

you compare me to your honey cakes, I may just boast to my men what you think of me.'

She nodded, both embarrassed and elated he understood, but more than that, he seemed... pleased by her clumsy words.

His eyes darted over her shoulder and his throat moved as he swallowed. As if he had clumsy words to say as well. 'Then inspect me as you would a cake. Look closer, can you see my flaws?'

Not clumsy words at all, but heated ones. Inspect him? She could barely lie beside him. She vehemently shook her head.

'Then let me inspect you.' He traced along her thigh, his fingers almost fitting into the grooves caused by the ceiling pieces that had trapped her sister.

She often did what Rhain was doing. When the muscles underneath felt raw or fatigued. But it wasn't the same now. In fascination, she watched his fingers skim her leg.

When she looked to his expression, he looked equally fascinated. When his darkened gaze returned to hers, she saw his questions, his innate curiosity.

'You can't feel here, can you?'

He could tell? She shook her head.

'How about here?' He skimmed his fingers along where her scars looked like broken spiders' webs.

'Some,' she whispered, intent on watching him, his expressions, his look of wonder. Watched his hand which trailed over her hip and along her torso. She felt the slight brush of his knuckles against her inner arm, but along that side just under her breasts. Nothing.

'Not there.' The scars were too deep. She remembered the pain of those well.

His brow furrowed as if puzzled. So she watched his fingers to determine what piqued his curiosity as he traced from skin that could feel to places that felt nothing. Back and forth.

'How about here?' He traced one finger along the jagged bits of her, the softened, flattened scars before the smoothness of her natural skin. There wasn't a perfect line from where she could feel and where she could not, but he seemed to want to know the parts.

'I can't feel. Not everywhere.'

He looked up then, his amber eyes lit as if by fire. 'I can't understand it.'

His tone was baffled. His expression fixed on the gentle swipe of his fingers as if he tried to figure out some complex recipe. As if there was something wrong with her.

Restless, she moved to sit up. He grabbed her hip and pulled her back down. 'Don't think that.'

'You don't know what I'm thinking.'

'Yes, I do.'

'That I'm some sort of aberra—'

A kiss, forceful and brief. 'Wait.' Swirling amber. Raspy whispered words. 'Watch me.'

He skimmed his caresses along the twisted skin, over her hip and down her thigh.

There she felt the caresses as inadvertently some of his fingers slid against less scar tissue.

With his hand now on the inside of her calf, he trailed along her unscarred leg and over her hip. Where she could feel, she felt hot. Where she couldn't, she watched the mesmerizing strokes of his palms, the arcs of his fingers and the heat flared more.

'Are you looking?' he said.

She felt and watched and noticed everything. The intimacy of the cold, damp room. The hardness of the floor made soft with their clothes. The room lit by the lone torchlight mounted by the door behind them. How the light highlighted his hair, illuminated the golden tone of his shoulders, encased the flexing muscles of his torso.

He shimmered and comforted her like honey, but he was so much more than that. She wanted to tip the balance of the scales, but these scales were vast, all encompassing. They held so much more than she could ever dream.

'Helissent,' he said, his voice holding some taut amusement. 'Are you thinking of baking again or are you watching?'

Unable to tell him all the words she wanted to say, she answered, 'Both'.

He let out a soft breath. 'It's not you I find I cannot understand. It's me. I don't understand because when I touch you, I feel *everything*. Like here.' He pressed his hand against the faintly puckered and twisted part of her. The part that was most pieced together. 'And here.' His hand low on her belly, where there were no scars. His warm palm radiating heat, his spread fingers creating an insistent pressure inside her.

'I feel everything. *Everywhere*.'

She shook her head. His fingers weren't scarred. Why wouldn't he feel everything?

'Now it's your turn not to understand. Let me show you.'

He did it again to her, now watching her eyes, watching her reactions. His hand trailing the same path, but fingers widening, pressing more as if he couldn't help it.

'I feel the soft textures of your skin under my fingertips, your tremors vibrating against my palms. I see your flushing along your chest, your neck. How it contrasts with the colors along here.' He traced with a fingertip between her breasts to her navel. 'How your scars changed your color to this soft violet that reminds me of the dawn. But I feel your skin elsewhere, too. Watch me.'

He shifted, and knelt between her legs. With both hands he caressed from her ankles to her inner knee and around the outside of her thighs. He rested his hands against her hips, feathered his fingers along her waist.

Then he did it again. This time watching her, this time, she saw his gaze heat, then heat again. His lips curve, the look of wonder darkening. Darkening again until she could only sense the amber in his eyes like a fire behind that lit her.

She shivered.

His lips curved like he saw something more that pleased him. 'You felt it elsewhere, yes? Not just from my hands, not just from your skin. But here in the thumping of your heart, in the flutters just under your skin, in the hitch of your breath.'

She did feel those things and more. She was being touched after years and years of nothing, and now it was almost too much.

'I understand,' she whispered, as his eyes searched hers, and he gave a rueful look.

'Yes, but not nearly enough,' he answered as his hands swept stronger lingering strokes.

Until she felt a want far past the sweep of his hands on her thighs and hips. Beyond the glide of his fingertips on her belly.

She quivered. 'I understand,' she said more forcibly.

'Not yet.'

When he lowered his head, when he cupped an ankle and drew it to his mouth for his kisses, for his tongue. She wasn't prepared for the flare of heat, like being speared with pleasure.

'No, no, stay,' he coaxed when she tried to escape. 'You have unsurpassed legs, Helissent. Is this what baking gave you? This strength, these lines?' He kissed her calves, caressed along her thighs. His kisses trailing higher the way his hands went.

Her left leg suffused with pleasure, he began on the other. 'Do you have any idea how many times I imagine your bare legs? Your height against mine?'

He kept kissing and stroking until she ached with need. She couldn't stand it when he gave the first delicate swipe of his tongue behind her knee, when he wedged himself between her legs to caress further, to kiss higher...

'Rhain!'

He gave a humorless laugh. 'Do you know how often I've imagined this?' he murmured against her skin. 'It's my turn to make demands, to give you no choice.' His fingers fluttered to the very core of her.

Images of him with the pommel of his dagger, the caressing strokes of his palm. All of it she felt now against her skin.

'So sweet,' he whispered. 'So ready for my touch, for my tongue. To taste you now…'

She gasped, her back arching. His hands at her hips anchoring her as pleasure overcame her.

Rhain knelt between Helissent's legs and knew he'd never be the same. None of it was pretend. All of it real.

So beautiful. Her body gathering in her breath, her neck and cheeks flushed with desire. A sheen to her skin that he brought there. Her eyes closed, her neck still arched.

The flames had taken away her modesty, and he'd reveled in her open responses. Every kiss, every touch, every taste glorious. Responsive as no woman had ever been.

Soon she would open her eyes and see what she had brought him, too. His body shaking, his breeches pulled taut. The sharp pain welcomed now because he could focus on it instead of her softness.

She humbled him, but now, all too acutely, cold reality crept in. He was unworthy of her. Unworthy in every way, both inside and out. He should have been a knight, noble, who didn't cave to his needs. He should have left her alone in the cellar.

So weak when it came to her, but he must find whatever strength he had left and walk away.

Surely, she would know now her capability of bringing a man to his knees. That she was worthy of love and desire, surely now she would let him leave.

A curve to her lips, she murmured as she sat up and he schooled his features.

'The inn is completely quiet,' he said. 'You could go undetected to your room.'

'Aren't we…?' She pulled her knees to her chest, and looked forcibly at him. 'I know what happens with men and women. I know there's more.'

He'd hated himself in the past. Felt shame his brother carried a burden that was never his.

He was the one, who was vile, and tainted on the inside. Each burning pulse of Devil's blood through his heart a reminder of his past, of how he could never truly have her.

She smiled at him, a glow to her skin, to her eyes. An inviting warmth. She was happy, and he wanted more with her.

From the firm line of her jaw, and her piercing eyes, she wasn't going to let him simply walk away as he needed to. As she needed him to.

So he'd have to do more than merely leave. He'd have to take away some of her happiness. To do so, he'd lie to her. A mercenary lies all the time; this should be no different.

She was different.

He couldn't do it. How could he be cruel when they shared so much? Cold sweat sheened and ice flowed under his heated skin. He turned the craving for her inward until it pained him. He needed to suffer. Outwardly, he needed to pretend that he could leave her.

After all they'd shared, he must lie to her to keep her safe…from him.

'This was all pretend, remember?' he said.

'I…no, it was real. I know it was.'

He shrugged. 'Because I gave you pleasure? You're only one of the many women I've lain with. I gave them all pleasure.'

She frowned. He stood, his body racked with need, with want for her. He watched her eyes stare blatantly at his need.

'But you didn't lie with me. I didn't get to touch you or—'

Each word she gave slashed his insides, all phrases he said burned his throat. He wanted her touch, wanted so much more. But she was determined, and he needed to keep her safe, from Reynold, from him. So he forced his words out, like they were knives. 'Why would I want that?' He almost sneered at her scarred hand.

Then he yanked on his tunic. Shocked he could get it over the knives he'd buried in his own heart. Wrapped his belt around him, tightening it until it felt like a noose around his neck.

His shoes he merely picked up. His body suddenly too weak as if the bits of leather and lace were boulders ready to crush him.

He wanted to be crushed and hung and stabbed as Helissent then said, 'So all those words about my scars. All your…kisses, and touch, what were they?'

'You know how curious I am. I wondered what your skin felt like, how it would respond. And you satisfied that curiosity.' He shrugged. 'Maybe I am no different than those men Rudd introduced you to.'

She gasped then, her eyes sheening in the flickering light. Her shoulders jutted back, her chin raised as if he'd rejected her.

He had to reject her. He couldn't stay here. He wanted to show her what she meant and he made it all worse. She made it worse by asking for more.

He clenched his eyes—no, this wasn't about her. It was all his fault. She didn't know how much worse it could be if he made love to her.

Kissing, touching and tasting her wasn't the first mistake he'd made in the heat of a moment. He'd done that in London and it cost him his life.

He wouldn't stay and be the cost of hers.

When he got to the door, he stopped to see her one last time. Even sitting vulnerable and exposed, she looked steadily at him. He still couldn't tell the color of her eyes. And as his gaze lingered, he could barely grasp the emotion behind them.

Then he closed the door, knowing that all that waited for him was disappointment, regrets and death. Maybe he could beg Reynold to torture him before his death. He deserved far worse.

Helissent sat for only a few moments after Rhain left. The cold dampness of the room amplified now though the torch flared brighter with the closing of the door.

It was quiet, like those caves behind Agnes's hut. Earlier this evening, she'd sought sanctuary here, but no longer did the room feel comforting.

It was good she didn't need comfort any more. Quickly standing to dress, Helissent felt a lightness and a determination she had never felt before.

With Rhain's last words, she should have felt hurt, but couldn't. Not when he'd given her a gift no one else had ever given.

He had made her believe with his touch and kisses that she deserved more than her shame. Just as the innkeepers showed her love, just as she carried on because of that, she would find a way for Rhain now. Despite what he said, the cruelty of his sneer. When he looked back at her, she saw the truth in his eyes.

It was him that needed comfort. He said those words because…oh, she didn't know why, but she knew she didn't believe a word he said in the end.

She loved him. Of that she was certain. He needed her and she'd been willing to give herself to him.

He needed peace, needed the warmth she gave him. What she didn't know was why. She desperately wanted to know why.

He said he didn't deserve her, but he was wrong. Somehow, some way, it would be her turn to show him.

Chapter Nineteen

Rhain walked in the dark morning mist. Two days. Two muted days where he'd avoided the inn and avoided the markets. Kept away from anywhere Helissent could be.

He'd failed her; couldn't face her. Coward that he was. What could he do or say? There were no words or actions to make it better. Not when his only action, to leave her, was the right thing to do.

He should have walked away in the garden. Should never have sought her company. Certainly should have closed the door when he saw her in the cellar.

But something in him wanted to make it right, to ease the pain he saw in her hazel eyes when he walked away. Show her how much she was worth. What a fool to show her the way he did with kisses, with his tainted body. He had to stop. It was the only way to show her what she meant to him. How he would never hurt her.

But by stopping, he made it worse. She lost that light, that belief in herself.

And he ached for her. Past the tension and need racking his every nerve, his very blood. The kisses he could never steal from her again still seared. The courage and softness of her skin fevered him. Anguish bit at his heart.

It was of no comfort that he wouldn't live long like this. Not when he remembered the last look she gave him before he closed the door.

He found Nicholas checking the perimeters of the inn. At this time of the morning, only the bakers were awake and, unfamiliar with York, Nicholas strolled slowly through the thin grey light. Rhain pulled his hood tighter against the heavy mist and hurried to catch him.

'Couldn't sleep,' he said, purposefully striding noisily up to Nicholas. Part of his friend's sight was diminished, but not his hearing, and he was fast on dagger throws. The longer they were away from London and Guy's death, the more alert Nicholas had become. It was no surprise to see him up this early, walking around the buildings and checking the security.

'I slept fine enough,' Nicholas replied. 'It's when I'm awake that I remember the trouble tailing us.'

Rhain couldn't seem to forget. Days in York and no sign of Reynold or his men.

With Nicholas's words, it seemed the wait was over. 'You didn't just wake up. You heard something.'

Nicholas gave a curt nod and they walked to a darkened corner of a building. 'Just now. I was here to receive information, but it's not news you're wanting to hear.'

Rhain's eyes went to the inn where Helissent slept and his eyes professionally scanned the narrow mid-terrace structure for weakness, or any signs of danger.

'It's not her you should worry about,' Nicholas said drily. 'It's you.'

'If Reynold's near, I have to worry about her. The man's as rich as the King, he doesn't have to be near to send someone to kill her.'

'He said he'd give her safe passage.'

Only to York, which wasn't enough for him. 'But not keep her safe.'

'He doesn't truly want her. This is personal for him. He's going to want the man who killed his brother.'

'It's personal for me, too.'

Nicholas exhaled. 'Does she know that?'

'No, and she won't. I was kind to one other creature and look what happened to her.' He wouldn't risk Helissent by being close to her again. Reynold could kill her with as little thought as Guy had the dog.

'This conversation is moot anyway.' Nicholas looked over his shoulder. 'He's here, a little over half-a-day's ride outside the North Wall. He's holed up in a country house with some fortification. It's so well lit at night, you could probably see his men walking the perimeters simply by standing on top of the wall there and looking for mass movement.'

Foreboding flooded Rhain's veins, but not surprise. He'd been waiting for the time he'd meet with Reynold. But how he was about to meet him was a surprise. He always imagined Reynold would attack by stealth or by force. Not sit like a king upon his throne and wait for the attendance of the man he would soon behead.

The ramifications of Reynold's comfort and protection weren't lost on Rhain. No, the only thing he lost was any time left. Unerringly, his eyes went to Helissent's building. 'Not even hiding.'

'No, he expected you travelling north to Edward's camp. Probably has been comfortably whiling away his time until you travelled his way.'

Reynold was daring; he'd give him that. He had to respect a man who didn't hide. He rubbed the hilt at his side. 'It's not even arrogance that he displays himself, is it?'

Nicholas shook his head. 'The moment we left

London this was all set. By the time York's gates were closed behind us we were firmly in his trap.'

'Just *me* in his trap.'

'Are we still arguing this? I was there, too.'

Nicholas was right. It was a vain hope that Reynold would be a reasonable man and let Nicholas live. Unlike Guy, Reynold's reputation was calculating, cold, but rumors weren't facts. The fact was: Nicholas was present when he had gutted Guy.

Still Rhain did hold to one hope that might be possible. 'Not the others…not Helissent. They weren't anywhere near us that night.' Which meant Reynold, without losing any pride, could let them go.

'True, it's not about them or her. But it's not up to just us either, because we can't kill him by ourselves.'

'Then we plan to go around him. He's has too many men; we are more mobile. Maybe backtrack south.' He could wait out Reynold for as long as it took.

Nicholas held out his arm and unfurled his left hand to reveal a small crumpled note. 'Remember that secret meeting I had with the secret source?'

Rhain took the note. 'It wasn't a secret?'

'He never showed. I was met by one of Reynold's men.'

Rhain read the one sentence. Then read it again before he, too, curled it tightly in his fist.

'So Reynold's declaring his wait is over.' All his intentions to ensure his men into Edward's profitable employ were lost.

They could find their own employment and yet, for mercenaries, they were loyal. He wanted to do better by them. Perhaps he could give them enough money to compensate for this one extremely ill-timed lack of good judgement.

However, killing Guy wasn't his only lack of judgement. What would become of Helissent? He'd brought her to York. The innkeepers were overjoyed with her. She could have a happy stable life here. Just not with him. His time was up.

'He may leave her alone,' he said.

'He may,' Nicholas said, his words agreeing, his tone heavy with doubt.

'By tomorrow night, I'm a dead man.'

'Without a doubt,' Nicholas confirmed.

If he was dead, so was Nicholas. 'I'm sorry,' he said for the thousandth time.

Nicholas laid a heavy hand on his shoulder. 'What did I say about taking in stray dogs? There will always be trouble. But this time, Reynold will be taking us in. Whatever happens, at least we can give him some trouble to remember us by.'

Rhain clasped the top of Nicholas's arm. 'Like a couple of stray dogs, then.'

* * *

Helissent could not catch her breath, could not move her legs. They didn't feel like they had the strength to hold her up much longer.

No, the only thing that did that was the building she leaned against, but even that was poor support. When Rhain and Nicholas continued their walk, she slid to the ground.

She had been returning from the kitchens, leaving her bread to prove in the warmth, when she heard their voices on the other side of the building. Her bread was safe.

But she wasn't, and neither was Rhain or Nicholas. The damage was done. Damage. Danger. So much danger.

Rhain had talked of what happened with the puppies. That Guy had a powerful brother after him. He'd warned her to stay away from him.

But she thought some solution could be found without...death. But Reynold had come for Rhain.

Stray dogs did cause trouble. She understood a bit now the joke between Rhain and Nicholas. Somehow they meant themselves.

How she didn't know. Both of the men were silent on their pasts, but there were snippets on Nicholas's as if he, too, had some personal pain he was trying to overcome.

If she knew Rhain and his band of mercenaries at all by now, she knew this. He protected strays.

She was one of them. Homeless, he took her in, protected her, fed her. Just as he did that feral pregnant dog. Just as he did the men he worked with, the men he called his friends.

Men, scarred, burned and damaged, just like her. She lifted her hands before her. One roughed from work, but passable, the other…the other had held her sister.

She had nightmares still of that ceiling falling. Of clutching her sister's hand, while the smoke overtook them both. She hadn't let go, not ever, and that was why it was badly scarred. The healer always told her she was lucky she could move it.

Maybe she was lucky. She was alive and Rhain needed her. At least now, she knew how to show him he deserved more.

It was a risk, and one she needed to take. What had Rhain called Reynold? A madman, with more slices, burns and intentions to kill than any other man he had met.

Well, she was a woman who had suffered worse and her intent was to save Rhain.

Chapter Twenty

'I trust the trip wasn't too arduous.'

Helissent pivoted towards the voice coming from the darkness of a long unlit hallway. A very male, self-satisfied voice.

For the last hour, she had stood in this ante-chamber, too terrified to take advantage of the rich furniture or appreciate the numerous stacked books that the room boasted.

She couldn't see who addressed her, not even a shadow, but she lifted her chin and gave her most level stare. 'There was a surprising ease to the whole affair.'

Getting out of York's gates was far more troublesome than gaining access to Reynold's grounds. After asking many questions, she was directed to the grand manor house that was surrounded by guards and a newly spiked fence and gate.

There was no traffic on the road to hide herself and by the time she approached the house four stone-faced men flanked her, took the burden of her packages, her cakes and the purse of silver she'd stolen from Rhain's room.

'What happened to your cakes?'

'What makes you think I had any?

'Your reputation precedes you.'

'Your soldiers took them.'

He gave a tsking sound that reverberated in the dark hallway. 'Pity, I would have liked to taste such confections. I have heard much about them.'

Cold. Arrogance. But it was his self-satisfaction that kept Helissent cautious.

Of course, he knew more than she did. This man had spies everywhere. However, it didn't matter that he knew because she had one certainty. He threatened Rhain and she meant to stop him.

'I could make you more.'

Her eyes adjusting to the darkened hallway, she could just make out a shape of a tall, lean man. He leaned one shoulder against the wall and his ankles were crossed. A confidant cat to her mouse.

'That is a most generous offer. Do you do this to prolong your life?'

'You won't kill me.'

'Your cakes are that good?'

'Because my being here doesn't accomplish what you want.'

He stood straight now, but still in shadows.

She sensed he didn't do it for the same reason as Rhain. This man before her liked the sunlight. His voice was too refined and relaxed. It reminded her of hot summer days.

'And you know this how?' he said.

'I just do. Just as I know you've been standing in that darkened hallway almost as long as I've been standing in this well-lit room.'

He paused. It had been a guess, but since she arrived she'd felt as if eyes were upon her. She was used to people watching her. It was almost like another sense such as sight, hearing, taste or touch.

'You know we can find out more about each other simply by sitting like civilized people in the chairs here.'

He watched her, but why she didn't know. He knew almost everything about her. What did he expect to find by observing her? The only thing she could think of was her scars. He wanted to see her scars before she saw his reaction to them.

She had been counting on seeing his reaction to her disfigurement; an advantage she needed if her strategy to save Rhain was to work. But now she realized his standing in the dark was almost as good.

Because his standing in the dark hallway without guards, without company, told her something of him, too. He was a man used to observing and standing on the outside.

'Ah, you're making an assumption that I am civilized.'

He stepped out of the darkness then. His voice made her think of summer, but his looks were anything but. Dark hair, almost black, blue-grey eyes and skin darkened by days in the sun. But there was something else about him.

His clothes were all black, as if he was in mourning for his brother whom Rhain had killed. A reminder that his revenge against Rhain was justified. How would she react if someone killed her sister? She, too, would hound the murderer to the ends of the earth. As it was, she had killed her sister and she haunted and hated herself for it.

'Of course you are civilized,' she said. 'Or else you would have killed me the moment I approached your gates.'

'I enjoy the fact he told you of me, you know. It proves everything I surmised.'

Nicholas was right, they did have spies everywhere. While she was here, Rhain and Nicholas could be fighting elsewhere.

Reynold was a man to make such strategies. Civilized. Cunning. Shrewd. She felt like she was baking in the dark, with ingredients she couldn't see.

But she didn't need to see. If Rhain was right in his description of Reynold, she personally knew the ingredients he was made of. Which was why she was here.

A curve to his lips that made the grey in his eyes colder. 'As for reaching my gates, I could have killed you in Tickhill when I realized you were no mere passenger in Rhain's little band of misery.'

Days had gone by since then. Days where this man plotted and planned, where he grieved for his murdered brother, and yet…he had held his hand.

'I am a mere passenger.'

He shook his head slowly, his eyes locked on her with certainty.

'I came to York, which was always to be my home,' she added.

'Was it?' He seemed amused by something, and stepped further in the room. The door to the right creaked open and in came three servants carrying trays of refreshments and arranged them on the table.

Such luxuries she wouldn't have taken for granted mere weeks ago when all she had was her own skills in trying to make the dull fare palatable.

Now she had Tickhill, and more fine food at York, but it didn't stop her curiosity about the array in front of her.

'Afraid if it's poisoned?'

'Just becoming accustomed to things I never dreamed of before. I should have you know, when I become accustomed to things, I keep them.'

'Ah, you mean my brother's murderer. You won't be able to keep him. Not when he come's for you.'

'No.' She shook her head slowly, the way he did. His lips quirked in acknowledgment.

This was a strange conversation and certainly one she was ill prepared for. It wasn't just her lack of communication skills.

It was the difference between the brothers. Guy stamped the head of a nursing dog. Reynold invited her in, gave her reprieve, comfort and food. Now he watched her as if she provided him amusement.

'York was to be my home. He was leaving me there.'

His smile was almost apologetic in its satisfaction. 'Yet, he told you of me and you came here.'

The way he said it, made it sound like she was significant. Rhain had warned her that simply telling her could harm her. Here was proof. 'That is no proof of anything,' she said.

'If you believe that,' he said, 'then why are you here to plead for his life?'

'I'm pleading for mine.'

'Yours? There isn't any threat on your life.'

'You are threatening my life, by threatening his.'

He made another tsking sound. 'And you call yourself a mere passenger.'

'I was a mere passenger, but I've realized a few things along my journey.'

He signaled to the chair behind her and she knew she was right about him. He was powerful, well guarded and alone. There were soldiers and servants everywhere in the great house, but no company for him.

He was a man who stood in darkened hallways and surrounded himself with books.

Now she was inside and he was providing opportunities to talk like she was a visitor. And he was curious about her. As she sat, she'd seen his gaze on her scarred hand and the side of her face. Nothing overt, but contemplative.

She found she did the same with him as he prepared their repast. She saw the scars and scrapes of a man who lived by a sword. Certainly, he was more refined, but there were similarities between Reynold and her mercenaries. It wasn't until he handed her a cup of wine that she saw the scars from burns Rhain spoke of. They were on the palm of his left hand, creating their own ridges and fissures that fanned around his fingers. It was as if his hand was held to a flame.

This man grieved and had known pain like hers. When she was done explaining, he would know why she was here.

She tilted the cup to her lips—again the heady smell of wine was almost as intoxicating as the sip she took. 'I would like to tell you of my scars.'

He set his own cup down, and gathered a plate, filled it with small bites from the selection. Methodical. Polite 'Do you intend to find if I have a heart?'

'No, I already know you do.'

'I threatened the man you're here to plead for, am now holding you for ransom and you think I am soft?'

'Just...hurt.'

'You know because you speak of my brother.'

'I know, because I speak of my sister. The flames that harmed me consumed her entirely.'

He set the plate on the small table next to her chair. It clattered as he lost his firm grip.

He did not get a plate for himself, but grabbed the flagon and his own cup and sat down.

'You don't have to,' he said, setting the flagon next to his chair.

She'd heard that before. 'It's my story to tell. Let me be the judge of that.'

He held the cup in both his hands and sloshed the liquid from rim to rim before he gave a curt nod.

As she talked, he courteously poured wine for her, wine for him. He graciously inquired about the honey salve. She watched him rub his thumb against the palm of his burned hand and wondered if he had similar concoctions or if he suffered through the pain.

When she got to her shame of not saving her sister, he set the wine aside and so did she. Then there were no more words left and Reynold stood, paced to the window.

'I know about pain and grief,' she said. 'I'm also beginning to know about something else.'

Keeping his back to her, he answered, 'Are you saying if the murderer of my brother was murdered, that "something else" would be gone?'

'Yes,' she said.

She saw his shoulder rise and fall with a breath before he turned to her. 'You are interesting company, of that there is no doubt. But you also put me in a dilemma.'

She tried to hide the relief in her eyes by setting the plate of food he offered earlier on her lap.

'I can't just let this go,' he said. 'I won't.'

'I didn't expect you to.'

He narrowed his eyes. 'But you expected me to have some reaction. Knew it enough to risk coming here. How?'

'Rhain told me of your brother and that you had an uncanny ability to cheat death despite your many injuries. I know something of cheating death.'

Reynold's scarred fist clenched. 'Since you are so wise, what now must be done?'

'No compensation can make up for your brother, but I offer what I can.'

His brow rose. 'Yourself.'

'I am here. I can cook, bake—'

'You do not offer your virtue?'

She was used to mockery, but his had a artful edge to it. He didn't care for her virtue, he wanted to know how deep their relationship was. How badly he could hurt Rhain.

'I'm innocent, but why would I offer my scarred self?'

His eyes scanned hers, and though she didn't grow warm as she did under Rhain's studying gaze, Reynold's gaze held that same tenor.

'Why indeed. It's a pity you're not from a wealthy family,' he said instead. 'But Rhain is and I'm glad he'll be here soon.'

'He won't give you money.'

'I must have some compensation.'

He hadn't said it yet, but she knew then he'd let them go. He treated her like a visitor and now bargained like a market vendor.

'You smile?' he said. 'Because you are pleased with yourself.'

She nodded her head.

'Did you rob him?'

'I took every coin I could carry.'

The corner of his mouth curved. 'You were expecting this reaction as well.'

'Your wealth and greed are well known.'

He pretended to look around. 'Where is it?'

'Your men took that, too.'

He made a sweep as he sat again and grabbed some fruit.

'Ah. Then I just have to wait.'

'For what?'

'They are probably checking your cakes for poison, your bags for traps.' He bit into a fig. 'Money, cakes and entertaining company. It's going to be difficult letting you go. But I am right when I say he'll be here. Until then, enlighten me as to why he is worth saving?'

Rhain wasn't coming for her. She'd seen the finality in his face as he left the cellar. She knew he'd lied with his parting words, but she had no doubt he believed them. That was why she was here, to buy them more time.

Eventually Reynold would get tired of talking to her and let her go. She just needed to wait him out.

* * *

'She isn't in the Cathedral.' Nicholas strode up the stairs, but Rhain didn't stop scanning the fields beyond the wall. 'Nor in any kitchens in any part of the town.'

Clenching his hands against the rampart, Rhain wanted to wrench it from its mortared hold and hurl it. He wanted to rip the entire city apart until he found Reynold. Then—

'Steady,' Nicholas said, 'we're doing what we can.'

Rhain cursed against his helplessness, until Nicholas's words stopped him short. 'The men have been looking?'

There was no money in it for them, no prize. He knew who they were and what they did for a living.

Nicholas nodded like he was reassuring a madman. 'They're a bit attached.'

So was he and he felt like a madman.

Frantic hours of searching the city, of asking questions. Of trying to figure out how a woman of Helissent's appearance could go unnoticed. Because she did and he knew with certainty she was no longer in York. The city was huge, but the right questions with money always led to information. Any trail on her was cold.

Almost a full day and he came to the terrible

conclusion. 'He's taken her. What are the men's thoughts?'

Nicholas crossed his arms across his chest. 'You've never asked that before.'

'And you're avoiding the question.'

'That's because you'll not like the answer. As I said, they're attached. Especially Carlos now that her honey salve healed his wound.'

He didn't want to talk of Carlos now. 'You act as though I'd be angry at her.'

'You would if you guessed what they have.'

He wanted to growl. He had no time for guessing; no time for Nicholas's jibes. To think at one point he'd wanted to save his oldest friend. Right now he wanted to chuck him and his men over the wall.

More, he wanted to grab his sword and rush off to save her. What he needed to do was make another plan since his intention of saving his men and Nicholas was no longer viable.

But he couldn't think, not when she could be dead, or tortured or—

'It's true then, isn't it?' Nicholas said.

'What's true?'

'You intended to just hand yourself over,' Nicholas said, his brow drawn. 'When? Last night when we made the pact?'

'Why bother with asking this now?'

'Because you look half-crazed with Reynold

taking Helissent and half-frustrated because you've been thwarted from your every desire.'

Rhain wanted to turn his back on his oldest friend, but it was too late to hide that truth. 'What else did you think I would do?'

'I don't know whether to be honoured or swing my fist.'

'Try,' Rhain bit out. 'You had to know I would save you.'

'For that endearment, I'll let you know what the men think now.'

Scraping his hand against the brick, Rhain welcomed the cold sharp pain. It was either that, or gutting his friend. He didn't need any word games when Helissent was outside the safety of the city's gates.

'Is it possible,' Nicholas said, 'Helissent went to him? You told her about him.'

'To make her stay away. She wouldn't know he was outside the gates. Unless…'

'Unless she overheard us last night,' Nicholas said. 'The conversation we had is right off the path of the ovens.'

'This is what the men think?'

'The men don't think she was taken. There was no sign of a fight or a struggle. No one heard or saw anything. The city's large, but you planted her in a very public area. Kidnapping isn't likely.'

It couldn't be true. 'What do you think?'

Nicholas lifted one shoulder. 'That you're well matched. After all, you were rushing off to save me and now she's rushed off to save you.'

Rhain's heart thumped harder. Rage and frustration warred throughout his veins. What Nicholas suggested was impossible.

There'd be no reason she'd run into his enemy's grasp. No reason…except she'd run into a burning house to save her sister.

Nicholas didn't know the story, but he did. *He* did. And he didn't know who to direct his anger at, Reynold or her.

But he was about to find out. Anger fuelling him, he released his sword. Fear making him reckless, he rushed down the steps and out the gates.

Chapter Twenty-One

A bellow broke out from the courtyard below and Reynold crossed to the window.

Helissent rubbed her hands against her skirts, then jumped when the door banged open and a man carrying her bags strode in. Dropping her precious cargo on the table, he whispered in Reynold's ear before darting a glance to her and closing the door.

Silence again, except the calls from outside. Did she imagine the sounds of swords clashing? The shrill scream of horses in pain, the cries of men?

'Ah, yes, he's come to rescue you. Do you want to see?'

She was compelled to, but the sounds froze every one of her limbs.

It was her eyes that darted for any kind of weapon she could use, as her ears all too acutely heard sounds outside that couldn't be as horrific as her imagination.

For Reynold stood too calmly with his hands clasped behind his back and a genial curve to his lips.

She breathed in raggedly. Forced reason through her panicking imagination. Until she heard only the angered calls and the clanging of gates.

Then she could move and stand next to Reynold to look out at the courtyard below.

Days without seeing Rhain should not have dimmed her memories of the cellar, of the garden. But it was almost a physical blow to watch him stride through the gates.

Even from a distance she recognized the broad jut of shoulders, his long legs. His innate grace of nobility though his clothes were marred, his scabbard empty and three men surrounded him.

When they reached the doorway below, she saw the unmistakable jerk of his chest as he suddenly took in a breath, then he tilted his head and stopped. One of the men grabbed his arm before he yanked it out of his reach. In that moment, she thought he would look up, but instead he continued into the manor.

Soon she would see him. Even now she could hear the additional voices down below and the ascending footsteps.

She was expecting him, but not expecting the full brunt of his anger.

For when he entered with two guards on either side of him, his eyes slid across the room, across her and settled on Reynold.

He was angry. Had he noticed the money she took? Had he felt forced to come here as if she gave him no choice?

He knew nothing of her and Reynold's discussion, or that Reynold intended to let him go free. He was now trapped in his enemy's home, just awaiting the noose, the sword thrust into his gullet, the axe against his neck.

Moreover, she had no guarantee Reynold would hold to their verbal agreement. By leading him here, she may have killed him as certainly as if she'd swung the killing blow.

He must hate her.

She hated herself at this moment. The loathing in the pit of her stomach was never ending. This man, who given her honour, was only trying to save his men, and she returned his kindness with death.

Shame swirled with her emotions. By her actions, she'd failed again.

She should have thought of this. Maybe written a note, but what guarantee did she have? Reynold had said it was a risk coming here. It was.

Despite everything, self-hate wasn't the only emotion flooding her. So was love.

Staggered with the emotions, she released the

hold of her gown and shifted her shaking legs. Prayed they wouldn't crumple beneath her.

All the while his attention remained locked on Reynold.

Seeing him again, even like this, after he left her in the cellar, she felt every longing, every want.

Reynold was taking in both of their reactions like a cat in the dairy. He didn't look like he'd honour the agreement between them since his entire countenance had changed. From a civilized man to calculating one.

'It took you long to get here,' Reynold said. 'I thought you were smarter than that.'

'Let her go, Reynold, you've proved your point.'

Reynold's lips curved. 'That's interesting—you think I took her? What do you make of her coming here on her own?'

Rhain didn't move, but his standing grace faltered for just a bit. Eyes steady on Reynold, he said, 'The facts are the same. You have me now.'

'I've had you since you killed my brother.' Reynold rubbed his hands, the sound softer than a clap, but loud in the tension of the room. 'In the meantime, why don't we share some repast?'

Rhain moved then and the two guards moved as well. 'Enough, I co-operated.'

'You co-operated because my men took your sword.'

'Is that what you think?' Rhain said.

One of the guards leaned over and whispered in Reynold's ear. His brows drew in and a scowl scoured his face before he burst into laughter and waved the guard away.

'Both of you, out.' Reynold pointed to the door, and the guards left. 'You've made your point and a clever one it is. So while we eat, I'd like to hear your version of how you bested the men at the gates.'

'I'll stay,' Rhain said. 'She's going.'

Reynold lifted a brow. 'What does the lady say to that?'

She wouldn't have any of this. She knew Reynold, or she thought she did. He was showing Rhain a different side to him. One she didn't recognize and one that terrified her.

'Let him go,' Helissent said.

Reynold chuckled. 'I'm hungry and my men have kindly brought up your famed honey cakes. I'd rather eat and hear tales instead.'

Rhain seethed with anger, with worry, with every frustration he thought he possessed and mostly with some unknown emotion he didn't know he had.

All of it made thinking nigh impossible, but it was the only commodity left to get Helissent out of here. So he stood, he breathed, he tried to clear the haze of rage at this man, who wasn't anything like Guy.

One step on to his grounds told him that fact. Reynold's guards were good, but no match for him or his men. He'd only allowed their escort so he could observe Reynold's surroundings to find any weaknesses in case he needed to escape with Helissent.

Instead of weaknesses, he saw the discipline, the order, the training of the men. Gone was the lasciviousness, the jests, the disgrace and uncleanliness of Guy's camp.

When he stepped into the entry, he expected more of the same starkness, but instead of the austere surroundings, simple comfort was in every clean rush, tapestry and cushioned chair.

And there was Helissent, merely sitting and enjoying a visit with his enemy. Reynold, who now stood with a smirk like a fox in the hen house.

While Rhain stood powerless, vulnerable, and with the woman he had promised to protect in as much jeopardy as she could be and stubbornly refusing to leave.

This had gone on long enough. 'End this, Reynold. We both know what you want and cakes are not it,' Rhain said.

Reynold shook his head. 'No, I don't think you are aware of what I want. Of how greedy I am, or of how inconvenient a predicament you made by killing my brother.' Reynold clasped his hands behind his back. 'But I can see how uncomfortable you are with the surroundings and I find that extremely poor for the digestion. Therefore, I will put you at rest. I do intend to exact my revenge, but I'd prefer to do it all after I try her cakes.'

Rhain forced his eyes to remain on Reynold as they all sat down. He'd made his mistake with Guy and wouldn't underestimate his enemy this time.

But Helissent's attention remained on him and her worry made it difficult to concentrate. Her fear, her emotions too turbulent for him to determine with the brief glances he allowed himself. But they were enough to make him all too aware of his empty scabbard.

He needed to continue this charade as he found a seat and accepted a plate of honeyed cakes that he knew were delicious, yet tasted like sawdust.

The wine was easier as they exchanged pleasantries, and he drank deep.

He could die tonight, but most likely, Reynold would want to make a show of his death. A theatre, a speech, missives sent to the King and to his family. With certainty, and soon, Reynold would decide what happened to him. He didn't care. He knew the moment after he killed Guy, he was a dead man. He'd accepted his fate.

But Helissent shouldn't have to endure Reynold's clutches. Shouldn't have to suffer through his toying with them. Hours, minutes, seconds passed and they scraped away Rhain's control until he felt nothing but raw agony.

When Reynold decided to make a public spectacle of him, what would he do with Helissent?

As Reynold forced the conversation to continue, he no longer guessed why, he knew it was to cause him further worry. Helplessness.

He felt helpless and it wasn't only because he and Helissent were puppets to Reynold's whims.

He felt helpless with his feelings for her. He cared. He cared too much and who was he to save anyone?

Yet, he had to try. He had to keep trying… until tomorrow when he'd most likely be dead. Then all of this would be over.

But what would happen to Helissent? He didn't know. He'd done all he could do…but not all he wanted.

No, not nearly all he wanted. It scoured him to ignore her. To give her even a moment of hurt, but Reynold couldn't know the depths of his feelings. He wanted her with some burning need he'd never felt and could never extricate himself from.

Years of women, loving them, easy, shared

pleasure. But this…this wasn't easy, this seared him. Days of watching her, travelling with her, then finally knowing her.

She was everything he'd ever wanted. Need, want, desire, love. What a fool. He'd watched his brother falling in love and laughed at him. Told Teague some anecdotes that were meaningless.

Meaningless because he knew nothing until Helissent. Now he knew what love was. His heart beat with it, his lungs filled with the air from it and here they were.

She'd risked everything coming here. How could he do anything less?

As Helissent and Reynold conversed, he tilted his cup only to find it empty. Just like his bravery, and courage.

He lied to himself because he risked nothing by coming here. He was already a dead man.

'Well, the rumors on this are true as well, your cakes are absolute perfection.' Reynold chose another. 'I don't suppose you'd share the recipe with my kitchens?'

Helissent glanced at Rhain, who scowled at his cakes, frowned at his wine, seethed at Reynold, but ignored her.

What else could he do? She had come here, given Reynold the power, and he was lording it over them. She tried to carry on a conversation, but she could hardly comprehend what Reynold was saying or what she replied over the buzzing of fear in her head.

But she heard Reynold's request for her cake recipe and knew the answer to that. It had taken months of her life to gain that knowledge, and no recipe would save Rhain. 'No.'

Reynold merely shrugged. 'Shame, I would have liked to taste those again after you go.'

Rhain sat forward in his seat, his eyes narrowed. 'She's free?'

'She was the moment you arrived. But, alas, I find I can't quite let her go yet. Though I realize it reflects poorly on me since she and I had an agreement.'

'What agreement?'

'Oh, the telling of it will be far sweeter coming from her lips.'

Rhain wanted to slam down his goblet, then slam his fist across Reynold's smug expression, but it wouldn't be enough. How many hours had Helissent been here and how much did she give of herself in this agreement of theirs?

He knew Reynold wanted his life and he was here to give it. 'You have your cakes and your delay. What more do you want?'

'Your manners are slipping, Rhain of Gwalchdu.'

He didn't give a damn for his manners. His brother kept a cooler head, but Rhain had never had patience or been capable of keeping silent for long.

And despite everything, he was curious. Reynold kept him here, but as the conversation continued, he knew it wasn't only for his death.

Reynold drummed his fingers against the table. 'As to what I want, the pity is I don't know. Can't quite put my finger on what it'll take to appease me. You have killed my brother—what do you have to equal his worth to me?'

Ah, Reynold wasn't after a simple beheading. He wanted information first. 'I came here. Respectively, you know what I offer as a skilled mercenary who has travelled to many warring countries and to many whispering courts.'

Reynold's congenial smile flattened. 'That's enticing, but not enough to set her free. There are those who witnessed her arrival. I couldn't simply let her go and appear…soft.'

Reynold was greedy. At least that rumour was true. Rhain had nothing left but some information and his life. Yet as he looked at Helissent, he wished he did if only to…

'How about this?' He pulled out his mother's necklace. For five years the necklace had dictated his direction, but it wasn't a direction he wanted any more. The intricate silverwork, larger than life before, now seemingly insignificant in this moment, now not nearly enough to save her life. How could a mere necklace save her life?

'No,' Helissent said. 'You can't.'

He could. He would. The necklace meant nothing to him compared to her.

'Why can't he?' Reynold asked.

'No reason,' Rhain said. 'Other than it's a costly, unique bit of silver. Will this be enough to let her go?'

Helissent vehemently shook her head.

Rhain didn't spare the necklace a glance as he handed it to Reynold, who eyed it speculatively. It was a fine bit of jewelry and a precious item of his mother's, but Rhain didn't feel the loss he thought he would. He only felt the hope that it would be enough.

Reynold's eyes slid to Helissent. 'This has value to him.'

'Yes.' She lifted her chin. 'It was his mother's and he carries it everywhere.'

Reynold locked eyes on Rhain, who saw no need to deny it. 'It's true.'

Reynold tossed the necklace in his hand like he could feel the sentimental weight. 'This I will keep, then.' Reynold pushed his chair away from the table and stood. 'With this and the gift you graciously bestowed on me earlier, my dear, I think this concludes our visit.'

Rhain offered his arm for Helissent to rise. 'She's free?'

'As are you.'

Rhain's eyes widened. 'What are you saying?'

'Did you think I wanted to keep you, and what? Torture you for information, then kill you?'

Rhain didn't deny it.

'And what will that gain me?' Reynold said. 'If you're alive, you owe me your life and hers as well. Though you have little wealth now, I suspect you'll come into more as time goes on. Who knows what fortune will come my way and what I could extract from you?'

Rhain welcomed the tight grip Helissent had on his arm. It was the only indication that he wasn't dreaming.

'Plus, it wouldn't be courteous after the generous favor you bestowed upon me.'

It was Reynold's smug tone he'd had enough of. 'I gave you no favors.'

'Of course you did. You think I don't know the caliber of man Guy was or the deeds he had done? I never liked or respected him.' Reynold clasped his hands again. 'With his death, his land and property was split between my other two brothers and me. Between that and what you generously gave to me, I am now an extremely wealthy man.'

Two facts were clear from Reynold's state-

ment. He wasn't a fool and his greed might sur-
pass King Edward's.

'We'll be off then,' Rhain said, attempting to
find his courtly manners again though he wanted
to gather Helissent in his arms and run her to the
safety of his men.

'One more thing,' Reynold said, his eyes on
Helissent, whose grip now shook against his arm.
It was the only indication that these moments
were straining her. Otherwise she held firm, her
chin determined.

Reynold gave a curt nod, almost like a bow
before he said, 'Rhain killed my brother, my
lady. But this agreement we made today will
hold firm; you have my word on that.'

Helissent gave a soft hitch to her breath and
her eyes brimmed with tears. For some reason
she trusted Reynold. What was their agreement?

'I am surprised by your choice of a woman,'
Reynold said turning his gaze to him. 'She's too
soft hearted for a mercenary's life.'

'Brave enough to face you.'

Reynold's lips curved. 'Ah, yes, I noticed that,
too. It's probably why I couldn't leave it at that.
We've had such a lovely visit; I'd like her to think
better of me.'

Rhain pulled Helissent close. After everything, she allowed him. With some satisfaction,
he watched one of Reynold's brows raise.

'You are an enviable man.'

'When haven't I been?' Rhain said, letting Reynold know if not by words then by tone that Helissent was not to be threatened again.

Reynold's eyes became cold. 'Still, you're easily found if I should envy too much.'

Rhain felt Helissent stiffen at his words and he squeezed her elbow to keep her silent.

Reynold was only letting Rhain know that he was still a threat, as if he'd ever forget. Reynold had the perfect excuse to kill him and no authority would deny him. But Rhain understood Reynold better now. He was a cunning enemy, but one he could respect.

'I'll send you missives of my whereabouts.' Rhain stepped back and Helissent stepped with him. They were now effectively out of a sword swipe. 'After all, you may have need of my superior mercenary skills.'

Reynold noted their distance. They might be out of one man's reach, but his power was far spread. For now, they were safe. Rhain only needed to get Helissent out of Reynold's direct clutches.

Reynold chuckled and waved his hand. 'Go. Before I change my mind.'

Gripping Helissent's hand, Rhain pulled them out of there before he got her killed.

Chapter Twenty-Two

Feeling light-headed, dizzy, with her arms and legs starting a trembling she couldn't control, Helissent blinked against the flaring torches in the night.

Rhain held her hand tight and pulled her close. Her trembling only increased.

'I'm sorry,' she said.

A muscle popped in the side of his jaw. He wore his hooded cloak, but his hood was down. The full radiance of his face, of his golden hair and amber eyes reflected and shone against the torches' weak flames.

He was so beautiful. So worthy of the light.

Outside the gates, Nicholas stood alone with three horses. Had Rhain come for her alone?

'Where are the others?' Rhain said.

'The others are still in the trees.' Nicholas nodded his head at the platforms. Reynold's men had their bows raised, arrows notched, but loose. 'But we need to get beyond these men.'

Not left alone. Rhain hadn't been abandoned. Relief and worry warring inside her. More trembling, more weakness, she hadn't felt this walking into Reynold's camp, she couldn't comprehend why she felt this way now. They were safe and alive.

But too close they came to bloodshed. If Rhain had men in the trees, he expected trouble.

Nicholas held her before Rhain pulled himself on his horse, and lifted her until she was settled in front on him.

Giddy, she glanced at the other horse with its empty saddle. Felt relief as Rhain wrapped his free arm around her and pulled her close.

She had her trembles under control, but not her chattering teeth. Rhain stiffened with tension. He was angry.

'Why—?'

'Don't say a word. Not one word, until we get through York's gates and within my lodgings. Even then you will wait.'

He was angry.

She hadn't asked to be rescued or for him to put himself in danger. No, this had to be about the silver which was Reynold's now. What was done was done; he'd have to live with his anger.

They flew through the gates and paid the tolls. Rhain dismounted and gathered her in his arms. He didn't set her down until he entered his lodgings.

She looked at the fine room. Large enough to hold attendance. Chairs, tables, a bed the size of her room at the inn.

He started pacing immediately, his hands yanking through his hair. 'How could you go there? How could you risk it? My God, when I think about what that man has done in the past. I told you what he's capable of and you still went!'

'I didn't ask for you to come after me,' she said.

'Not to come after you? At what point did it occur to you that I wouldn't?'

She hadn't believed him that he didn't care for her. That he hadn't felt something for her. But coming for her was something else. He'd told her that Reynold wanted to kill him, she was never at risk. He was. 'I didn't tell you I was going. I purposefully did that so you—'

'So that I what?' he interrupted. 'Sit back, sleep, eat, go the other direction? As if I ever had a choice to go another direction when it came to you! Since the first moment I saw you, I couldn't look the other way,' he said. 'When Rudd put those three extra flagons on your tray though your arms were already shaking? When he called you a troll? Do you think I have time to sit in every inn that feeds me? Do you think I just throw extra coin at every scrap of food I get? That money was for you!'

He was angry, but it wasn't any anger she was familiar with. Not like Rudd, nor like Agnes. She wanted to hear more of his voice, more of his words. Her heart wouldn't stay in her chest. 'I thought it was for my cakes.'

'Your cakes! I wasn't there for something sweet, it was for *you*. I recognized your voice that night long before I saw the men and Rudd. How could I recognize your voice when I barely heard it before? Everything I've done since then was for you. So what do you do? Go to my enemy, come to some agreement that I still know nothing about and I don't know why. You could have died!'

He moved restlessly around the room, his breath was abrupt from his speech, his eyes almost pleading.

'I'll tell you why,' she said.

He'd come to Reynold's to save her. Her love was rapidly blooming, like when she doused too much ale to flour. She felt as though she needed her hands on her chest to hold it in.

'When you bake, sometimes you forget the cakes are in the oven. You get distracted by someone yelling for more ale, or you're wanting to know what rosemary does to a biscuit, or some such emergency that keeps you away from what's important.'

She hoped she was making sense. She'd run to Reynold, trying to save Rhain from his shadows. She knew why she loved him, but the only other thing she understood was baking.

'When you do that,' she said, 'when you keep the cakes too long in the oven, they burn. If you're quick, sometimes you can save them. But often you don't have the time to find something to protect your hands. You just have to reach in the fire and yank them out.'

He stood stalwart, silent, and his eyes roved over hers. His breath was steadier now, almost as if he forced the air calmly through his lungs so he could hear her words.

'It's worth it, though, to save the cakes. The price you pay either by some burns on your hands or by losing a purse full of silver. You're worth it.'

He adjusted his stance. Just a bit, just enough, so it was she who stood still to hear every word he said. 'Are you, by chance, comparing me to a cake again?'

She nodded, unsure at first and then more emphatically. 'That's what I was doing when I went to Reynold. I was yanking you out.'

He released a breath. 'Because there wasn't time to save yourself or think things through.'

When she nodded her head this time, her

brimming tears flew from her eyes, so she wiped them, which made his puzzled expression more clear.

'But what do cakes have to do with silver?'

'With the purse of silver I took to pay him to leave you alone. I assumed that's why you were angry with me.'

'You thought he'd leave me alone because you paid him with silver?'

'No! That's ridiculous, that's like saying the cake is going to be delicious because you took it out with your bare hands. Taking it out of the oven means it's not burnt. But that's a far cry from being delicious.'

He opened his mouth to say something, then closed it again.

She cursed her silly useless words.

'To be delicious, a baker has to know the ingredients,' she said. 'How much and the quality. That's what makes a good cake and that's why Reynold's going to leave you alone. I understand about ingredients.'

'That is convenient for you, but I am not a baker and I am no longer following this conversation.'

'It was his burns, Rhain. You told me he'd suffered from swords' wounds and fire, and nothing killed him. I know about withstanding that kind of pain. I appreciate what it is like to lose a sister as he had a brother. Reynold suffered through all of that. He carries similar ingredients to me!'

'Are you comparing the most powerful and corrupted man in the country to flour and honey?'

'Well, yes. I thought it would be easier to understand.'

'To you.'

'I can see that now.'

'Am I to conclude you talked him out of killing me and going after my men and family?

'Yes—' she pointed to him '—long before you showed up, and then I didn't know what he was going to do when you did. He already agreed to the silver; I couldn't offer him anything more. I think he was—'

'Toying with us.' He threw up his hands. 'I have never been so terrified in my life when I realized you were in his hands.'

'I thought you were angry about your silver.'

'I didn't know about it until now. How did you get into my— Never mind that for now. I thought I was about to lose you. I was angry, and frustrated, and terrified. I was also trying not to pull you into my arms.'

She knew how he felt then. 'I thought he'd kill us both until you gave him the necklace. Oh! Your mother's necklace!'

His eyes softened. 'I don't care about the necklace. Not any more. I would have given every bit of my property and stitch of clothing to get you back.'

She saw Rhain's face when he'd handed the necklace over. He hadn't even looked at it, but she couldn't believe it meant nothing to him. 'What about all your searching? You could return to London now. You were close to finding the answers.'

'Answers I don't need. No, more than that. I wasn't asking the right questions. I was searching, but I thought I needed to know my past. I just needed to know my future. You're my future.'

A smile tugged at his lips, even as his brow furrowed. 'Tears, Helissent. Ah, you've a soft heart and I'm only going to hurt you.'

'No, you came back for me. We're safe. We can be together and—'

His smile disappeared. 'You're my future, Helissent, but I'm not yours and can never be. I'm not a savior, remember? I'm not…right for you.'

Because he was perfect. He hid himself to cover his beauty and he came from wealth and had earned his spurs. What was she? Homeless, penniless.

He stepped back and growled. 'You do not see it. Everything that is wrong with me is inside.'

Somehow she knew he was about to tell her something worse than Reynold. 'Please don't.'

'Don't what? Tell you the truth, that you risked your life for nothing? Because you did.'

Rhain paced. She deserved to know. It was time now. It was time before she ran off to save him. His heart still hadn't recovered and it might never. He could have lost her. He was angry, desperate and he didn't deserve her.

Knowing why he didn't tell her was no comfort. Especially since, the moment he did, he'd lose her. Truly lose her. That utter look of joy she had when he arrived at Reynold's had hit him like a divine force straight to his heart.

Though he'd ignored her, Reynold, with his smug look, knew what she meant then. Reynold, who let them go. Now he had to let Helissent go.

'It's a long tale and one only a few people know. Not even Nicholas knows this.'

'Then don't. It doesn't matter.'

'It does with you.'

Helissent slowly sat on a chair, her eyes never leaving him. Eyes that he still couldn't say what color they were. But he watched how they lit when the sun shone on them and how they darkened with passion. He only wished he could see their colors in all the changing seasons and years. Years he would never have with her.

'My mother wasn't the Lady of Gwalchdu. My father wasn't the Lord either. Her name was

Ffion and she was the sister to Lady Gwalchdu. I thought she was my aunt. I still think of her that way. I still think of Teague as my brother instead of my cousin.'

He exhaled, shook his head as if dislodging those thoughts. 'Ffion was also… She was also sister to God, having joined the abbey. Having grown up thinking I was the second son, I went happily to Edward's court and trained. When the time came, I returned to Gwalchdu no more knowledgeable than when I left.'

Rhain paced the room while Helissent sat. His body still shook from Reynold's threat, from Reynold's unbelievable grant of freedom. Now this. A story he never expected to tell. But Helissent was unexpected and she deserved to know.

'I don't care if you're noble born or not,' Helissent whispered. 'I wouldn't care if you're noble. Why would I? It makes it—'

'Easier?' He turned to her then.

She nodded. Her eyes looked determined, but hopeful. Of course they would. If his separation from her was only as simple as nobility, he might even feel a shred of that hope.

'Just wait. That part of the story I've reconciled with long ago. I was a second son. I had a brother who deserved to be first born. My skills are enough to earn any spurs, nobility or not. No, the fact that my mother wasn't my mother doesn't cut me. In fact, there's almost a blessing in that. You taught me that blessing.'

'I did?'

He nodded. 'I never knew Lady Gwalchdu, who died when I was born. I had a chance to know my mother. Remember those garden stories, the journals and the smell of lavender? I was telling you of Sister Ffion, my true mother. Though she never told me who she was, she spent time with me, taught me some gardening and healing. You've shown me that those are happy memories, despite that I never wanted to remember them as such…despite what I must tell you next.'

He wanted to pace again and just stopped himself. There was nowhere to go with this tale. 'All her life, my mother suffered a terrible illness. She had seizures. Remedies were tried, but nothing made it better. Rumors began that she had the Devil's own blood in her. Teague, my brother… cousin…paid the Church to keep quiet and took the rumor for himself to protect her.'

'It made him greatly feared on the battlefields.' Rhain let out a humorless laugh. 'He wasn't only protecting his aunt, he was protecting me. But we didn't know that then. We didn't know who she was to me or what she wanted.

'But she let us know, when I returned to Gwalchdu. Teague began receiving threatening messages. At that time, there were many Welsh people unhappy that he'd sided with the English in the fight for Wales. The messages weren't that unusual. The timing was.

'Plagued by this, he and I searched for this enemy, only to discover it was our aunt, my mother. She wanted Teague and his wife dead. Teague wasn't pure Welsh, I was. I had returned to Gwalchdu, and she wanted me, her true son, as ruler.

'When I discovered what had happened, when I tried to rescue them, my mother took poison and died almost immediately. But not before revealing I could find my father with that necklace. That's what I've been doing, trying to find the pendant, trying to find my father.'

'All in vain, all to no consequence.' He shook his head. 'My mother died by her own hand. Went mad in the end. Mad because she suffered from seizures from her Devil's blood.'

Rhain breathed deep, walked the room again. Slower this time because the more difficult words he still had to say. He still had to let Helissent go.

'My mother is dead, my father unknown, and it's likely I'll never find him. I have no need to now. I think I had some childish hope that if I did find him, I'd find some great man, from a strong lineage with powerful blood running through his veins. Strong enough to counter whatever ran through my mother's. What runs through mine.

'So you see, despite everything, despite that you rescued me, I can't have you. We can't get married. We'll never have children.'

Helissent felt her tears; felt the constriction in her chest.

His expression stark. Utter desolation. Vulnerability. This was the source of his pain. Why he prayed in the garden and why he pushed her away. 'Do you believe all this?' she said.

'I *know* all this,' he replied.

Though it shouldn't, though more had to be said and understood, something eased within her when Rhain said, 'Despite everything.'

She knew what the 'everything' was and she would fight for it. She only wished she had her mother's spoon to either wave or hit Rhain with to make him see. All she could do was stand. 'Well, then, I know something as well. You're a fool, Rhain of Gwalchdu, mercenary of unsavory mercenaries.'

'No doubt that, too,' he said with a voice full of derision, which she understood now he pointed at himself.

'But no more fool than me. You think you deserve pain, deserve no future, because of your mother?

'I was that way once, too,' she continued, 'but then I met this mocking man who kept to the shadows, who was somehow kind to me. I met these surly mercenaries, who asked for my advice. Then I came to York and I saw others living with injuries, some as bad as my own. I knew not all of them could be merely accidents. Some of them had to be on purpose like mine.'

'On purpose?'

'I've carried a shame all my life, Rhain of Gwalchdu. It has scalded my every action and thought.' She rubbed her hands along her skirts, shook them out as if there was flour there. Wished her feelings were as easy to brush away. 'When my mother and I ran to the house, I promised her I'd get my sister free. The look she gave me was the last I ever saw of her.'

Fear shortening their breath, skirts raised to their waists, their bodies bent forward with purpose. Her mother had looked at her with pride, gratefulness and determination. Love. Helissent swallowed the tears building, this wasn't the time for tears. 'She believed me. She believed my promise and I broke it when I tripped. I can't help but think if I hadn't, we would have made it.'

'That is why you show your scars to strangers, so they could see them and you could hurt yourself.'

'Partly. I broke a promise, but I was also a coward.' She spun away from him then, didn't want to see his eyes. 'When the ceiling collapsed, my sister and I were trapped. I was able to free myself, but not her.'

Silence. While she waited for her words to sink in. Waited until she could finish her thoughts.

'You didn't leave her though you could,' he whispered.

Helissent closed her eyes on Rhain's steady words. He was still seeing her as courageous. She shook her head. Not ready to finish her thoughts. Her tears shook with her and she wiped her face.

'And you think this is shame?' he said.

He drew in a breath and she knew he'd argue his point. But she hadn't made hers yet. She turned around then, but still couldn't look him in the eye. 'The Church teaches us it is wrong to cause our own deaths,' she said. 'The innkeepers' perseverance in saving me and kindness taught me it was wrong to, even for a moment, have had such a thought.

'But I held my sister's hand, held her eyes as long as she held mine. Even when hers had closed, I held her hand. When I realized I'd broken my promise, when I realized my entire family was gone, I laid down with her. That's when the blackness overtook me, too.'

Utter silence then, and she still didn't raise her eyes to his. Didn't want to see what she knew was there.

'You may be more a fool than me, Helissent from a village of no name.'

She swallowed, clenched her eyes, then looked up. 'No doubt a fool and overflowing with shame from broken promises and weakness.'

His eyes… Warmth, incredulousness…compassion. 'Not weakness. My God, I thought you brave before for rushing into the fire. But there is no word for what you did. You stayed in the fire. You didn't abandon your sister. She knew you were there for her until the end.'

'And then I stayed because I was a coward. Because I wanted to die so I didn't have to face my failures or my shame.'

He shook his head wildly. 'Not shame. *Grief.* Your entire family died. Your sister right before you; you were feeling devastation and loss.'

She tried to catch her breath, tried to tamp down familiar feelings of being broken. It was easier now. After all he'd shown her, he'd made it easier now.

'I see that now. I didn't see that then or most of my life. All I felt was shame and regret.'

His brow furrowed, his eyes going beyond hers like he was seeing something else that troubled him more than her shame. 'You have regret that can never be changed,' he said.

'It doesn't have to be,' she said. 'I'm seeing it differently now. I'm no longer scalded by regrets because I have been reminded of something far more substantial. Far more hearty and sweet.'

'Your cakes?'

Mockery again. She knew why he did it and wanted to soothe the chaotic thoughts behind his amber eyes. 'Didn't you love your mother?'

'You think a fool has no feelings?' He turned and traced the design on the back of the chair, his fine fingers usually elegant, now restless. 'Yes, I loved her. Even in the end when she tried to kill my brother. It's one of the reasons why I left.'

So many similarities between them that they shared, but he couldn't see all that yet. She had to make him see. 'Did she love you?'

He silently drummed his fingers against the scrollwork. 'I may have been the only one she loved.'

'So she went mad, was ill, but still someone loved her...and she loved in return.'

'It was not enough,' he said, his voice warning her.

His eyes were full of remorse, almost like he hadn't rescued her from Reynold and she had died. But she felt very much alive because love was enough.

'You think I don't know the power of love when it's been shown all my life? I failed my little sister. I didn't get her out of the burning house. She screamed. Like a coward, I tried to die so I wouldn't feel the pain of failure. When I was rescued, I believed I deserved to live with the agony of shame. But being with you taught me something else. I might have failed my sister and broke my promise to my mother, but I never failed at loving them.

'We're alive and I'm not failing now. I want you. I want all of you, Devil's blood or not. And I want your smiles that you feel you shouldn't give. So I'm staying by your side and making you cakes and ignoring your mockery and banishing your shadows.'

'Keep me there, Helissent,' he choked.

'No, there's too much light in you.'

'There's not. Stop looking or all will be dark.'

'Then why did you take me from the village; why did you kiss me?'

He looked down at the chair, at his hands clenched there. 'Though I pretended otherwise, it was never for the cakes or the parchment or my curiosity. It was for you. Your bravery, your sweetness.' A curve to his lips, 'Those legs.' He looked back up, his eyes holding hers. 'And so I am to be plagued with your demands even now?'

'You shouldn't be surprised.'

He came around from the chair to stand in front of her. 'No, you're a woman who went through fire for her family, and travelled with unsavory men to find a better home. A woman who insisted I take her to York even if it threatened her life, and faced my enemy to save me. I'm not surprised by your demands.

'But even so, even so, I can never give you what you need. I can never be what you want. What I want to be for you.'

She smiled then, because she knew she had him. He hadn't said the words. But she knew it. It was all in the ingredients. She simply had to measure her words carefully now and balance the scales.

'You want to be with me,' she said.

'How can you not know?'

'I know because you make me believe I'm beautiful and brave. I want to make you believe that you're beautiful and brave, too.'

'I thought my beauty and bravery were already established.'

His mockery again. 'No, I'm trying to make you understand. You've shown me nothing but love and it's because you've been loved. Your mother loved you.'

'She tried to kill my brother...my cousin.'

'She was ill, but it doesn't mean that there wasn't love there. You talked of her sharing the gardens with you.'

'She was younger then.'

'Was it possible her illness caused her madness?'

'That is what Teague argued. It's why she's buried in sacred ground.'

'He did that for you.'

'There was always affection between us.'

'Despite that you were a handful and far too arrogant with far too many women after you?' She could use mockery as well when it suited her.

His mouth curved. 'Despite all that.'

'You have affection for me despite my scars and my shame?'

'Never despite your scars or your actions. You have no shame and I have more than affection for you. I love you.'

He might still be warring against love, but she was winning; he was coming into the light. She just needed a pinch more words.

'That's because love has nothing to do with perfection or beauty. It has to do with acceptance.'

He closed his eyes on that. 'Is that how you did it…is that how you went from the dark caves to the fires to bake?'

'Agnes, the healer, was blunt, brisk and very efficient. I was more of a challenge to her than a person. But John and Anne, they gave me so much. I carried my failure to save my sister, but they showed me that there was still love. However, I didn't learn acceptance until you.

'You and the men treated me differently,' she

continued. 'As if my scars didn't matter. The pain I was used to, by being stared at with horror, disappeared. Then, in the cellar, I listened to your words of deserving. It's how I've been letting go of the past. It's why when I learned that the parchment contained only numbers, it didn't hurt as much. I was being accepted, being loved, for who I am. It's why I was able to tell you how I laid in the fire next to my sister. I could never do that before. But I'm letting the past go and you are, too.'

He opened his eyes. 'No. The past is in my blood. It's here now.'

'It is, but how you look at it can be different. I accept your Devil's blood and your perfection. And despite your words, you are letting go of the past. You let go of your mother's necklace, as I let go of the hope in that parchment.'

He shook his head as if he couldn't believe her words and she pushed into the hold of his arms, felt them go around her, but not near as tight as she wanted.

'I will only hurt you,' he said. 'There could be rumors. If we married, if we are together, our children may suffer.'

'Will you love them any less? Will you not give them the chance to find what we have?' She leaned her head against his chest, reveled in the smell and warmth of him and braced herself for the words she had to say next. 'Then you're not only a fool like I was, but a coward, too. You're laying down in the fire while it consumes you. Denying yourself a future because you carry shame and regrets.'

He stiffened and she dug her fingers into his tunic so he wouldn't pull away.

'If you do this,' she said, 'you deny not only yourself a future, but the future of our children. The future that I want to see. Not perfect, but good. Truly good and full of light.'

Beneath her hold, his chest stilled as if he held his breath. Beneath her ear, his heart increased. He was listening. His heart was listening. She just needed to yank a bit further and he'd be out of the fires he'd put himself in. Then they'd both be in the bright light they deserved.

'You say you love me, despite everything,' she said. 'You cannot expect me to honor your love for me, without also understanding and honoring my love for you. I love you, Rhain of Gwalchdu.'

He pulled her tightly to him then. Gripped the back of her gown and just held on. Tears poured from her eyes as she rubbed her cheeks against his chest. His heart true, his grip strong. She felt in that moment as if he was yanking her out of the fire. That somehow they had saved themselves.

He brushed his cheek against her hair as if he,

too, had tears. 'I may need a few more cakes to understand this kind of love you're showing me.'

Pulling away, she looked up to see the tracks on his cheeks. He was beautiful, perfect. No more shadows, or almost-smiles.

She smiled just as wildly back at him. Freely, no longer covering her mouth, and watched his eyes brighten before they drifted to her lips, then back up. His mesmerizing eyes now bringing a welcome heat with them.

'How many more cakes?' she asked, wanting to see and feel that promised heat.

'Thousands,' he said, taking her hands and leading her to the bed behind him.

'Only that few?'

'That many. That many and for ever.'

She laid on the bed and watched his amber eyes darken to honey and fire. 'We may be here for a while, then,' she said against his lips.

* * * * *

If you enjoyed this story, you won't want to miss these other great reads from Nicole Locke

THE KNIGHT'S BROKEN PROMISE
HER ENEMY HIGHLANDER
THE HIGHLAND LAIRD'S BRIDE
IN DEBT TO THE ENEMY LORD

MILLS & BOON®

HISTORICAL

AWAKEN THE ROMANCE OF THE PAST

A sneak peek at next month's titles...

In stores from 24th August 2017:

- **The Major Meets His Match** – Annie Burrows
- **Pursued for the Viscount's Vengeance** – Sarah Mallory
- **A Convenient Bride for the Soldier** – Christine Merrill
- **Redeeming the Rogue Knight** – Elisabeth Hobbes
- **Secret Lessons with the Rake** – Julia Justiss
- **Winning the Mail-Order Bride** – Lauri Robinson

7/04

MILLS & BOON®

EXCLUSIVE EXTRACT

Georgiana Knight accidentally auctions her innocence
to ex-soldier Frederick Challenger. In order to protect
her reputation, she must marry him, but if Frederick
hopes to tame her he'll have to think again...

Read on for a sneak preview of
A CONVENIENT BRIDE FOR THE SOLDIER
by Christine Merrill
the first book in the daring and decadent series
THE SOCIETY OF WICKED GENTLEMEN

Mr Challenger dropped to his knee before her. 'Miss
Knight, would you do me the honour of accepting my
offer of marriage?'

Georgiana had heard the phrase, 'without a trace of
irony'. This must be the opposite of it. The proposal was
delivered without a trace of sincerity. And yet, he did
not rise. He stared at her, grim-faced, awaiting an answer.

'But, I do not want to marry you,' she said, staring
back at him incredulous.

'Nor do I want to marry you.' If possible, his expression
became even more threatening. 'But as you said before,
if word of this gets out, I will be called to offer for you.
I see no other way to save both of our reputations.'

'Your reputation?' Did men even have them? Of
course they did. But she was sure that it did not mean
the same thing as it did for girls.

'If you do not marry me, I will be seen as the villain

who threatened you, a seducer of innocents. Bowles, on the other hand, will be cast as your rescuer. In either case, your future is set. You will have to marry one of us to avoid ruin.' The statement was followed by the audible grinding of teeth. 'Please, my dear Miss Knight, allow me to be the lesser of two evils.'

The idea was insane. 'But then, we would be married,' she reminded him. 'For ever,' she added, when the first statement seemed to have no impact upon him.

'That is the way it normally works,' he agreed. 'You must have understood the risk when you undertook this desperate mission. As I told you before, if you do not marry me, then you shall wed Bowles.' He looked at her for the length of a breath, then added, 'For ever.'

'For ever,' she repeated. It sounded so final. Eventually, she had known she would have to marry someone. She'd just never imagined it would be to a man who had never been willing to give her the time of day, much less a proposal.